The Heart of Stone Adventures

Fool's Proof

Power's Play

Doom's Daze

Praise for **Fool's Proof**

The inevitable comparisons to Terry Pratchett are accurate.
—Andrew Shanahan, author of Before And After

A wonderful read for fans of the fantasy-comedy genre in the spirit of Monty Python.
—Sydney Rappis, Reedsy Discovery

A cleverly plotted, twisty novel with a gratifying conclusion.
—The BookLife Prize

Replete with satisfyingly unpredictable twists and turns.... those who appreciate humor and satirical inspection are in for a treat!
—Diane Donovan, Midwest Book Review

A book and a writer to look out for.
— Jim Webster, author of the Tallis Steelyard series

I absolutely loved it. If this is Eva Sandor's first venture into this genre, then I personally can't wait for the next one.
-John Derek, Netgalley

FOOL'S PROOF

Eva Sandor

ISBN 978-1-7350679-0-2 (Paperback)
978-1-7350679-1-9 (eBook)
Library of Congress Control Number: 2020913119

Cover illustration and book design by Eva Sandor
Linen texture courtesy of kuesı - www.freepik.com

Printed in the United States of America
First printing 2020

Published by Huszar Books
Visit us at www.huszarbooks.com

to my parents

UMAN-BEINGS *(also known as Hewmen, abbrev: Men) are bipedal, but lack feathers, beaks, or the power of flight.*

Uman-beings possess a rudimentary yet serviceable spoken language, grammatically similar to our own and thus not difficult for any enthusiastic pet-keeper to learn. In addition, certain male Hewmen are able to utilize a system of notation which bears a surprising resemblance to our Scratchmarken.

The social organization of Uman-beings also mirrors our own. The best-studied Hewmen (those whose large sandstone hive is to be found near our Noble Stronghold) appear to have their own version of a royal family, court, peasants, and so forth.

Indeed, scratches the eminent scholar Colo the Elder, "If imitation be flattery, men have praised magpie kind since the dawn of days".

—Colo the Younger,
A Hatchling's Guide to Animals.

NO NOTE EVER SOUNDS, *without some note in echo.*

—Grandmaster Bharr,
Observations.

CHAPTER 1

THE GUARD WATCHING OVER THE evening market was a big, tall, strong wench of exactly the kind who watches over markets the whole world round. She had the standard town emblem sewn on her sleeve, the typical ill-shorn hair stuffed up under her helmet's molded brass curls, the all-too-common dribble of spit in one corner of her mouth from the big clod of maidenroot she chewed. It had lost its flavor, though perhaps not its effectiveness at preventing brats; she hooked its herbal cud out of her mouth with one finger and flung it into the mud beside a cattle trough, looking up just in time to see trouble coming— a street jester, shoving the crowd aside in his zeal to make some complaint.

With a yawn she pulled a bolt from the pouch slung beside her crossbow: a small blunt one, enough for a man. And now here was the jester.

The long striped tassel of his hat hung limp. His face glowed red with indignation. Something far more annoying than the summer flies, the stink of livestock for sale, and the wall of rain clouds threatening the sunset had worked him up.

"Hoy. Guard. There's a penny-poacher over there, do you see him? Him! The one with the bird! Get him off our territory. Damn it deep, it's already hard enough to make a living around here."

"So whata ya want from *me*?"

"Shoot him with a stinger bolt, for Ye Gods' sakes. Or something. Can't you see he's stealing our audience? Look. Look! They're putting coins in his hat— and that's no street-license hat. He's obviously some rich man's private Fool. So what's he doing out here, poaching from the likes of us? Shoot the greedy wight! There are laws!"

The guard's watch was over at sunset. She glared down at the street jester.

"Till a town officer gets here, *I'm* the law, fella. So go on back and juggle ya balls. I've got work here. Someone's tryna—" she craned her neck—"I dunno, do a suspicious."

Before he could reply to this, a great din erupted from the market square. Something black and white flashed up out of the crowd, then plunged back down into it, screeching and cursing as if the voices of a dozen angry sailors had somehow come together in one throat. A mass of men surged toward the guard and she could see that every one of them belonged to the Public Amusements Guild, with his tassel and his baton and a tag with writing on it pinned to his shoulder. They were chasing somebody. Somebody in a drab, old-fashioned linen smock like the kind a monk would wear, and ridiculously oversized women's workboots, and a hat whose beautiful embroidery and numerous bells made it shine out like a well-polished lamp among cheap candles.

The Fool under it had a face so unexceptional the guard really couldn't have described it. But Great God Almighty, the man had flair! Even as he ran for his life, he was able to turn a very accurate handspring, kick his booted heels together and shout a few bars of some song that went "Help Me, O Help Me, Woman Are You Blind". The guard watched him and his pursuers sweep past, fascinated, and her finger lay motionless beside the trigger of her weapon until she realized it was too late to do anything at all. The fellow complaining to her had been swept away with the strange parade. Nothing was left but footprints in the clay road that led down to the river, where a weird little ferryboat shuttled people to the Whellen Country.

Vendors began striking their tents and packing away their wares. The wind kicked up and everywhere the evening turned a soft and sparkling gray. Rain gathered on the brim of the guard's helmet and dripped down her neck as she put the small crossbow bolt back in its pouch.

She gave a contented little snort. The Whellen Country!

She had been raised to want no truck with that place, nor with the crazy old hag who ruled it, but somehow she found herself wishing she were there. She wanted to watch the rich man's fancy Fool, as he learned the hard way that he ought to keep his jingles out of other people's business.

ONE BY ONE THE CROWD of squalid street-license hacks on the riverbank quit making their threats and obscene gestures. Malfred Murd, seated on the downstream gunwale of a departing ferryboat, leaned out from the knot of other passengers for a final glimpse of the knapsack which had hauled his meager belongings and his still more meager bankroll from one pisspot of a town to the next for all these weary months, and—what was infinitely worse, worse to the power of hundreds, of thousands— a final glimpse of his hat.

Even now, as some cut-rate provincial gagflogger dared to set it atop his lousy head, the hat had dignity. Sunset kissed the tarnished engraving of its bells, caressed its matted velvet, and whispered endearments to its faded comical embroidery of roosters laying eggs and nullicorns dancing with very un-virginal hunters. But the towering scrawny oaf seated beside Malfred elbowed him, and he had to turn away for a moment and then— just like that— when he looked again the hat was gone.

The magpie Corvinalias was still diving into the crowd after it, over and over, doing a fair imitation of an enraged falcon, but Malfred knew it was useless. His midsection felt strangely full: not of food, certainly, but of more than its usual bitterness. What else could happen?
Oh, right. It began to rain.

He sat and got wet as the other passengers all reached into baskets and boxes and bags. Everyone else had a waxed canvas hood or an oiled silk wrap or at the very least a cone of braided straw. The fellow who'd elbowed him now kneed him, and shouldered him, and ankled him in the process of unfolding a set of freakishly long, lean, sinewy, tanned and windburned mostly-naked limbs. The wight had a bag around his sunburned neck, so he was clearly a flyer— that is to say, a long-distance roadgoing foot messenger— but he was the most ridiculous one Fred had ever seen. Most flyers were quick mannish little wenches, who sped between the carts and wagons of road traffic like dragonflies between cattails. But this one reminded him of a big-nosed, sad-eyed and frequently-kicked male greyhound, which opened the bag and drew out a long, long oiled-silk rain poncho that flapped and fluttered and stuck to Malfred's wet face.

"Hoy, Stilts. Do you mind? I'm not your deep-damned clothesline."

The flyer muttered a reply in the thickest Yondstone accent he had ever heard: it couldn't have been more of a caricature if a goat had yodeled it from a stony mountaintop. A dozen juicy Yondy jokes were on the tip of Malfred's tongue and he saw his chance to make a couple of brass pennies before the trip was over, but then he realized that, without his hat, the other passengers couldn't know he'd ever been a Fool at all. So he held his tongue, wondering miserably how he was going to pay the ferrymaid.

But there was no ferrymaid. No oars, no scull, no sail. Only the craft moving straight as a shot across the rain-roughened water, passing buoy after buoy. Malfred's hair stuck to his forehead and his smock became a great damp floppy awning and the twin blister factories that served him as boots let rain come in— for although twenty years of professional acrobatics, dancing and stunts had left him as brawny as a common laborer, the boots had been made for Lumpy Lettie, the royal family's head charmaid, and his legs simply weren't thick enough to fill them. He turned around on the bench and knelt, drawing his feet up behind him and getting the seat of his breeches wet too. He sighed and stared down at the turbulent river.

This was probably a winchboat. He had seen such things before; on the Isle of Gold there had been plenty of winches, powered by ponies or oxen or workers' strong backs. There had been a clever system by which food and drinks could be winched up to the royal chambers in an ornate gold-trimmed rosewood crate. There had been a water mill and seven windmills. Keep thinking about machinery, he told himself. About rain. About anything, anything except what the hottest hindmost Hell you're going to do with no license, no money, no hat and no future.

A black and white speck was following the boat, pulsing and flashing through the gray veil of rain, drawing ever larger and closer. With a fierce grunt of effort Corvinalias made a final wingbeat and flung himself aboard, landing hard on Malfred Murd's shoulder. His long black claws dug into the linen of the smock and he clung there, sputtering and trying to wipe his eyes and beak on the ragged stubble growing on his pet's jaw.

"Ye Gods, those low-rent fools can fight," he gasped. "I had to brawl like a gull back there. Broke two toenails and bent one of my remiges. I got a couple of licks in— I think I bit a piece off some poxy wight's ear— but it was no use. They took the hat and all your shinies, Fred. I'm really sorry."

"*You're* sorry?" Fred burst out. "What am I supposed to do now? Look. Look. I bet I can do the whole Topsy Turvy routine right here and no one'll give me so much as a half-penny." Without warning, he stood on his hands and began wriggling his legs as if they were two actors performing a puppet show. His smock flopped down over his head and he coughed at its musty stink. Not a soul laughed, although he did hear a yelp from the Yondy flyer as one of his boots hit something. When Fred turned back upright he expected to find every face in the boat glaring at him with disapproval, but for some reason most of them were smiling. One or two of them even winked at him and hoisted imaginary cans of drink to their lips. That gave him confidence enough to lean across toward the wench who sat on the opposite gunwale and say: "Did I give you a laugh, goodwife? How about giving *me* a couple of brass pennies? For the fare."

The woman shook her head. "Ain't gotta pay any fare. Not till tomorrow. A holiday ain't over till the midnight bell." A few of her neighbors gabbled and babbled in approval. They spoke of taverns and barrelmusic and picturebooths and coinpuppets and dancing under a wyrmlight lamp; a tavern was the only one of those things Fred had ever heard of. He turned to Corvinalias.

"Well? Are you going to explain what you've chased me into *now?*"

Corvinalias purred soothingly. "Fred, Fred. Don't get angry. I didn't chase you, you know that. I only ever make travel suggestions— it's those other Uman-beings that chase you. Shhh, shhh. It'll be all right. I'll catch you a nice big juicy mouse. Or a frog. Or a lizard. Or a whole pile of locusts. And then I'll— whoa." Corvinalias's supple neck whirled his head around as if it were a flag in a sudden change of wind. His gaze was upon the Yondy messenger's bag. "Did you see that?"

"See *what*?" Fred's voice had an edge to it now. He was becoming agitated. Corvinalias purred some more.

"It's all right, it's nothing. We magpies can see all kinds of things Umans can't. It's— well, all right. It isn't nothing." He hopped higher on Fred's shoulder, pressed his beak against Fred's ear until the whiskers around his nostrils bent, and whispered: "It's shinies. That fellow's bag is full. Of. Shinies."

Fred couldn't help but gaze at it himself. *Really? Someone trusted a bagful of coins to this dolt?* Oh, if only one or two of them would fall out. And oh, if only those were more than just brass pennies. Oh, my God, be good to me, and make a few fall out that are moon-marbled silver, or glistening gold.

But the passengers began to shift themselves closer to the gangplank stored in the bow; the giant bony flyer stood up and a gust of wind plastered the tail of his poncho to Fred in a great damp slippery slap; fine soft gravel hissed along the hull of the boat and someone flopped the gangplank down; everyone swarmed off the ferry and Fred's god was not good to him at all. Nothing fell out of the Yondy's bag. Indeed the fellow vanished into the crowd that was flowing from the waterfront toward some kind of noisy glow. Fred was about to demand that Corvinalias tell him just where in the furthest foulest hell they were, but before he could the bird cried "Jackpot, Fred! Meet you later!" and launched himself away.

FRED LEFT THE FERRYBOAT BEHIND and drifted through the streets. Very clean streets, he couldn't help but notice, paved with limestone cobbles so uniform they might have been tiles on a floor. No bothersome puddles here; instead the well-drained cobbles simply glistened in the rain, reflecting a galaxy of lamps on posts. He gazed up at the lamps for quite some time: whoever could afford them all? Even the King didn't send his servants out to hang this many lamps, and certainly not in a midsized street full of commoners. *Were* these commoners? They were all so well dressed, and as clean as the cobbles... then Fred heard a hissing, and smelled something burning. He pulled his foot hastily out of a gutter in the middle of the pavement where a dark-gray cable rushed swiftly along. It had run smoking against his boot and as he stood cursing at the long, charred scar it had left, someone grabbed the collar of his smock and yanked him out of the path of a wagon, clamped to the cable and trundling along at what would have been a brisk round trot if there had been any horses. The people in the wagon all turned back and stared at him as if *he* were the oddity.

Fred heard music, and jogged toward it, thinking to ask the piper or the fiddler or the dulcimer-drummer what the situation was like around here for illicit busking. But there were no pipers, or fiddlers, or dulcimer-drummers— only lit-up pavilions full of people dancing:

skipping and jigging and kicking up the Dizzy Dan around fellows who stood turning cranks on the sides of kegs. He had no idea who played the music. Nor any idea why children were lining up to put their eyes to a hole in a crate, or what was inside it to make them laugh or scream or applaud.

Neither could he guess who this woman might have been, with her face on all the banners hanging limp and wet about the town. They were crude folk art and not realistic. Every year the Royal Family had proper portraits done; Fred had fumed at the way he was always shown sitting off in a corner, with his thumb stuck in a pie or some such nonsense, but at least those portraits had looked like them. These showed him only that the woman was old, and had some kind of gray tiara on her head. One of the banners had writing on it, but the letters were sloppy and Fred really couldn't tell what HPE XSSHN DA was supposed to mean— if that was what it said. But then he turned a corner and found himself in a square dominated by a big coaching inn. Under the eaves of its long veranda hung a banner which had clearly been painted by a professional scribe: ALL OUR PRAISES TO HER HIGH HONOR, DAME ELSEBET DE WHELLEN! HURRAY FOR YET ANOTHER PROSPEROUS YEAR!

It took Fred aback. He actually froze in mid-stride and looked around. He was in the Whellen Country? But then where were all the slaves, groaning at the bars of some dread gigantic capstan? Where were the bitter lakes of sweat and tears? Or the furnaces, belching filth as they poured forth shoddy brittle tin and cloudy glass? Come to think of it, hadn't these de Whellens been extinguished, or at least brought to heel like their co-conspirators the de Brewels, who— let's not kid ourselves, thought Fred, remembering the tribute they paid the Crown— were still rolling in gold?

This couldn't be right. He ran his wet hands through his wet hair, flummoxed. If this were the Whellen Country, why then, he'd be a blue-arsed ape. He'd be a rubber pumping bucket. He'd have a seven sided blister on his little pinky tooooooe...

There was. There was something by his pinky toe. Fred whipped off his burned boot and shook it and, Great God Almighty who is beyond and between and within, it was a coin. Hell's holes, a coin!

It was a single brass penny, dull and greenish in the lamplight, warm and stinky as a sweaty foot, but Fred could not have been more excited if it had been a wish-granting magical gem. His mind began racing, thinking of what he might buy with a brass penny. A drink, by his god, that's what he wanted. He strode toward the inn, boots squishing. But the closer he got, the more it bothered him that the patrons going in and out looked clean and prosperous, laughing under their lacquered rain hats, gesturing with hands full of rings. Fred knew what he looked like. Dodging another cable wagon, he scanned the street for the shabbiest people he could find. Some bedraggled travelers trudged by; he watched them go until he spotted others who looked worse; and by this means Fred soon came to know that off the square, behind the prosperous inn, there was a seedy one where strangers like him took their custom.

It wasn't really even an inn: only an open shed and some stalls meant for travelers' beasts. No glass lanterns here, no cheerful pavilions; just a few rickety tables and some smoky rag-wrapped torches, stuck into sockets in the ground. Low-budget drinkers sloshed through puddles on the gravel floor and dodged drips from the leaky roof. The emblem of a Brewel Country throwball team was painted on one of the inside walls, but visitors had carved so many species of genitalia over it, as well as one or two misspelled cursewords, that it was hardly legible. Fred gripped his brass penny more tightly and set himself to figuring out the least poisonous thing he could order.

"Sherry Lorroso," he heard someone say, and a laugh burst from his mouth. Who knew he still could laugh? Really, it was just too absurd. Lorroso.

But after Fred's laughter died he felt like weeping instead, weeping for one last taste of that exquisite dark nectar the King's butler used to bring up from the cellar in quaint bottles thick with dust, and pour into red crystal glasses on an old, old, historic bronze tray. His body moved of its own accord, sleepwalking toward a crooked square window where a sullen innkeeper rattled crockery.

"Another Lorroso here." He ordered as if in a dream. He didn't know how much it cost. It didn't matter.

The moment Fred took the dirty glass mug, someone tapped his shoulder. "New in town, are ya?"

A bumpy-faced fellow whose hair was longer and dirtier than the wig balanced on top of it leaned conspiratorially against Fred, who flinched in reflex.

"Well? Are ya? New."

"Mmm-huh," he replied. He didn't know where to look as he tried a sip of the sherry. He gagged— it tasted like distilled horse piss. The fellow was still leaning on him.

"Where from?"

He forced himself to keep sipping, and the fellow leaned harder, until Fred said, "South."

"Silver Bit? Oldmarsh? Coastwall?"

The fellow's bumpy face was inches from his own, his breath ranker than sweaty boots, his insistent stare making it obvious that he could, and would, lean on Fred all night waiting for an answer. Fred set his jaw, squirmed the fellow off his shoulder and said, "Further. Now go away."

For one blessed moment the bumpy fellow was quiet, eyeing Fred's diminishing drink. But then he was at it again. "Ain't no land south of

Coastwall. Not till opposite shore of the Midland Sea. I know, for once I used to be a sailor."

Fred twitched as he downed the last of the reeking mug and set it down with a thump. "Oh, there's something before the other side all right." He turned away— but not before he saw the bumpy fellow snatch up the mug and lick the inside of it, his tongue inching against the glass like a big pink leech.

The fellow gave a belch of surprise. "You don't mean the Isle of Gold? Really! You were a servant at the King's Palace?"

Fred flicked a dismissive hand, which did in fact wave the fellow's stink away for a moment, so he did it again, harder.

"Well me, I come from Coastwall, come up here to get work as a poet."

That actually got Fred's attention. "You. A poet."

"Oh, aye, I've as good as got my license—guild just wants a written sample. Now, truth is I don't actually know my letters. What I do know is a wight back in Coastwall who's a scribe and he fixed me up." The fellow tapped one grubby finger on the side of his greasy nose. "Wrote it down neat as you please, under the table like. Meanwhile I know my poem by heart. I bet you can't top this: 'Dear Dame Elsebet. You're the greatest yet. Fifty years you've ruled here fairly, trouble has come rarely. You are wise and strong and skilled. Put me in your Guild of Poets.' "

During his months of exile, Fred had let a lot of his standards slip. Shaving every day had soon given way to shaving every week; paying some hostelry for a tub of bathwater had become jumping into a cattle trough when the farmer wasn't watching; human meals like soup and sausages had turned into whatever vile tidbits Corvinalias brought him, jabbed on a razor and charred over a skimpy fire. But everyone has some depth to which he will not stoop— and Fred's was letting this blister think he could beat him at poetry. In twenty years with the Royal

Family, he had composed poems beyond counting. He hadn't written them all down, but they could have filled a book: intricate, winding fourteen-line sonettos with not a rhyme in them, but only the whisper of agreement; lilting, looping mirandelles with their interplay of repeated words; doublets, heptoons and punchy little snap-songs that could be taken as bawdy or pure, depending on the listener. Grudgingly he decided to give the bumpy fellow a sample of the latter:

"A clever young scribe from the Fen
said 'mistress, come sharpen my pen.
And if you should think
it has run out of ink—
why, sharpen my pen yet again.' "

That one had occasioned a lot of giggling and raised painted eyebrows among the Old King's even older sisters. It was a classic. But the bumpy fellow only turned out his sticky lower lip, narrowed his eyes and after a maddening delay said, "I don't get it."

Fred took a deep breath and, wrapping the tail of his smock around his hand, picked up the vile mug. In pointed silence he strode back toward the innkeeper's window, hoping with all his heart that distilled horse piss cost less than a penny.

But the fellow followed Fred, grabbed his shoulder and whined, "Hoy, seeing as how you're rich, can't ya get me a drink too?"

"No. And I'm not rich."

The fellow became insistent, tugging at Fred's sleeve. "Sure you are. King's servant musta got a fat pension—whatever the King touches, it's gold, ain't it? On the Isle the buildings is all gold. I seen 'em from the deck of my ship. "

"Go squeeze a boil," growled Fred, yanking his sleeve out of the bumpy fellow's hand.

The fellow scowled. "Hoy. Watch it. You don't want me to get cross, do ya?"

"I do. I want you to get 'cross the yard. To the latrines over there, and shove your thick head in." Fred thought that was good and witty. He strode away.

But the fellow got revenge. He waved his arms overhead and boomed out: "Hoy, mates! This rich fella says he just bought a round for the house! And he's getting the next one, too!"

A frenzy swept the shed. Some of the squalid customers converged upon the window, ordering more; others simply downed their drinks and fled, leaving their tabs unpaid. The bumpy fellow was one of these. He slipped away as smoothly as a braised eel, leaving Fred squarely in the path of the meanest-looking barmaid he'd ever seen.

CHAPTER 2

THE ANCESTRAL HOME OF THE de Whellen family was built upon foundations of old limestone, but anything old about it ended there. Whatever leaky, creaky ancient timbers and thick chilly walls it had once shared with other nobles' palaces had been torn down. Instead it burst forth in breathtaking translucent geometry: gleaming walls of glass and mirror that soared up and up into the skies, aqueducts and tunnels that brought in water and heat and coolness, stately domes of crystal and wrought metal, smooth white gravel roadways that wound through parks and courtyards cleverly planted to look more natural than nature, and a stableyard as magnificent as many a temple. Tonight, as it did every night, Whellengood glowed from within, lit by thousands of wyrmlight lamps that flared to life with the sunset. But this had been a special day, a once-in-a-lifetime day, and soon it would close with a great feast— this fiftieth Accession Day, anniversary of the rule of Her High Honor Elsebet, Domina of the Whellen Country.

Dame Elsebet rushed into the sparsely furnished elegance of her suite, thrust her heels into the bootjack and pulled off her riding boots. Her maids had not heard her enter. Before any of them could lift a finger, she slipped the boots over a pair of cedar lasts and began rubbing them with the sleeve of her long doeskin glove.

"No no no!" cried the maids. Over the course of half a century, those cries had become a kind of ritual music, with a ritual dance to accompany them: one maid with a shoebrush snatched the boots away; others followed Dame Elsebet as she eluded them, removing and folding her own coat, her blouse, her breeches; some managed to hold her back from filling her own bathtub, though just barely. And although Dame Elsebet made her usual sighs and groans, insisting that she could do this all herself, she knew how this would end: the maids would overwhelm her with their menacing armament of gear for hairdressing and maquillage.

"Oh, pocks! Not this again!" she protested, as they redrew her eyebrows from faded silvery arches into dramatic dark brown wings, hid the creases of her rugged tan skin with creampaint of surreal ivory, amplified her lips from pink to crimson. She said nothing until they reached her hair— then she really had to call for a breather.

"Ladies! Who wants to join me in some tea?" Dame Elsebet hopped to her feet, almost as quickly as she had at the age of twenty. But a flurry of hands pressed her back down.

"We have some ready, Medame," said the oldest maid, and signaled to the youngest, who hurried into the chamber wheeling a little cart. Set in its very center, without a coaster or a tray or even a doily, was a plain cylindrical glass of ice-cold tea, completely unadorned except for the beads of sweat that clung to its smooth colorless sides. It was a truly handsome object.

"That's new," said Dame Elsebet. "What a handsome glass that is."

"Only it *isn't*!" squealed the youngest maid, jumping up and down. "It's your present from the Alchemists' Guild! Prophessor Lembick says all the glasses at the feast will be like this one. He said that when you're done drinking, you should hurl it to the floor as hard as you can. Oh, I can't wait to see! Go ahead, *hurl* it! As hard as you can!"

"Very well," said Dame Elsebet, and swung her arm so hard its leathery muscles shook like a bowstring. The glass bounced and rolled across the travertine floor, but when the youngest maid sprang up and fetched it back, it wasn't broken. Not even chipped.

"You see? It isn't glass! It's something new! Prophessor Lembick said they can also use it for—oh oh oh!" the other maids tried to cover up her mouth, but she had given away the secret of their own surprise gift: a shawl, which the oldest maid held out to her mistress with shy fanfare.

"This is from *us*, Medame. We hope you like it..."

The youngest maid simply could not help butting in once again. "Really, really, *really* hope you like it, because there's a trunk in the other room with forty-nine more of 'em inside. Ow! Stop pinching me!"

The shawl was feather-light and water-smooth. Its surface was a continuous pattern of hearts and cogwheels in various sizes, interlocking and repeating, fascinatingly seamless. Dame Elsebet wrapped it around her shoulders and said: "How beautiful. Is this made from the fleece of the vicanna? Such a rare creature. I once saw a wild vicanna, so close I could have touched it, in the high fastnesses of northern Yondstone."

No, no, no, crowed the youngest maid, it was not. It was spun from the exact same material as the glass that wasn't glass. And the weaving loom had put the pattern in all by itself! Yes, all by itself, with nobody at the controls, oh Medame you should have seen it go. And every one of the fifty shawls was dyed a different color with something the gentleman from the Textile Guild had said was made from tar, if you could possibly believe that, gooey old *tar!*

In the excitement, Dame Elsebet thought the maids might forget about her hair and just let her pin it up in the sort of net she wore while riding. But of course that was folly. More hands than ever attacked her with brushes, combs, switches, bun rolls and extra braids until they had turned her head into a towering snow-white configuration. And then on went her hose, her shoes, her undertunic and her long, heavy robe with its elaborate sash. This garment was made from silk the color of the River Whellen: its threads flowed and played together in a harmony of green and gray, blue and brown, and across the entire back of it, embroidered in a thick mat of golden beads, was a cogwheel encircling a salmon-pink heart.

The sleeves were long and broad and hid her hands to the palm.

"Ladies," said Dame Elsebet, staring at the sleeves as if she could see through them. "My gloves, please."

Everyone knew what the gloves were meant to hide: two perfectly matched grayish-blue ruins, like veins slowly dissolving in tears. Fifty-one years ago they had been a lovely teeming lacework of birds and beasts and flowers, the finest wedding bracelets ever painted into a bride's skin, the masterwork of a great artist; any other woman would have kept them touched up, for wedding bracelets never went out of style. But Dame Elsebet would condone no such desecration. The blurs stayed, but were never spoken of, as was her widowhood.

"All right, then, ladies. Am I sufficiently groomed? Has my mane been brushed enough, my coat polished, my tack arranged just so? Am I ready to enter the arena?"

"You only need *this*, Medame." And the oldest maid, the one who had been with the Domina through everything, reached out to her mistress's brow. Into the hair she pressed an arc of intricately marbled crucible steel.

"You are ready, Your High Honor. Long may you reign."

CHAPTER 3

In the brightly lit corridor, with the rain rattling down upon its skylights, Dame Elsebet pushed out her left elbow and raised her voice with as much cheer as she could muster. "Lorenz," she called. "Let's get on with this thing." Her brother was not late; he emerged from one of the guest suites opposite and strode to her side.

"The girls are almost ready," he said, straightening the overlap of his fine lambswool collar. "It's their husbands who aren't. One can't find his glasses and the other one spilled ink on his knee." He gazed up at her hair with an expert's eye. "You could win a show at the Northern Cattle Fair, brushed and glued like that."

He wanted her to laugh, she knew. So she did, but it was a weak imitation and it didn't fool him. He squeezed her elbow and said no more.

He means well, Dame Elsebet told herself. He wants me to follow his example. He has let it go, and imagines that letting it go will do me just as much good. Lorenz Whellen did indeed look at ease. His hair still had considerable brown left in it; laughter remained in his keen dark eyes. Dame Elsebet pressed the steel of her coronet a bit more closely against her forehead as they stepped into the Grand Salon.

Her vassals were enjoying themselves, she was relieved to note. Some were laughing at jugglers and conjurors; some were drinking from portable wine fountains; some took turns cranking one of a dozen brightly painted music barrels while others danced to them. A few of the women who had gone riding with her still wore their tall boots, and that did make Dame Elsebet smile. Removing wet leather could be quite a challenge.

Her entrance had been seen. At the far end of the salon, a great organ sang out with its array of reeds and pipes and horns: *Heart of Stone, Heart of Stone, lend us your endless power.* Within Dame Elsebet's lifetime, this song had become the anthem of the Whellen Country, and when her guests began singing it, spontaneously raising their arms and swaying, she was forced to fumble inside her sleeve for a handkerchief. Lorenz gave her his own. "Come on, Elsie. Let 'em see you cry. They're tears of joy. Right?"

"Right," she said, raising her hand to open the feast. "Forty-five years— the first five were yours, not mine. Don't you ever, ever, *ever* imagine I will forget your bravery, Seigneur Lorenz de Whellen."

"Hoy, knock it off with that." He squeezed her elbow again as they drew up to the head table.

There was food. Oh, so much food: Dame Elsebet lost count of the dishes that poured from her cooks' imagination. There was drink: wines and meads and brandies made from every fruit and flower that grew upon her vassals' lands, and she knew that down at their tables they would be arguing— playfully, she hoped— over whose holdings produced the best. The tableware itself was stunning, colorful, inventive. Even the rain on the dome of the Grand Salon was welcome, a soothing noise like that of a waterfall, and it pained Dame Elsebet more than any words could say to look upon such happiness and prosperity, knowing that unless her gambit proved successful all of it would end.

The King doesn't care, she felt rather than thought, about the unbreakable glass that sits at every place on all of these tables. The machine that wove my new shawls? He would burn it rather than let his court wear anything made in the Whellen Country. He would smash every wyrmlight lamp on every post, tear the cylinders out of the music barrels, even stoop to cut the cable of the automated ferry across the Greater Good. Rather than bring our works to the rest of his Kingdom, he would throw all of this away and keep the world threshing grain and drilling rock by hand, condemn them to hand sewing and hand smithing, to lives of sweat and tedium, just for the sake of showing that, wait three generations if he must, the de Whellens would not escape punishment.

She gripped the edge of the table. *Oh, my very own God, if only I knew whether everything is still going according to the plan.*

Her thoughts jittered between the mystical and the practical. Doktor Lively must be aboard the ship, she told herself: I have a bond of the soul with him, and if he has fallen ill or somehow hurt himself on the way to Coastwall, my very being will surely cry out with a premonition of doom. Is *this* a premonition of doom? No, no, damn premonitions! What I want is that messenger. He's supposed to come back and tell me it went all right; when he gets here... suddenly she felt faint, and on the edge of the table her glove twisted into the cloth and her unbreakable glass toppled and spilled.

"Lorenz. I just had the most horrible thought. What if that nice young fellow— you know, the one tall enough to see over even the biggest crowd? What if... well, if he broke his leg?"

"Then I think you'd have to put him down," replied Lorenz Whellen with exaggerated gravity. "You know messengers pine away in captivity." When she only blinked at him, he picked up her fallen glass and handed it to a passing servant. "Now listen. You can't do this to yourself, not tonight. Tonight is—"

"Tonight it's crucial that I *know*! Unless I am sure Doktor Lively is safely underway on that ship..."

"What's crucial is to have patience. Say you know the ship sailed. What then? After that it's out of your sight. A whale could eat it, and you wouldn't know. Lively could fall into a gold mine on the way to the Palace, and you wouldn't know." He trapped his sister's madly fidgeting hands between his own. "You insist on doing this thing, Elsie, but accept that you won't *know* whether it succeeds or fails until the Face of the King shows up in your major-domo's office to tell you whether your nieces will have a 'de' in their names." He took one of the beautiful napkins off the table, unfolded it and pressed it into her hand. "It isn't bad, I promise you. Being a commoner, working the land. Look at the girls and their families—"

Dame Elsebet did not apply the napkin to her tears. Instead she applied it to the floor. She sprang to her feet and her voice shook with a mixture of ferocity and despair. "I have no doubt it suits you to drop your 'de'. It's perfectly clear the youngsters are all fine without it. But the *machines*, Lorenz! The brilliant gentlemen who made them, the good people who run them! Our country, sir! Its capabilities, its future! It is in peril, mortal peril! And you advise me not to..."

Some of her vassals were looking at her. "...not to eat any more lamb. Why, damn you for a haughty cattleman, Lorenz, I'll eat more lamb and like it."

"Hear, hear," said one of the vassals, who raised no fewer than eight breeds of sheep.

But now that Dame Elsebet was standing, the eyes of the room were upon her. The vast, great, suddenly very quiet room. She scanned the Grand Salon in desperation. No tall Yondy messenger had sneaked in through a side door. Her heart was racing. Then she remembered some of the breathing exercises Doktor Lively had taught her, to be used in those terrible moments when the memories flooded in. Surely they would work just as well to banish *this*. She breathed. And breathed. And then a lovely idea came to her. As though she had meant to do so all along, Dame Elsebet took a step back and turned to face the wall of glass behind the head table. She spread her arms wide, knowing that it would make the de Whellen arms on the back of her robe flash and gleam and glow. "Grandmother's tree," she began.

She did not have to speak too loudly. Her voice echoed from the glass. There was a scramble as a few servants lowered a canvas drape to cover the wyrmlight chandeliers. Now everyone could see through the wall of the Grand Salon and there behold a massive blueneedle tree, jutting in solitary majesty above the lamplit walkways of Whellengood's central garden.

"Everyone here knows Grandmother's tree. When she planted it, Annelyn de Whellen was a newlywed. Of course, young though she was, she *had* already done a few things besides gardening." A rueful chuckle rose from the crowd behind her. These were Whellen Country nobles; all of them knew that the history books on the Isle of Gold were false, that Annelyn de Whellen and her equally young de Brewel sweetheart had made an innocent choice, for love. It had never been their intention to start any kind of war. Dame Elsebet let the silence fall again.

"I have a painting of her, with that tiny stub of a sapling. The garden looks very strange: a huge empty circle, waiting for a giant to grow. But you see it did. Now. I'm sure I don't have to tell you that this is a metaphor for our country, and for the foresight of Grandma Annelyn in knowing that what were then only a few simple shacks full of gears would become the technical marvels we now enjoy." She turned to face her listeners. Without the echo on the glass she would have to speak up; Dame Elsebet gathered her courage, the way she used to gather it when she couched her spear and legged her horse and made ready to withstand the shock of collision. At this thought a wisp of memory clawed at the edge of her consciousness; she breathed it away and forged on.

"You all know what Lorenz and I are. Our grandparents... our parents... then us. Ours is a third generation and so, as of old, a decision will be made—" an unhappy murmur began in isolated parts of the room. Lorenz shaded his eyes and Dame Elsebet saw his hand shaking. But she felt strangely powerful. *It's all right,* she wanted to tell him. *I'm in control of myself.*

"—a decision will be made in the Royal Palace. Oh, I'm sure that to the King it won't be much of a decision at all. Renew our title for another three generations, or not." Dame Elsebet forced her crimson lips into a smile. "He probably puts more thought into ordering breakfast." The unhappy murmurs were replaced by polite laughter. "It is of course my duty to live as long as I can, and so delay that decision, but someday it must come. And yet, my dear friends, I have a feeling. The strangest feeling. I have a feeling that something will soon make the King realize what he has in us, will convince him to come down on the side of progress, of creativity. I have a feeling— no, it is more than a feeling..." Careful. As if from outside herself she recognized the warning signs of the other danger: the hounds running riot, the landslide. Doktor Lively had taught her to breathe that away, too. Steer the middle path, the middle path, between despair and delirium. The middle path shone wide and clear before her; never had her mind worked with such ease. Lorenz was right: her fears were groundless, her worries useless. All would be well.

"...it is more than a feeling. It is a conviction! You see, our Whellen Country is like that tree," announced Dame Elsebet, pointing, not in the shout of a lunatic but in the grand tones of an orator. "It's still growing. The King cannot stop it. It grows from our land, our waters, our Heart of Stone, and human decisions are just so many raindrops falling upon it. No rainstorm could ever harm such—"

A massive explosion rocked Whellengood Hall.

Guests, servants and entertainers all cried out as the wall of windows became a single blinding block of light, black-burning-white, a sun bigger than a thousand suns. For a moment the tree stood silhouetted in a searing halo; then boiling sap burst from it with such force that the windows rattled under a hail of sticky drops. Glowing blue needles showered upon the domes overhead as the thunder rolled and rolled, and in the garden's place of honor nothing remained but a blistered spire of charcoal, burning like the wick of some monstrous candle.

The rain put out its flame.

CHAPTER 4

Alvert Dragonsson was sorry he'd ever pulled this pockin' slippery poncho thing out o' his bag. It were a bother, and a trial, and a irkable frill, for a fellow who'd never worn one before.

In Yondstone he had worn a boiled wool cap and goatskin britches. That had been quite some time ago, before Ma had come down to the lowlands and taken up work hefting a delivery pack. A rover, she were, running where there weren't no roads, with her freak of a pup behind her, a boy growing so tall that his goatskin britches soon hardly covered his bony little behind. Then Ma had become a flyer— more money in it. Flyers' bags mostly just held paper, but paper was worth more than coins to gentlemen as could read. And naturally, havin' no other skills, Alvert had become a flyer too, though he fit in among them about as well as a crane fit in wi' kestrels.

To what he owed his new position with Medame, he did not know. He'd knocked his freshly-shaved head on the doorframe as he entered the major-domo's office at Whellengood Hall; his ears had been ringing as the gentleman with the glasses and the shiny black wig examined Alvert's Guild license and he had not quite understood what was happening when the gentleman pushed a book at him and said mark here. The gentleman had been most displeased to repeat himself, and had called Alvert a lot o' the same names Ma used to call him, but in the end Alvert had left Whellengood Hall wi' a bag around his neck, a right fancy beautiful bag, plain on the outside but inside all needleworked in thread o' gold.

And he had gone down to Coastwall, not runnin' as a flyer ought but in right rich fancy style, on one o' Medame's fast riverboats along wi' the Doktor gentleman and ten knights. The knights had scared him a little. They had stern faces like Ma, plus each one a sword and a dagger. At the great big huge shiny white castle they'd put him up in a dorm wi' other servants, but Alvert knew his job was to be at the harbor the very next mornin' to watch that ship, the *Longwing*. Watch it run out on the tide, bound for the Isle o' Gold, and then fetch back a paper for Medame that proved what he'd seen was so.

Only somehow he hadn't seen it, an' the only paper he carried now probably didn't say it.

Oh, Alvert had been at the harbor on time. In fact, he had been so nervous about missing the appointment that he'd left Brewel Hall in the wee hours of morning, begging one of the de Brewels' servants to row him across the great mouth of the broad brown Denna and leave him at the harbormaster's shed. He loitered there till dawn in the brackish night breeze, was forced to make a few spirited explanations to Brewel Country constables, and endured the attentions of several prowling guards who chewed their maidenroot at him and wanted to know how tall he was lying down. But the sun had risen, and it had climbed, and Coastwall harbor had filled with the most immense crowd and all the ships that floated upon its waters came alive and their boats hoisted up and their sails fell down and their whistles blew and they slid right out past the customs hulk and the lighthouse and into the Midland Sea, and Alvert had never seen the knights, the Doktor gentleman, or even the *Longwing* anywhere.

This was bad enough. His shallow concave guts had roiled. But when he'd gone back to the harbormaster's shed for the paper, that was when Alvert had flat out wanted to die.

There wasn't any paper. How could there not be any paper?

The harbormaster repeated himself, over and over, using many of the same words Medame's major-domo had used. Sure it was a bad thing that there wasn't any paper, any passager manny fest, he called it. But some sky-high Yondy lummox asking for it over and over again wasn't going to make any manny fest appear out of nothing. He had just better get used to the idea that there wasn't any, and either wait till they found it or go on back to... where again?

Tears had run from the corners of Alvert's round gray eyes, slime from his big long nose. He had a lot of brow to wrinkle and a lot of jaw to tremble, and the great angular lump in his neck had gone up and down. But then there was a little bit o' miracle. Beside the quay, floating in a spiraling eddy of trash, he'd spied a bunch of pages. Alvert's arms were just long enough to reach them, and his heart boomed like a big goatskin drum when he saw that there was a picture of a bird, an especially long-winged bird, stamped in one corner. He ran straight to a scribe's booth, knocking over three or four cursing dockyard wenches. "Is this from the *Longwing*?" he had yelped. "Is it a passager manny fest?"

And it was. From the *Longwing*, anyhow. As for the other question, it took the scribe no more than a glance to see it was no passager manny fest but rather something else, a cargo manny fest. The gentleman didn't even need to check the other pages, though he took the silver coin Medame had given him for the return run's food and lodging and didn't offer Alvert any change.

But none of that mattered. The moment Alvert had them papers in his bag he hit the Trade Road, a-scorchin' shoe leather as if a bear were after him— which, in Yondstone, was actually not an uncommon occurrence.

He had gone back up through the Brewel Country at a short-way pace which, especially in summer, bordered on the unwise. His dinner was the tea in his leathern bottle and his inn was a haystack; at last he was flying up the road by the bank of the broad brown Denna, leaving footprints the way Whellen Country sewing machines left stitches, passing through villages from respectable to wretched, stopping only to ask other flyers for a sip from their leathern bottles. When the Denna met the Whellen he turned to follow it, and the day grew darker and more humid, and the clouds began to cover the sunset, and in the town of Bogg across the last river before the Whellen Country there had been some kind of disturbance among the street Fools. Alvert had given this a wide berth and reached the ferry without incident, thinking how lucky he was that it was Accession Day— he had no coins left for a ticket. At this time, it finally began to rain, so he put on this poncho, which were very nice o' Medame to have given it to him, but oh were it ever an annoyin' thing, the way it would flap its pockin' self in every little wind and the way it hung down between his legs and bunched all up in his beans. When the poncho tangled itself yet again and almost tripped him onto the neat limestone cobbles on the streets of Good Market, Alvert lost his patience. He stopped in his tracks, took the bag from around his neck, set it on the cobbles and was just about to slip his foot through the strap to keep the precious thing safe when a deep-damned fluxin' boil-blistered scabflap of a pus-weepin' bird swooped down and stole it.

Stole it!

Why, *why?* As the wretched animal shot up into the clouds, cheering and gloating, Alvert saw that it was black and white and that explained it all. A magpie. A thievin', sneakin', loud-mouthed braggin' magpie.

He wove madly through the crowd, the poncho streaming from around his neck like a battle standard, knocking down whole families lined up for a little fun at the eyepieces of picturebooths, upsetting barkers cranking their music barrels, spilling the punch from topers' cans and crashing through the expensive machinery of a coinpuppet show so that when he scrambled to his feet he was covered with paper stars and the scales of a tin firewyrm. He left the puppet-master shouting after him in fury; he could still make out the magpie, flapping ponderously overhead, its claws hooked tight into the bag's waxed canvas.

Alvert was gaining on the bird. Yes, he was! The creature was growing weary, it was starting to fly lower, the bag was sagging down. With his eyes on the prize, Alvert reached up with every possible inch of his long, long arms, sprang like a high jumper— and a massive bolt of lightning tore the sky.

For a moment, Alvert was blinded. Maybe that's why he didn't see the bull just there ahead of him, before he crashed into it like a stone from a catapult.

CHAPTER 5

"BOILSORES! LOOK WHERE YOU GOING!"

Alvert knew this thing he'd hit was a bull. For one thing, it smelled like the milk cattle he'd known in his youth, that grazed near prosperous villages lower down the mountains. Its bellow of surprise also sounded bovine. But there the resemblance ended, for this creature was far larger than any cattle beast he'd ever seen, broader and darker and richer-looking. The exact same could be said for the woman who sat astride it, shouting down at him.

"Careful my rain tent, stupid man!"

Indeed there was a colorful canvas roof overhead. The four servants carrying the poles at its corners were hard pressed to keep it upright, because the great bull had been startled into a furious bout of bucking. Alvert fell on his rump in terror as a storm of hoofs slashed the air far too close to him. Yet the woman sat completely unperturbed, swaying with the animal, patting the brute's neck the way a child pats a puppy. When it finally settled down, she let it lower its enormous sharp-horned head to snort at Alvert as he cringed there on the cobbles.

"Shh, *ipo.* Stupid man here did not.... ahhh?"

The woman stared at him. Her round, dark golden face wore an expression nobody ever had when they looked at Alvert. It lasted only a moment, though; one moment, and then she was giving him the kind of glare he was used to.

"Why you jump in middle of street like some spring toy? Get up, ah. You hear me? Up, up!" and she was bending low, extending one of her hands.

Alvert had never in his life seen anything like her. She was majestic. Her hair swung down, long and smooth and black as a bottomless cave. When her mouth moved, he saw that four of her teeth had been filed sharp, like the fangs of a puma. Her dress had more flowers on it than an entire valley in spring.

"Get up. Follow me. I wish to offer you food." She tossed her head as if daring him to question her plans. "Eat it or do not. After that, you deal with Her High Honor missing bag."

"How did you... ?"

She pulled him up. Her grip was like a farmer's.

"How I know you Dame Elsebet servant? She has mentioned tall new man. I also see you have no bag. You know you must file lost message report immediately, ah? Do not worry. Grand Constable of this town will be there, where food is."

They walked along together, man and beast and magnificent woman, under the artificial sky. The roar of the rain on the canvas above him, the swaying of the bull as it strode, shook loose one of Alvert's few pleasant childhood memories.

It had not begun that pleasantly, to be sure. He had run to Coastwall beside his Ma, and a sullen silent journey it was, until they crossed paths with another messenger: a towering, whip-thin fellow who, it transpired, was Alvert's father. Then the trouble began. Ma and that fellow quarreled every stride of the way, until the skinny boy between them was nearly deaf; once in the city they roared at one another in the street and tore at each other's hair and, surprisingly, shared a room at a dismal flyers' hostel, where they bent to the evening with gusto, hurling articles from the room at one another. What began with a light barrage of knick-knacks escalated quickly and when Ma heaved the entire washstand— complete with basin, pitcher and towel— at Alvert's rediscovered Da, the boy had slipped away and run down the grubby streets to the great, breathing, copper-green sea.

He'd heard the sea was deadly, and fervently hoped he'd heard right: wouldn't that just show Ma once and for all? But as there didn't seem to be any pier handy to leap from, the boy had waded into the sea instead... and felt its enormous kindness. Over and over the sea lifted him high, set him gently down; it stubbornly refused to kill him, and instead swept him along with great surges of joyous force, proving that there were things much stronger than misery.

An echo of that feeling filled him now, as he was swept along beside the golden giant on her lofty beast. Too soon, they reached an inn with a long, long sign that Alvert couldn't read hanging under the veranda. The woman threw one of her legs lightly over the bull's withers and dropped to the ground as gracefully as a petal falling off a flower; wordlessly one of the servants reached out for the golden ring in the creature's nose and then it, and the rain tent, were gone. The door of the inn opened wide for the woman before she had so much as stepped up to it, and a whole mess o' gentlemen rushed forward to greet her.

These gentlemen definitely looked like they could read. They intimidated Alvert: one was richer than the next, with hair combed just so or wigs that cost more than a wagon, many with their own servants orbiting them. Through their ranks the woman glided, and they moved aside for her. Alvert kept himself in her slipstream as they entered a private room that smelled like flowers and spices and furniture polish. Inside, yet another clutch of important-looking gentlemen leaped to their feet around a long table.

"It is my honor and pleasure to finally meet you, Medame! I am newly employed by the bankers who financed your recent expansion into—"

"Perhaps you remember me from our dealings some years ago at the Southern Cattle Fair. I was the gentleman who offered to purchase—"

"Medame, allow me to congratulate you upon your acquisition of that excellent piece of river frontage north of Coastwall! As I said to my partners—"

Someone pulled out the huge red leather armchair at the head of the table, and the woman sat; Alvert tried sitting on the windowsill, but the woman indicated otherwise; instantly a servant was folding him down into a seat at the corner of the table nearest her. At a gesture from her, a fancy gentleman even moved aside for him. He could not comprehend what was happening, but the empty place around his neck where the bag had been felt like some kind of abomination. He should not be here. His stomach twisted in a slow knot and sweat began to trickle from the nap of his recently-shaved hair.

He opened his mouth to ask permission to leave, but— ask who? Everyone was occupied with talk, talk, important talk. He tried getting up, but every way out was blocked by servingmaids hauling in cart after cart of food and drink. The talk intensified: a great clamor of bargaining, of offer and counter-offer, of proposal and agreement; of hiring and firing, descriptions of merchandise and customers, of subcontracted shipments and new equipment, routes and rates and schedules. Eventually it dawned on Alvert that he was in the presence of the Ox-Train Queen.

No flyer in any part of the Kingdom was unfamiliar with her fleet. It blanketed the Trade Road and all its major arteries; practically all the shipping that wasn't waterborne traveled in the Ox-Train Queen's wagons, hauled by her renowned oversized brown-and-gold oxen. She was as much the mistress of the roads as the de Brewels were masters of the Midland Sea. Alvert stole a sidelong glance at her and remembered what she had said about reporting his lost bag to the Grand Constable; for some odd reason, he recalled that he had been looking at her foot when she said it. Now, her feet were under the table, bare and golden on the shimmering silk carpet. His own big, dirty, wet feet in their cleated goatskin shoes looked like trespassers. He should ask her about how to report the bag. When he looked up, three servingmaids were surrounding him with platters of melon and sliced ham.

"You like it?" the golden woman asked him— quite earnestly, it seemed.

Alvert glanced at the food. His guts gave another nervous twist, but he nodded politely and said "Aye, Medame."

The Ox-Train Queen clapped her hands together, clearly delighted. "Gentlemen!" she said. "Tomorrow I meet with Her High Honor on matter of steel railway proposal. Let us put all in order tonight, no matter how long it take. Paper, ah? And drinks!"

A scribe leaned out of the crush and pushed pen and paper into the Ox-Train Queen's hand. The roar of talk began once more, and Alvert was genuinely entranced to see her hand dipping the pen, moving it, the ink spreading behind it into shapes he knew were writing. He'd never seen a woman write before; for a moment it made him think that maybe he could have learned to do it, too. But o' course not. How could he possibly have done that, up in the steeps in a village where nobody even knew proper numbers, instead counting their flocks on the joints of their fingers? He looked back at the table and the platters were gone, off on their way around the room.

Cart after cart of drinks went around, too. While Alvert scanned the room with his heart pounding, trying to figure out which gentleman was the Grand Constable of The Municipality of Good Market, and whether a bird counted as a citizen for the purposes of reporting a stolen bag, he took one of the sweat-beaded pewter cans from a drink cart and sipped it. Some kind o' tea, he thought. Very tasty. His stomach stopped hurting so much. He drank a second can and the gentlemen's faces somehow seemed friendlier; one of them looked as if he might not mind being spoken to. Alvert decided to ask him about the Grand Constable, the moment he finished a third delicious can o' tea.

With the fourth can, Alvert listened along to a conversation and was surprised to discover that he had something to add to it. He did so, and nobody swatted him like his Ma used to, or called him names, and that made him so happy that he took a fifth can off the cart, although this one felt a bit slippery somehow and he had some trouble holding onto it. Soon he found himself agreeing voluminously with certain people who, it seemed to him, were absolutely correct, and heard himself arguing with others who were obviously wrong, and all the while it was growing steadily more difficult to stay upright, or to hold subsequent cans.

Then, in a bit of a surprise move, the beautiful silk carpet filled his field of vision. Its pattern was far, far too complex to look at. Looking away, however, failed to help; the room was sinking downward in a nauseating fashion, and while it did suddenly snap back up into view whenever Alvert concentrated, it soon became as inexorably wavy as the sea, only not so kind.

A tiny, reasonable voice that felt as though it originated from somewhere far behind his face told him he ought to go. He ought to be up and on the road. Why wasn't he on the road? Oh, the bag. The bag! He leaped to his feet— or tried to. But the table stopped his head with a fearful bang and then he was lying on a slowly rotating planet while everything around him faded down into soft, blank silence.

CHAPTER 6

THE MEAN BARMAID WAS PRACTICALLY on top of Fred, gesturing at all the empty mugs the fleeing drinkers had left strewn about. She looked as sympathetic as an executioner. "I hope you've got more money, because *I'm* not payin' for all these. A lousy penny don't even begin to cut it."

"But that old wretch was lying! I never agreed to buy..."

"Pay up now, big shot, or I call a town officer!"

"Who here wanted an officer?"

The barmaid turned to look, but no one was there— only a magpie, which fluttered hastily through a hole in the roof. When she turned back, the shed was empty and Fred was gone.

He ran so fast he practically left his boots behind. He crossed the gap between the shed and the prosperous inn with the barmaid's shouts in his ears and getting louder every step. He rounded the corner of the inn, plunged through the door and found himself in a crowd of what seemed to be wealthy merchants.

These gentlemen glowed with health and cleanliness. Instantly Fred felt more at ease; this was his kind of company. Or at least, he thought so until one of them noticed him and recoiled.

"Hoy, Reeves. put this grubby wight out." The merchant's servant stepped forward and pushed him, somewhat gingerly, toward the door.

"No! Wait! I'm the entertainment!" Fred grabbed some meatballs from a nearby diner's plate and began juggling them. Herbs and sauce splattered around the room. He grinned maniacally, trying to sell it. "You should see what I can do with eggs. Reminds me of a story..."

"Get him out of here!"

Something shot through the partially open door and abruptly a magpie attacked the merchant, screeching and pecking and calling him and his servant foul names in multiple languages. Other guests, offended by the disturbance, leaped to their feet and tried to catch the magpie. Fred planted himself squarely in the middle of the fracas and, making cryptic gestures with his arms, boomed "Hocka, bocka, dominaka! And.... *ta-daa!* I've conjured up a magic bird— what fun!" He bowed, backing across the room, desperately looking for somewhere to hide. "You've been a great audience, I mean that..."

The merchant lost his temper. "Stop it, you!"

He swung his open hand at Fred's ear, and although the blow was feeble and missed its mark, the mere fact that it had happened stabbed into Fred like an arrow tipped with poison.

In his banishment, Fred had certainly been knocked about. He'd endured plenty of kicks and whacks and shoves from street rabble in struggles over possession of a prime corner, or for half a dropped bun— but never in his memory had he been dealt this sort of condescending pop. He had seen Lumpy Lettie give such blows to her kitchen help; it was an established form, a specific gesture to be understood as a rebuke from superior to underling. He rounded on the merchant with a furious rush of wounded pride and one of his hands scrabbled at the other to yank off the glove he wasn't wearing. But before he could issue a withering challenge, he slipped on a squashed meatball and crashed to the floor, grabbing a tablecloth and scattering all the platters upon it as he fell.

"Ah! What happening over there?"

At the back of an adjoining room, an enormous figure rose from a red chair.

Of course Fred remembered her. Who could forget someone like that? No, the impressive thing was that *she* remembered *him*.

The magnificent woman studied him for only a few seconds. Her expression changed from displeasure to delight as she came over and pulled Fred to his feet.

"Ah! Little monk boy! Yes, it is! Ha! Well, you not boy no more." Turning back to her colleagues she said: "It all right. I spend a minute with this one."

The mutterings, the whisperings that followed did not faze her. She invited Fred to come sit at her table in the private room, and that seemed to settle it: the strange, bird-herding juggler was someone from her past. The Ox-Train Queen's past was known to be colorful.

She watched Fred hook a passing platter and snatch a generous slab of ham from it, as well as several thick slices of melon and a folded spicy pie. While he crammed these into his mouth, the woman gestured at the assembled dignitaries and said: "Well, as you see, I make success. Biggest overland shipping business in whole world, is mine. All start from that one wagon and little calf, you remember?"

Fred remembered. The "little" aurochs calf had been the size of a moose, and growing.

She reached across the table to pluck at the fabric of his smock. "Aw no, Monk Boy, this still same shirt you wearing twenty year ago! Well, at least you grow into it. But so dirty— what's you trouble? No job?"

Corvinalias hopped onto the table between them. His feathers bristled with indignation. "He had a job! The best job! Better than *your* job, whoever *you* are! He was hand picked to be the young King's very own Fool! And—"

Fred's hand flashed out and pinched the bird's beak shut. "Don't listen to him. He says dumb things."

The woman's hooded black eyes gave a merry twinkle. "You got pet bird, Monk Boy? I always want one. Bird! What you name?"

Corvinalias answered the woman, but his eyes were on Fred. "I'd say it, but my name's not a dumb thing."

"Hoy, don't sass off to her!"

"Nah, is fine. Bird, I am Ata Maroo. Lately I got nickname 'Ox-Train Queen'. That because business is good. I knew you friend here when he was, hmmm, I say thirteen. That right, Monk Boy?"

"You have a good memory—"

"And you name, now I thinking, was Malfred. Yes? Malfred... Murd. You were cute little boy, Malfred. And funny. Smart. What happen after I drive you from monastery to city?"

Fred lowered his eyes. "That. That would take all night to tell."

"Well, I can see end of story pretty good. You need job."

"Yes," Fred sighed. "I need job. But it's impossible— I've been blacklisted. I *was* pulling in a few coins on the sly, here and there, but now nobody even knows what I am... if they ever did, said the Fool, bitterly. Close curtain."

Ata Maroo pushed one greasy lock of hair away from Fred's forehead as if in search of the promising child she had known. But only a strange miserable man was there.

She rapped the table with her knuckles. "That all right. I give you simple job to do, not Fool Guild job at all. How much money you need?"

Fred gave a wan ironic chuckle. "How much have you got?"

"I have got more than most entire town, ah? So listen. You do small thing for me tonight. Do you know how to groom bull?"

"No."

"Do you know how to dry and store rain tent?"

"No."

Ata Maroo's mouth formed a determined line. "So what you know how to do?"

"Jesting, clowning, tumbling, juggling, general acrobatics, funambulism, comedic monologue, poetry recital, poetry composition, play-acting, classical dance, tableau vivant, and miscellaneous amusements not specified."

"I do not need those."

"Really. And here I thought any decent shipping fleet would have an acrobat on staff."

"You make joke, Malfred, but I hope it is not joke on me."

"Of course not."

"Because it take *real* fool to make fun of old friend trying to help you."

Fred stared at the table in silence. Finally Ata Maroo patted his shoulder.

"It all right. I do not mean to make you feel worse. I know how it feel to be lost and alone."

"Is that a fact? Because you *do* look so lost and... wait! Don't go! I'm just—" Fred gave a yelp of fright. "Ow! Something grabbed my foot!"

A gurgling noise came from under the table. Ata Maroo bent to see what it was, and when she sat back up there was a vertical line of worry between her brows.

"This not good," she said. "Stupid man who is drunk under table, work for someone very important. *Ai!* It is my fault for not watching him. He need where to sleep. Not in my room— that look like funny business— ah yah! All right, Malfred, I know what job you do for me. You move stupid man into stall next to my bull, son of calf you remember. In return..." She pointed over Fred's shoulder. The mean barmaid from the drunkards' shed stood inside the door, gesticulating to a neatly dressed gentleman who was clearly the owner of the inn. She glared daggers into the private room, daggers aimed directly at Fred.

"...in return I pay *her*," finished Ata Maroo. "Deal?"

CHAPTER 7

FRED HAD DONE PLENTY OF comedic double-takes in his time. But when he looked under the table to take stock of the job he'd agreed to, he did one that was completely genuine. *Really?* The damned drunken wight he'd agreed to drag out of the inn, across the limestone courtyard, and into the barn turns out to be that sky-high, big-nosed, goat-cheese roadpounder with the ridiculous rainflap, from back in the winchboat? Wow. Of course, he'd never doubted it was a strange world.

And in his time he'd done a lot of strange things— but for sheer clumsy floundering it was hard to beat the task Ata Maroo had saddled him with. The poxy wight's extensive limbs were determined to point in every direction except ones that might have made it easier for Fred to wrestle the poncho out from around his neck, unfold the thing, roll the miserable drunken oaf onto it and pull him out of the silent inn, with the night guard looming over him, chewing loudly and staring pointedly at the oaf's very short knitted pantaloons. That last part had kind of hurt Fred's ego, but he told himself that no wench could be so crass as to eye up a monk.

At least the bull hadn't given him any trouble. The creature had looked like a mountain. Even lying on its chest, chewing cud much like the guard with her maidenroot, the brute was so big that it gazed down upon Fred as he stood in the barn aisle gathering his courage. He tried to push Alvert head first into the straw-bedded stall, but he bent at every joint rather than go in. So at last Fred had pressed his lips together into a pale white line, told his God he didn't want to be judged just yet, and backed into the stall pulling the poncho and its load. Still chewing, the bull had turned its lethal head with a ponderous majestic gravity and touched its slippery nose to Fred's face, an action which nearly gave the straw more to absorb.

But in the end Fred remained there, beside the monstrous coffee-brown beast with a streak of golden hair running from its withers to the root of its tail, stayed because where else was he to go? The stall was the cleanest place he'd slept in for months. And at least with the drunken flyer beside him, he wasn't alone.

Buildings were bad for Fred to be alone in. No matter how large the space, how airy and bright, still the moment the door shut and left him to face a room alone, the world would start folding in around him. The walls would bulge, the ceiling would dangle, the floor would rise; no matter how often he told himself that none of it was true, still he would feel himself being crushed, smothered, buried. Over the years this malady of his had forced him to keep company with many he would otherwise not have tolerated, who were in fact far more of a trial than the drooling lummox sprawled in the straw.

Fred sighed. He sat. He may have slept. A thin gray light glowed through the window of the stall. Some swallows chattered in the loft. And then— from exactly what shadowy part of the barn, Fred couldn't tell— Corvinalias crashed down into the straw with the flyer's bag.

"Hoy, you should be glad you can't understand what those scissor-tailed yobs up under the roof are gabbing about. I swear... Fred! Is that fellow awake?" Corvinalias flung himself on the bag belly up, with his wings spread wide and his legs thrust out, claws ready.

"I think he might be dead."

"Dead men don't snort, Fred. Can't you hear him? No? I suppose birds can *hear* things you can't, too. Well then...hoy! Careful! You'll spill the shinies!"

Fred shoved the open bag back at Corvinalias. There were no coins in it— only a clump of papers that looked as if they'd been wet down and wrung out. The shiny stuff he'd seen was only embroidery.

"Well, I'll be damned three layers deep." Corvinalias pecked repeatedly at the embroidered lining, as if one of its round motifs would come off in his beak. "Aw, pus."

Fred gazed at the embroidery. He had seen it before. Where? It was something recent, he sensed it. Something he hadn't seen until he came into the town. He ran his finger over the interlocking teeth of the pattern, thickly sewn in gold and salmon-pink thread. Then he recalled Ata Maroo saying, *stupid man who is drunk under table, work for someone very important*, and just like that he knew.

He knew, he knew, he knew. This bag was worth shinies all right. Maybe barrels of shinies. He grabbed it and was on his feet in a heartbeat.

"Fred! What's happening?" Corvinalias raced out into the courtyard after him, clearly exhausted but burning with curiosity, half hopping and half walking and from time to time fluttering weakly to catch up. Fred said nothing. He walked faster and faster. He even started to run, slinging the bag around his neck as if he were the flyer. "Where are you going?" shouted Corvinalias, and in the pink dawn some bluebirds sniggered at him.

Fred stopped. He pointed. Corvinalias saw it. In the middle of town, where the Accession Day festival had been merriest and the most banners still hung, the crude cheerful likeness of Dame Elsebet de Whellen smiled down from windows, porch roofs, lamp posts and fences. The artists might not have known how to spell, or how to paint a face. But they could certainly paint a golden cogwheel around a salmon-pink heart: the de Whellen family arms.

"This thing is worth big money," said Fred, and his voice was husky with anticipation. "Reward money."

"Good thinking! But I bet you'll have to wait all day for that fellow to wake up."

Fred was stuffing the bag hastily down the collar of his smock. “I’m not taking it back to him, you piebald pinhead.” Now the bag was hidden; Fred simply appeared to have a potbelly. He jutted his chin up at the banners. “I’m taking it to *her*.”

CHAPTER 8

THE MIDLAND SEA —SHE OF the brandy-black deeps, womb of classical culture, crossroad of empires— mingled with the mouth of the broad brown Denna— Old Mama River, Carrier of the World— pretty much in the front yard of a little place known as Brewel Hall.

And Brewel Hall was being turned upside down.

Officers and investigators tramped mud across the inlaid marble floors of the treasury. Servants scuttled along behind them, picking up their candle stubs and empty tea mugs and pipe ashes. The Treasurer himself, looking sick and frightened, paced back and forth in a vast gallery. Some of its delicate tall windows were open to court the morning air, but they were all well protected by iron grids— delicate, intricate ones, to be sure, but protection nonetheless, for this gallery was the treasury's inner sanctum, lined with cases where the de Brewel nobility kept their particularly valuable valuables.

Impressive though their stock of these was, it was dwindling. Every year, the King's representative would sail from the Isle of Gold to Coastwall, capital city of the Brewel Country. The representative would visit Brewel Hall at an inconvenient time of his own choosing and demand to view its treasures; then, singling out a particular bauble, he would wonder aloud whether His Majesty might ever own anything so wonderful. In this way the Royals avoided using the unpleasant word "tribute", and the de Brewels avoided admitting they were in disfavor with the Crown. Their part in any alleged uprising— some generations before— was thus swept under an exquisite, hand-knotted silken rug.

But this morning the Treasurer's fingers, looped through his candleholder, were shaking; so was his voice. "Nothing is actually missing," he said. "Nothing except a few monetary notes. A few bundles of notes. From the strongbox. Yes, there *is* a hole in the strongbox. But nothing else is actually missing."

"What's that?" An officer of the law, perched at the top of a folding ladder, paused in his minute examination of the top one of the display cases. "Something else is missing?"

"No, no, no. You misheard. Nothing is actually—"

"Right." The officer went back to his work. "You keep saying."

Dozens of officers had scoured every inch of the gallery, the treasury, the hallways surrounding them, indeed just about every part of the palace except the vast private apartments of the de Brewel family. The officers annoyed the servants; the servants hovered about the officers; the de Brewels and their houseguests shied away in their splendid chambers. The atmosphere was uncomfortable in the extreme, and nothing in Brewel Hall had ever before been acquainted with discomfort.

Into this vortex stepped the Grand Constable of Coastwall. The windows of the gallery began to glow pink and gold, a particularly flattering light. For an officer of the law, the Grand Constable was a handsome man. His face was not too extremely scarred; not very much of his hair had fallen out; his thick gray mustachio precluded any unpleasant view of teeth lost to fisticuffs. His uniform, halfway between that of a military officer and a diplomat, was martial enough to reassure the onlooker that misdeeds would be met with force, yet projected an air of eminently reasonable civility. He slipped off his boots before entering the crime scene and addressed the Treasurer.

"Inventory?"

The Treasurer hurried over and handed him a freshly written list. "Officers have checked everything. All cases have been opened, all drawers have been unlocked, everything has been counted and examined. Nothing is actually missing. Except some monetary notes. From the strongbox."

The tightly written dark letters made the Grand Constable's eyes hurt. He had learned to read because the job required it, but oh, for his old days as a simple thief-taker! Back then, all he'd needed to bring a crook before the magistrate were the right questions asked in the right places, a few reliable wrestling holds, and a good pair of manacles. Not all of this.

"I'll read it more carefully back at the Station House. How much were the notes worth?"

"Just... this figure. Not really so very much."

The treasurer pointed at a number which made the Grand Constable swallow hard. The de Brewels controlled trade on the estuary of the Denna, and upon the Midland Sea as far as the Perdoffino light. Their wealth was immense, yet the Grand Constable was still stunned every time he glimpsed the extent of it.

"Well, if anyone in town starts driving a solid gold carriage, we'll know why," he joked, patting the Treasurer's shoulder. "Breathe, there's a good man."

"The art objects and the... spellbound objects are all here," babbled the Treasurer, his eyes pleading with the Grand Constable as if he could somehow intercede with the de Brewels. "Only two of my guards were distracted. They have been dismissed. They didn't see who, how, the hole, the strongbox..."

"Get some tea in you," the Grand Constable advised. "I'll see you at the Station House later."

From down the gallery there was a soft cough and a click of heels. A servant with a quiet but strangely penetrating voice announced: "Their High Honors the Domina and Seigneur de Brewel."

The Grand Constable turned and bowed. "Dame Irona. Donn Felip."

Dame Irona was wearing a painting. That's the only way the Grand Constable could have described it. She was a tall imposing lady, and her robe was a vast heavy wall of silk, bolstered up by a series of knots and stays and some kind of framework which could only have been devised by a mind that saw the world in terms of sailing ships. A huge flock of gulls arrowed across the silk, each one of them picked out in gold and silver and pearls, and a slim silent servant girl, dressed so that she might blend in with her mistress, huddled close behind her. The moment Dame Irona stopped walking, the girl crouched to one side of her and held a jeweled gull, exactly like the ones on the robe except that it was three-dimensional, in a perfectly calculated spot as counterpoint to the flat visual behind it.

"Did they get any of the *objects*?" Dame Irona craned her graceful neck toward the gallery.

"No, Your High Honor. It doesn't seem they did." The Grand Constable glanced at the servant girl. Her face was blank with concentration as she moved the jeweled gull back and forth as if it really were flying.

"Well, that *is* a relief." Dame Irona put her hand vaguely into space and the girl instantly filled it with the lacquered handle of a large fan. The Domina opened this to reveal a painting of a cloud; she fluttered a breeze upon herself and nodded sharply down to her husband. "Just think, Felip, if they'd got the Cans. We'd have been in such a fix— I've heard rumors that His Majesty will soon... admire them."

"It's all right," Donn Felip assured her, patting her hand with his exquisite silk glove. But his brow was furrowed in perturbation. "I understand that we recently had assurance written on the strongbox, do you remember, dear? And the objects too, of course."

"Assurance! As if *money* could ever make up for it if someone stole the portrait of your great-grandfather! Or the Majestic Sapphire! Or the Twin Cans!"

"None of them were touched. It was only money."

"Well, thank Ye Gods for that. But to think— brigands— here among us, in our very home!"

The Grand Constable was about to speak, but he had to pause a moment. It would have been the height of rudeness for him not to look at Dame Irona's smooth, dramatically made-up face, but he was fascinated by the way the servant girl now put away the gull and instead unfurled a blue and green scarf upon the floor in front of her mistress. In a series of rapid well-practiced movements, she rippled the scarf so that its white reverse created a dynamic facsimile of waves upon an imaginary shore.

"I— ah— forgot what I was— ah. Your High Honors. I assume that you wish this matter to take the utmost priority?"

Donn Felip's narrow face assumed a scowl. "We do indeed. It is a very serious concern, for someone to have got into the Treasury like that. Yes. Make it your priority, and while you're at it, impose a full, complete, and total blockade on harbor traffic."

"Very good. But I would be remiss in my duty if I didn't point out that we *do* have a few other cases under investigation."

"Certainly. I appreciate that. But we don't want those other affairs to hinder you. Surely they can wait."

"Just so." The Grand Constable knew perfectly well that all other affairs *would* wait, whether they could or couldn't. His title might be pronounced 'Grand Constable of Law and Order in the City of Coastwall', but it was spelled d-e-B-r-e-w-e-l.

"I do so hope you find the cankerscabs who did this!" cried Dame Irona. "I'll make a seeping example out of them!"

She turned on her heel so suddenly that the Grand Constable didn't even have time to bow. Instead he gave a respectful nod to Donn Felip, and watched as the noble pair left the room. Behind Dame Irona the servant girl stood on tiptoe and flourished a huge disc of golden paper; theatrically she lowered it as her mistress walked away, and when it touched the floor she turned it over to reveal a slumbering dark-blue moon. A carved, painted door slammed shut and the de Brewels were gone.

THERE WAS NOT MUCH LEFT to learn, but the Grand Constable and the last of his officers spent a few more hours at Brewel Hall. An artist was brought in to draw diagrams. A scribe was brought in to take statements. Slowly the investigators worked their way out of the treasury. The Treasurer posted a new troop of guards, whose usual expressions of boredom had been replaced with ones of desperate vigilance.

The Grand Constable strolled around the gallery one last time. Truly beautiful things, these: a painting of a nobleman helming a ship, glowing with what seemed to really be the brilliance of the open sea. A green-and-blue striped sapphire as big as a small loaf of bread, carved all over with leaping fish. A pair of scuffed, old pewter drinking cans. The Grand Constable crouched closer, reached out and traced his fingers across the glass case protecting the last of these.

"Those have been examined," said an officer exiting the gallery. "I'm told they're in good working order."

These simple gray metal cans, of the sort to be found in any tavern, didn't look new or special. But in the Grand Constable's opinion, they might have been the most incredible of the de Brewels' possessions. The Twin Cans. They were magic.

He quickly corrected himself, of course: magic had been debunked. Men of education now agreed that there was no such thing— there were only phenomena yet to be explained, and Prophessors seeking to explain them. But was it not magical, were things like these not *spellbound*, to use the common old term?

Who had been the first to notice, wondered the Grand Constable, that these old cans could speak— that however far apart they were, and whatever might stand between them, anything said into one would shortly be repeated by the other? Over the centuries, the Twin Cans had sent messages in battle, passed whispers of love, and carried the news of commerce which had built the fortune of the de Brewel dynasty. But the family had long since cemented its position, and now these wonderful tools were locked away.

No Prophessor or engineer had ever been able to learn why the Twin Cans worked as they did. Maybe the de Brewels really didn't want to know: being unique, they were all the more valuable. The Grand Constable sighed. How valuable they would have been to *him*. Coastwall was a big city, full of crime and intrigue, with more and more each day as the population grew. Keeping it even moderately safe was thankless, frustrating, tedious work, and the de Brewels' whims often caused promising investigations to wither on the vine— he could think of several dozen that were withering now. Oh, if only he could speak instantly to faraway officers. Maybe even many of them at once. Then he could *really* get something done! But police work was not magic; it was only toil. And its reward was not treasure, only... justice. The Grand Constable straightened up and pulled the belt that held his truncheon smartly into place. His reflection floated across the glass in front of the Cans, and he knew he couldn't deny it: twenty-nine years on the force, and even the word still gave him goosebumps. *Justice*.

CHAPTER 9

THE ROAD OUT OF GOOD Market was slippery, sticky. It was the kind of clay that grabs every footstep, when it's been rained on all day and half the night. Nevertheless Fred strode along as fast as he could, trying to avoid the largest wagon ruts and the slipperiest, stickiest puddles.

A carved post in the town had pointed the way to Whellengood Hall, which sounded to him exactly like the kind of hall a de Whellen would find it good to live in. Fred hunched down so that hair might hide his face and the swinging of his arms might hide his precious pot. He was making not unreasonable time, given the conditions, but someone else was going much faster: a rhythmic slapping of footsteps grew louder and louder behind him, astonishingly rapid and precise despite an accompaniment of random gasps, retchings and moans.

It was the flyer. He swept past Fred without so much as a glance, legs whirling like a pinwheel. Fred hugged the stiff canvas of the bag protectively under his smock and watched the miserable wight go by.

"Hah!" shouted Corvinalias, perched on Fred's shoulder. "Good luck to that one. Hoy, I see some haystacks up ahead that look like a great place for rats. Do you want one? No? Well, pardon me for asking."

Within about a mile, the road became quite lively. Many of the previous evening's revelers were making their way home; others were going to market. Some were afoot; some rode or drove. They brought horses and donkeys and oxen, spare long spotted highcats and frolicsome packs of hounds. All of them trod the clay of the road, turning to and from their villages when smaller paths branched their way. About half a league out of Good Market Fred felt something warm puff on his back.

"Good morning, Malfred!" Ata Maroo leaned backward, and her bull slowed from its brisk trot down to the speed of a trudging man. "You see drunken flyer go by? I could not stop him. I went to barn this morning to get this one"— she patted the bull— "and man shoot out of barn like swallow with tail on fire! Maybe that because you put him in stall actually *with* bull, not stall *next* to him like I say... Ah yah, stupid drunken man will reach Whellengood before me."

Fred turned to exchange a look with the bull and stumbled over a tall, sharp ridge of clay left by a wagon wheel. These had been getting more and more frequent; they were a menace. He shaded his eyes with one hand and looked up at Ata Maroo through the glare of the midmorning sun. "Ata. My old friend," he began in his most winsome voice. "Would you mind giving me a lift? It just so happens that I'm also going to Whellengood, and this road's been so torn up by someone's mumping wagons."

"Malfred, you make two mistake. One: you have name backwards. My given name is Maroo."

"My dear, kind Maroo—"

"Two: it rude of you to use curse word for my wagon."

As she said this, they crested a hill. In the long valley that stretched ahead of them, where the road led on toward something that gleamed in the distance, camped an army.

A vast herd of enormous brown oxen had been picketed for the evening to graze and sleep; now brawny wenches with thick boots— and in fairness, some very large men as well— were yoking them in teams of eight, ten, twelve, before the wagons. These were no common farmer's drays but great wooden arks as big as houses, riding on ten-foot wheels, into which teamsters hoisted crates and nets and bundles of merchandise. Scribes buzzed from one wagon to another, dealing with documents. Watchdogs barked and teamsters' brats squealed, and at random intervals the blare of a signal trumpet cut the din.

As he and Ata Maroo drew closer, they could see the claws of the oxen's hoofs and the iron rims of the wagons' wheels churning the road into more of the ruts Fred had struggled with. Ata Maroo pointed down at them.

"You right about road, though. Shipping volume in this district way up and rising— but soil here is expansive clay. It already close to limit of shear strength. That mean it not support more traffic, even if we amend with angular gravel, ah? So Her High Honor give me permission to discuss a plan. I have many backer who see opportunity to put in steel railway, something like one Whellengood already have from river dock to loading dock. Except that one is cable power, mine would only be ox power." She paused. "For now."

"Aha, look. Here is my own wagon. You may ride it to Whellengood— Nadima will drive. But you tell her she is not to whip my team, ah? She is daughter of big customer, but between you and me, I am not sure I keep her much longer. I will meet you in Whellengood front courtyard this afternoon." With a quick nudge of her leg against one of the bull's gleaming sides, she turned and rode away, leaving Fred beside the enormous wheel of a particularly beautiful wagon, with a snowy canvas top and gray teak sides carved in intricate patterns. The oxen yoked before it turned big, smug eyes upon Fred and one of them shat decisively.

"Go on then, come on up inside, what are you waiting for, Paunch?"

A young woman with long, spiraling bronze coils of hair leaned out of the wagon, pointing vaguely at its outer wall. Fred considered how he ought to scale it; tentatively he set one foot upon a wheel spoke, took hold of a carving, and began to ascend— when without so much as a glance at him, the woman flipped a sharp heavy set of stairs out over the side of the wagon box. Only Fred's training in acrobatics prevented him from getting hit by this supposed convenience. The woman paid him no mind. She bustled about inside the wagon, cursing vehemently at no one in particular. At last she emerged holding a length of rope. "Come on, Paunch. Up the stairs, on the box with me and I'll drive 'em with this." She flailed the rope, not particularly skillfully, and its end sang. The oxen gave a sharp snort and began moving.

"Uh, Maroo said you aren't supposed to whip the team."

"Maroo, is it? Oh, ho. Are you Medame's latest lover? Just kidding. I mean, look at you." She swung the rope again. "And look at this, Paunch. This *rope* look like a *whip* to you?" She popped it at Fred, just enough to scare him. "Ya got any money?"

Not yet, thought Fred, but he shrugged and said, "Why?"

" 'Cause. Whattaya wanta bet that he's gonna—" she jabbed her finger to indicate a scribe, riding a donkey not twenty feet away from them. Then she waved the idea away. "Eh, never mind. Anyone can see ya haven't got half a brass."

Fred exhaled sharply. Once, he had worn fine velvet motley, sewn by his own personal tailor. He'd had his hat, and a queue wig made from the mane of a golden vicanna. His hands had been as clean and smooth as any donkey-riding scribe's. Cleaner.

"Tell ya what, Tub: I'll spotcha this one. Betcha that fellow says 'dammit' before you can count to three. If you can, I'll give you a silver coin. If you can't—" she winked and spat her minty-smelling maidenroot all the way over the first yoke of oxen "—you'll give me a kiss that burns your tongue."

"You're on." Fred didn't wait for her to get ready. "One..."

The woman's hand flashed out of her pocket and before Fred could even say 'two' a cube of unchewed maidenroot had hit the scribe right in the forehead. "Dammit!" he exclaimed, glaring, and the woman laughed so hard she nearly fell off the driver's seat.

Fred laughed, too. It was a good trick. But of course, he hadn't been tricked quite so horribly. Because, well, for all her scary ways... "You need to pay up," he half-whispered, in the voice he used when he played the Handsome One in theatricals. He knew some tricks, too.

She closed her eyes and leaned toward him. Fred closed his and did the same, opening his mouth a little, enough to give her a taste of his *holy hells I'm on FIRE!*

The woman rolled back and forth on the wagon seat, breathless with hilarity and holding up the cut half of a tiny, bright orange pepper overflowing with spicy white seeds.

Fred leaped off the wagon seat. It was higher than he'd expected and he landed on his knees in the mud— not the kind of properly turned vault he would normally have insisted upon, but the blaze spreading around his lips and down his throat and even into his nose had distracted him. He wiped his nose, accidentally touched his eye and cursed in pain as it watered. He stood up and took a step. One of Lumpy Lettie's ridiculous boots stayed behind, stuck in the mud. So Fred pulled his foot out of the other boot and, keeping dignity intact as best he could with his toes squelching, his eyes smarting, and his nose running, he turned and exited the road barefoot.

In the distance, across what looked like broad flowery meadows, stood some kind of shiny building. It could only be Whellengood Hall, so he made for it at an indignant, long-stepping walk, with the woman Nadima's laughter raining upon his back like arrows upon an ignominiously retreating enemy.

CHAPTER 10

For just how long Dame Elsebet had been riding, she could not say. The horse might have told her, for horses told her plenty of things— the sort of things they happily tell anyone whose mother set her in a saddle before she could walk, and for whom the smell of their coats and the sound of their grazing is life's own scent and sound. They tell their news with words made of touch, with movements, with warmth and breath, with stares and glares and gentleness. But horses do not understand minutes and hours, so Dame Elsebet could not know precisely for how long she had wandered, carried on the back of one of her numerous herd, without bridle or saddle or hope.

At first the horse had been frightened, of course. To be taken abruptly out of his stall, in the black-sky darkness where he still smelled rain, with the owner whispering harshly to the groom and leaping up upon him with no warning and no idea where they were going— that was frightening. Horses know when there is no plan, and there is nothing as terrifying as having no plan. Soon the horse realized it was upon him to decide. And so they wandered.

Timidly at first, because in the night lurked gruesome possibilities: lions, longwolves. But the grounds they walked were familiar, the footing below soft and wet; fur-foot monsters did not often hunt in the wet and so the horse slowly grew more bold. He explored the places he liked best, where there were delicious crisp leaves and grasses and those trees from which fruit sometimes fell. A few times he asked the herd whether they were still all right: he shouted back to them, snug in their barn, so loudly that his belly tucked up and his sides rattled and the owner lying on his back making those sad sounds was nearly shaken off like a fly. The herd had answered, far away and softly, so it was all right. The horse went on.

He walked while the sky turned gray, then pink, then pale blue, until the Big Light showed itself once again from the Early Side and the early air began to flow. The featherbugs came out of hiding, swooping up and down the sky and exclaiming in their peeping voices. One of the horse's friends came cantering out, wearing a groom. The horse nickered at his friend, but could say little more, because upon his back the owner shouted go-away with her arms and so his friend who was wearing the groom went home. Then it was quiet again, except for the owner's sad sounds, and for another long time they wandered, grazing slowly up a slope to a place where the horse knew the ground fell sharply away and riding ended. He grazed near the edge.

There!

His ears snapped forward and he dropped to a crouch, trilling his breath in alarm. The owner sat up. Down below the edge of the lawn there was noise, human noise. The horse shied away from it and turned to run, but then he felt the owner saying no. He asked why not. Her body replied that it was her decision now, and that he should go back and have a look, and that she would answer for it if anything went wrong. Reluctantly the horse agreed.

"I'll go! I'll go! I'm going now! Just, please— point those somewhere else!"

Dame Elsebet looked over the edge of the massive retaining wall, with a deep drop below it, that separated Whellengood from uninvited persons. Two of the archers who patrolled the grounds stood ready to fire upon... Ye Gods be praised.

"Ladies," said Dame Elsebet. Let him go."

Below her, the red-eyed barefoot monk raised his weary head in gratitude, and Dame Elsebet's heart filled, filled, filled and overflowed with wonder. Tears began to drip down her cheeks.

"You are here," she whispered. "You have come. I prayed all night to the Great God Almighty, and it heard me."

"What?" yelled the monk. "I didn't quite catch that."

"Silence!" hissed an archer. But Dame Elsebet had dismounted from her horse, wiping her face and saying to bring this fellow up. So the archers escorted Fred to a place where the stones of the wall formed a well-hidden narrow stair. Sweet-smelling thyme and rock roses crushed under his muddy feet as he climbed. At the top, the old woman met him.

"You have come," she said, taking his hands and holding him away from her in admiration, as if he were a child that had grown surprisingly big.

"Uh, yes. Yes, I have." The canvas bag hung reassuringly in its place and Fred decided not to mention it until he had some idea how much money he ought to suggest as an appropriate reward. Only then would he ask this old woman to show him to her mistress, the Domina de Whellen.

"You have been weeping."

"Again, you are correct." He studied her. Long white hair in tangled braids, weatherbeaten face, a naked horse following her around as a companion... Fred decided she must be a garden hermit. At that time it was very fashionable to have a garden hermit; usually it was an old scholar who'd agreed to grow out his hair and beard and live on the grounds in some sort of hut or grotto. The King had had four of them; sometimes when no one else was around, they would share their brandy with Fred and complain about the state of their grottoes. A female hermit would be just the sort of odd twist he expected from the Whellen Country. Maybe she wasn't a scholar, but more of a faded-glory warrior. That made sense; the archers *had* listened to her. "My, uh, dear lady of the sword—"

“Lance, twinstaves and broadspear, actually. I have never been truly adept with a sword. But let us not discuss sport, good brother.” She indicated the horse. “Will you ride or walk?”

“Walking’s good. I… say, is he going to bite me, or..?”

“He wishes only to smell you. Ah, see how he sniffs at your tears… how he recoils from them. Truly, horses are wise. He senses something is wrong. Perhaps he, too, longs to know what awaits.”

“Aha. See, about that…” Fred stopped himself. It was too soon to have this discussion. He fell into a mock distraction: think, think. She had called him “brother”. Roll with it. “…I shall not speak of, uh, divine portent until the time is right. I mean ripe.”

Was *ripe* more monastic? Fred couldn’t really remember. He’d only been a kid, after all, and— if he was being brutally honest with himself— never going to make it as a monk. He had demonstrated no religious inclination at any level; most boys passed their novice exams on the first or second attempt, but Fred had struggled fruitlessly for an unheard-of nine, his fingers forever stained with ink to no avail. Instead, he had pacified himself by performing japes and stunts and follies, until one day Ata Maroo was sent to fetch him away from the monastery altogether.

They reached the stableyard, and the hermit woman opened a gate for the horse, which bucked for joy as it raced to the barn. She waved weakly to a groom and turned away, pressing her back to the fencepost. “Let us not go in. Not yet. Please, tell me about the messenger.”

“Well,” said Fred, feeling his way along, unwilling to say anything that would lower the value of the bag nestled in hiding beneath his folded arms, “what do *you* think?”

“I fear he has met with an ill fate.” She set her jaw, clenched her gloved hands together and looked off at who knew what. Her face is good looking though, thought Fred. A little bit of the crazy eyes, but dignified— probably the de Whellens were able to get someone of noble lineage for their garden hermit. Some disgraced vassal, probably. You'd have to be pretty hard up if you were vassal to a pack of conspirators.

"...destroyed the great tree," she was saying. Gods, these hermits did love their trees.

"So I'm hearing that you're really worried. About a tree, about fate." She was nodding, yes, but Fred was running out of material and he had to make a move soon. He went with the messenger angle: "Worried about that Yondy fellow. The goofy-looking tall skinny one."

"Yes, yes! You have seen him in your visions!"

This was encouraging. "Oh, I did indeed. I saw him lying on the ground, unable to speak. He— he— was poisoned and the message was stolen."

The old woman gave a gasp of horror and covered her mouth. Wow, thought Fred, this is going to be some score. He wound up for the big finish. "What do you think, good lady of the, uh, broadspear? What would the ruler of this country give a fellow who brought her the message that this messenger could not?"

"Why, I would give you all that it is in my power to give!" she cried. "I would take you in, just as I took Doktor Lively in when he was a broken-spirited wandering holy man just like you! You must know how I cherished him, how I nurtured his learning, how I helped him train up his powers, until he became what he is now: the only magical healer that walks this Earth! Ask it, good Brother, ask it and I shall give it, only tell me... tell me if he is safe!"

Fred's head swam. "The messenger? He's safe. Kind of retching a lot, but..." *and what did this old woman mean by 'I would give'?*

"Not him! I mean Doktor Lively! Is he safe? Is he on his way?"

Fred decided he was out of his depth. "How about this, lady. If Domina Dame Whatever has, let's say, twenty golden coins, you can tell her I know where the bag is."

CHAPTER 11

For the criminal element of Coastwall, day and night are neither here nor there. Like everyone else in that maritime city, they go by the tides; stolen items and kidnapped persons, forgeries and corpses and codes, all appear and disappear on the schedule of the sea, as likely to be hidden from the sun as from the moon. Doings that in other cities took place only on the darkest, most inscrutable nights, might happen before lunchtime in Coastwall.

Also confounding the clock is the fact that certain Coastwall warehouses are always dark. Their windows have been painted over and their doors are kept solidly shut. The owners of such buildings say they specialize in the storage of delicate dyes and fleeting herbals— that the sun degrades them— or else simply that their patrons are discreet. But then again, it is well known among the fancy that some of these places have helpfully crooked owners; that the strong-arm folk at the doorways know the face, walk, voice and scent of every pig in Coastwall; and that for a price, approved persons can visit these timeless places, quite sure of being undisturbed.

Doors rolled open and rolled shut. Two lanterns flared. Two pairs of criminals faced one another in the gloom.

It appeared they were preparing to duel: one of each pair was clearly a subordinate, a kind of second. The lanterns were small and the seconds held them low. Neither crook really wanted to recognize the other, though they were in fact very well acquainted. One was a woman shaped like a potato; the other was a man colored like a ham. At last the man broke the silence.

"I'm sending it over." His voice was small in the long, dark distance.

The woman thought about it for a moment, then gave a nod to her second.

The crooks' lackeys crossed the warehouse, stalking by one another with glares in passing, like two dogs getting their backs up. Soon each was standing behind his principal's opponent, with knife drawn in case of treachery.

The man's lackey handed the woman a plain cotton bag. She reached inside and drew forth a plain pewter drinking can. She glanced at the man; he nodded; she held the can to her ear and his voice rang out, sharp and close, from within.

"You see I am true to my word."

The woman gave a pout and a slow nod, impressed. She put the can to her lips.

"Me hat's full off, O Gentleman. Benny prize, these articles. But how? A course, thaz na got to say." At the other end of the warehouse, the man's head moved; she could tell that her voice had leaped the gap between them. From her own can issued his reply.

"I don't mind bragging just this once. That strongbox affair at Brewel Hall stirred up some perfect cover. The place was just crawling with law— every pig who ever carried a truncheon must have been there. So who'd notice an extra one? Nobody, that's who. I switched the goods and hiked before the Grand Constable ever set foot in the place."

The woman gave an admiring chuckle. Again she spoke into the can. "Well done. But these goods, as tha calls em, these articles: thez much too well known to hit the platter within three hundred league a here. Benny luck that me buyer's further away."

"Where further?"

The fence's growl was so fierce the thief hardly needed the can to hear it. "Neh! Think I'm some kind a cork-brained oaf, dez tha? Jus' decoration? Might go ahind me back? Never, me benny wight!"

The seconds heard her tone and they grew agitated, saw one another glinting their knives, stared pleadingly at their masters. The thief soothed the fence with a gentle whisper.

"Nay, dear, ease yourself. It was just an idle question. The ship, the dock, the day— none of it's my business. Just tell me where to be when it's time."

"Word'll come the usual way," replied the fence. Then, giving the can's tame gray surface a respectful caress, she slipped it back inside the bag. The seconds crossed back to their principals. They doused the lanterns, and everyone vanished.

CHAPTER 12

IT HAD TAKEN FRED A few more moments to realize who the hermit woman was— and some pretty fast talking for him to convince her that the gods *did* sometimes forget to tell saviors just who it was they were supposed to save. Coming on the heels of such jabber, his suggestion of twenty coins as a reward had fallen quite flat.

"Ten?" he asked hopefully, when he dared to bring it up again. "Or, what do you say we make it silver. Do I hear twenty silver? Fifteen?"

"Good brother, are you testing me?"

"No! Uh, maybe?"

"If I gave you even the smallest coin, just to leave me and never speak of this again, would you take it?"

"Honestly? At this point I probably would."

Dame Elsebet smote her forehead— that's definitely smiting, thought Fred, that's really the only word for it— and exclaimed: "Then I have passed your test, good brother! I would never, *never* buy my freedom from the sacred responsibility I have toward my people! Terrible though that omen was, and fearful as the thing I must do may prove to be, I will be brave. Very well, then. Bring forth the message bag. You safeguard it beneath your vestments, I've noticed."

With a sigh Fred brought out the bag. In his mind, a pile of unspecified coins buzzed away like flies. He opened it and watched Dame Elsebet fish out the wad of mangled papers. Their eyes met and she patted his cheek sadly.

"Good brother, please do not feel I wrong you when I say this, but I prefer that someone other than yourself read these to me." Her tanned face turned a bit red. "It's not that I have reason to doubt you, but... this world is filled, I understand, with tricksters, impostors, opportunists. When I had those, those *years* of mine..." Her eyes fluttered closed. Fred had no idea what she was referring to. "...it is a miracle that no such... exploitative malefactor rose up against young Lorenz. I have forever remained on my guard, for *traitors*."

Dame Elsebet pronounced that last word with a strangely passionate emphasis. Fred heard the leather of her glove creak against her knuckles as she gripped the papers. She looked away from him and suddenly she seemed quite small. "Although to be honest, I am not sure I still possess the strength I would require to deal with a traitor."

"So... back to these," said Fred, gently peeling the papers from her grip. "Who do you want to read them to you, then? Young Lorenz?" whoever *he* was.

"Oh, no! Certainly not! No, I do not wish to burden him ever again. He already has his doubts about my plan to send Doktor Lively. Let me think... I have it. We shall ask my major-domo." She smiled a little. "I have a lever I can use on him, with which to swear him to complete secrecy."

From a tower beyond the barn, a bell rang and Dame Elsebet said: "Oh, blisters. If I don't go to my daily practice Lady Verocita will be on me with a thousand questions. Come, I will send her away, and the gentleman will meet us in the exercise salon."

JUST ENTERING WHELLENGOOD HALL ROCKED Fred's mind. He could not have been more in awe if he'd been practicing for it. *Damn me deep*, he thought, letting his awestruck gaze slide up the arrow-straight, sky-high walls of the clearest glass he'd ever seen, circle around shining pillars of some metal that looked brighter than silver, sweep across floors as smooth as calm water. Well, the Royal Palace had glass, and it had floors, he'd give it that much, but this... he had to tell himself that he was supposed to be a man of the gods, dammit, used to seeing the magnificence of the Divine— so he should stop goggling at everything. And then Dame Elsebet had apologized, saying there was no time to show him the *impressive* parts.

And of course the exercise salon was not a gymnasium. Fred wasn't even sure why he'd imagined it would be— after all, noblewomen exercised with steel. It was a combat arena, fully equipped with sand and benches and racks of weapons, and it was absolutely full of monsters.

The heads of monsters, stuffed and mounted, tiled three gleaming walls from floor to ceiling. They were the fiends that Dame Elsebet had sought and fought and bested, back when she was but a young maiden: firewyrms, ten of them, with razor-sharp scales and a multiplicity of horns, their once-flaming maws now wired firmly shut; fennemums and meldragores by the dozen; the dread ramphaleon; twenty bat-serpents, and a bhabairus with coiling tusks so long they transpierced its own brow. The most esteemed quarry of all was not there, of course— the nullicorn must not be slain. But Fred imagined that she had probably seen a score of them, that she'd sat in some forest when she was a virgin maid and they had walked right up and put their curling beards straight into her hands, and that Whellengood was the way it was because she'd been granted so many wishes.

Fred was studying an extremely terrifying and lifelike mount of a gorgriffin, about to ask Dame Elsebet whether it had really turned the feathers on its crest into stone and hurled them at her with its tail, when two people joined them. One was a knight: even though she wore a simple robe in place of mail, there was no mistaking her height, width and calm hardness of expression. The other was a man, a smallish gentleman of rigorous bearing with a geometrically perfect black wig and a pair of round spectacles.

"You have sent for me, Medame?" asked the gentleman in a voice much like his nose—sharp and to the point. This displeased the knight. "Wait your turn, Nick," she groaned. "You heard the bell. It's Medame's practice hour."

"Lady Verocita, I fear we must postpone our— oh, for all the heavens' sakes. Please don't give me those puppy eyes. Oh, very well. Set me up *one*, good lady, and that will be all for today. All."

While the knight bustled off to some cabinets against the far wall, Dame Elsebet put her hand on Fred's back and pushed him toward the gentleman, who looked him up and down and didn't have to say a single word for Fred to know exactly what he thought of dirty, muddy-footed threadbare monks. Dame Elsebet gestured at Fred. "This is brother... brother..."

"Malfred."

"Just so. Brother Malfred has brought me word of the messenger who has gone missing."

"He is no longer missing, Medame. I have sacked the fellow. He arrived empty-handed, stinking of liquor, asserting vehemently that a bird stole his bag and that he was unaccountably delayed while seeking to report it." The major-domo glared directly at the bag under Fred's arm. "*This* fellow most likely orchestrated the entire thing. Let me guess, Medame: he asked you for money."

Fred was about to deny it but Dame Elsebet spoke first. "He did no such thing, Nicolo. Now. I would thank you to read us these papers, and to speak of it to no one, or else I shall be forced to let it slip out that—" she did not have to stoop very far to glare into her major-domo's spectacles and whisper: "—you are really not as heartless as you wish to appear. I know you send severance pay, out of your own pocket, to the servants you sack. If I spread *that* around no one will be afraid of you anymore, will they, Nicolo Moktabelli?"

"You wouldn't!"

Lady Verocita stepped in among them. "The sheaf is ready." Into Dame Elsebet's hand she pressed a staff of wool-wrapped lacquered wood, which rose up and up over their heads and there terminated in a fearsomely long and wide, gently curving razor-keen blade. "And now, remember, Medame— hands *apart*. Faster isn't better if it means you miss." She mimed a few correct and incorrect strokes. Dame Elsebet ground her teeth together and vented an exasperated sigh.

"You see, she is perfectly relentless. A moment, gentlemen." Clutching the broadspear, with her teacher at her side, she stepped a few feet away. A tripod was holding up a sheaf of bundled wheat straws, roughly a foot in diameter. Fred was about to make some comment about "straw men" but it was swept away by a great, resounding grunt that burst from deep within Dame Elsebet's torso. In her hands, the staff and blade became a whirl of gleaming fury. Once, twice, three times a flare of reflected light swept past the sheaf, each time singing out a big, hollow note as though a huge harpstring in the air had been plucked— and a smaller noise, too, a crackling hiss like a serpent on fire. The sheaf remained perfectly still, until Dame Elsebet stepped away from it, wiping her brow. At that moment it fell from the tripod in three pieces.

Lady Verocita shook her head and turned pleading eyes upon her mistress. "Medame! You *must* let me set up a second sheaf, you simply must!" She ran to the pieces, held one up and pointed at it accusingly, as if she had caught it red-handed picking her pocket. "Your *kuaga-losha* cut was at least three inches short— it is your weak point, Medame, I am sorry to say, and unless you correct it immediately..."

"That will be all for today. The matter is closed. Leave us— I will clean this up."

Fred noticed the small smug look the major-domo shot the knight as she hurried away, muttering under her breath. But Dame Elsebet saw nothing; she was leaning on her broadspear, sadly contemplating the piece she held in the other hand, turning it this way and that to examine how her second cut had not, indeed, passed completely through the bundle of straw. Or was it straw? Fred craned his head and asked "What's that in the middle?"

"White oak," sighed Dame Elsebet. "It's supposed to represent bone. Or rather, the neck, if we're being specific." Her eyes met Fred's and they were weary and frightened. "Do you see what I meant? I no longer possess the strength to deal with a traitor. The *kuaga-losha* cut requires a certain bracing of the shoulders in order to develop the necessary torque, and without it I am afraid I wouldn't be able to complete the stroke that removes the head."

"Removes the head."

"Yes, the first and third strokes are ceremonial."

"Ceremonial."

"Yes. They punish the deranged mind and the depraved heart of the traitor, respectively. But if I botch the second stroke, why then..."

"Why then." Fred's skin had suddenly begun a most determined crawl, with a bonus cold sweat thrown in free of charge. When Dame Elsebet put her hand on his shoulder, he almost fainted.

The major-domo coughed politely. "Medame. You were assuring me that this, this Brother Malfred is delivering your message in good faith, and not simply holding it for ransom."

"Nicolo! How can you accuse him of such an act! Brother Malfred is here to help me. He knows perfectly well that simply to tamper with my business is a crime. It is endangerment of the realm, tantamount to treason—" They both turned to Fred in alarm.

"Nope, nope, it's nothing, my... my knees just gave out there for some reason."

My god oh Ye Gods oh Great God Almighty she might botch the stroke that takes off my head. Fred climbed shakily to his feet, unable to focus on anything but the message bag now in the major-domo's hands. Please let this end. Let him read that message and send me on my way. I don't need any gold, I don't need any silver, all I want is to feel the road under my feet and my head still on my neck.

In a hypersharpened blur Fred watched the gentleman open the bag. His neatly manicured hand went inside. He pulled the lump of papers out. He commented on its lack of a proper seal. He tut-tutted at the lack of a passenger manifest. This is a cargo manifest, Medame, he was saying, and has no proper authentication— why, anyone could have written it and anyone could have written oh my god.

Fred didn't know who had said oh my god. Was it him? His brain? No, it was the major-domo. He had really said oh my god and he was really taking off his spectacles and he was really looking up at Dame Elsebet and his face really had turned pale. "On the back," he was saying. "It's written in plainhand," he was saying. "It says, 'SEND HELP' ".

CHAPTER 13

SOMEWHERE OUT UPON THE MIDLAND Sea was a ship with the figurehead of an albatross, wings open wide, wings that swept back along the bow and merged unbroken with the long, long stripe of white that graced her sleek black hull.

The *Longwing* was a sweet sailer, narrow and deep, built strong to carry a vast press of sail. She was not comfortable, but she was fast, and though her crew was small, they knew their business.

At first the ship's owner had balked at the idea of so many passengers. The *Longwing* usually carried news out to the Warm Ocean, the Herb Islands, or even further; most of the time, passengers only got in the way. But he had been assured that these were not the sort who required comfort—they were knights, escorting an important gentleman to the Isle of Gold, and speed was of the essence. The day and time were especially fortunate, for the extreme strength of their outgoing tide. All was well. There was no reason to think anything would go wrong.

Yet someone monstrously wrong had stolen aboard among the passengers. Someone who put a knife against the captain's throat, demanding they sail immediately without sounding the slightest alarm, or else he would kill her. So they sailed, and before long he killed her anyway.

He gave no name, nor asked for any. Instead he invented names, such as the one he gave to the round-faced gentleman he called Sweetface.

Somehow, he had recognized Sweetface as a healer, and that amused him no end. He tied Sweetface's hands to a cleat, in order that the fellow not miss what was happening to the others in the sickbay. The sickbay, place of healing, where there were plenty of sharp things, and plenty of medicines that could just as easily be poison.

Before the screaming began, Sweetface had blamed the knights— *they should be protecting us*, he thought. But then he remembered the poison, and how the knights were nowhere to be seen anymore, and understood they would protect no one ever again.

Soon the sea around the *Longwing* was writhing with the massive forms of sharks and the sea-jackals that feed on their leavings. She no longer had her storied speed, nor any semblance of direction, nor much of a crew left anymore. She was only drifting, much as Sweetface was only waiting. Waiting his turn.

CHAPTER 14

"HOW MANY SANDWICHES WILL YOU wish to take with you, Medame?"

Dame Elsebet's major-domo was fumbling with butter, slices of bread, meat and marinated vegetables, heaped high on a hastily deployed portable table. His hands had clearly never held any implement other than a pen; he was the chief of Her High Honor's household staff, not a servant himself. Fred imagined Lumpy Lettie giving his a pop on the ear, for dropping a perfectly good slice of smoked mutton on the floor of Dame Elsebet's coach house.

"I don't give a pock, Nicolo, and unless you hurry up with them we won't be taking any sandwiches at all." She turned to examine the progress of a big hollow capstan, utterly stationary but whirring busily from somewhere deep within, that protruded through the limestone floor. From an opening on the side of this object emerged a stout, steadily rotating horizontal beam, and this beam in turn disappeared into a hole in the side of the handsome carriage before them. Like the capstan, the carriage was vibrating ever so softly. Fred found it unnerving, but the horses Dame Elsebet was harnessing appeared quite used to it. She patted the fourth horse's neck and rushed to pull a big lever on the top of the capstan. "Remember, you will speak of this to no one. Especially not to Lorenz. He would want to help me, and that will not do. He has a farm and two daughters and their families and his poor dear wife up North to look after."

"Yes, Medame," said the major-domo despondently, examining the lumpy asymmetrical sandwiches he had produced. "And what am I to tell your petitioner Medame Ata? She must have arrived by now. You were scheduled to meet with her at luncheon today, to discuss the railway..."

Now Dame Elsebet was rolling open the great double doors of the coach house; morning air flooded in and the horses pranced in their traces. "Pocks to the railway. Unless Doktor Lively is accepted, there will be no use for it. The moment Lorenz and I are underground, our people shall be thrown back to the Age of Flint! Every gearhouse on the Heart will be broken up, Ye Gods forbid! Tell her I am ill." She climbed onto the box of the carriage, gathered four sets of reins deftly into her hands and turned to Fred, who dawdled beside the still-humming capstan. "Brother Malfred, time to get in. Ladies!"

At her call, a pair of archers appeared. The major-domo barely managed to shove Fred into the carriage and slam the door before the horses sprang away. Sprawled on hands and knees on the carriage floor, even before he scrambled up onto the velvet seat, he could tell he was trapped. Left and right, each window showed him an archer in a jumpseat, ready to fire upon anyone who might try to attack the carriage— or escape from it. And the walls were covered with a crowded maze of interlocking cogwheels and driveshafts that he could almost feel clanking and twisting and shredding him between their teeth.

"No, no, no!" howled Fred, pounding the windows. The air was running out. The roar of the wheels was deafening, the sway of the springs uncontrollable. They were going to capsize like the dirty little boat that had taken him away from the Isle of Gold, only this time there would be no slightly bigger boat to pick them up. He would die here and they'd find a little twisted box in the road, full of cogwheels and arrows and his bones.

But then the carriage slowed down and the door flew open and by the time Dame Elsebet was beside him, Fred's lungs worked again.

"Should I sit with you?" she asked, and he managed to nod. A brief discussion between Dame Elsebet and the archers, and the carriage continued— as fast as before except that now, somehow, it was all right. The windows were just windows; one of the archers was riding post to guide the horses, and the other was up on the box; and the walls were just walls, whose placid meticulous fabric pattern was more soothing than otherwise.

"Do you want to talk about it?" whispered Dame Elsebet. Fred shook his head. "I have felt your fear and many others," was the last she said of the matter. She clicked something at the corner of each window and it slid down, letting a brisk breeze flood in and wash the last waves of horror away.

FRED DIDN'T SAY MUCH FOR a long time. Neither did Dame Elsebet. The carriage flew on and on, across farmland and through woods and up and down over hills, never slowing, and Fred realized that he had been daydreaming about vehicles on The Isle of Gold. The Isle had one large city and several smaller ones, and he had often travelled between these in carriages with wheels, and springs, and seats, and horses. The horses, he found himself recalling, had never gone this fast. Usually they had walked; at times they had trotted; once or twice he had pulled the stunt of whipping them up to a kind of scrambling gait, while certain people in the carriage cried out in fright— although Fred had never actually let it get dangerous, scab over it. He wasn't a madman. Whatever he had done, it was only ever in jest, and besides, certain people had it coming to them... suddenly Fred didn't like thinking about this anymore.

"How is it that the horses don't get tired?"

Dame Elsebet pulled a smoked-mutton sandwich out of a willow basket and considered it. "Would you eat half of this if I ate the other?"

"Sure," said Fred, and looked away when he saw that the knife she was using to cut it was the blade of her broadspear, which had been stowed in a neat sheepskin case.

"They're a breed that loves to run. But more important, this carriage has what my engineers call a booster mechanism." She wiped the broadspear clean with tea poured on a handkerchief and held the second half of the sandwich out to Fred. At first he thought he might actually not want it. But that was ridiculous. Of course he wanted it.

"The booster mechanism turns the wheels. So really, the carriage pulls itself. And whenever we're coming down hills, that restores its power. We bring horses because, first: running before the power carriage is excellent training for them and second: at some point, the mechanism *will* run out of energy— although every year my engineers tell me they're getting closer to making one which won't require horses at all."

That capstan back in the coach house, Fred remembered. It was what powered the carriage. So what powered *it?*

Slaves, he thought, frowning. She's probably got thousands of slaves, toiling away down in her dungeons— because after all, this woman is a de Whellen. She wants to remove your head with the second cut. Her people defied the King, or something, and how can anybody trust someone who defies the King? The actual king, of course, the old king wearing his crown and sitting slightly diagonally on his throne, drinking peppermint tea. That's the one you'd defy, if you were going to. Making certain people cry out in fright, just a little, wasn't defying. And neither was a perfectly understandable, fundamentally harmless, momentary outburst of... Fred decided he'd rather ask Dame Elsebet what powered the capstan.

"It is powered by something truly wondrous, Malfred, which you soon will see. The Heart of Stone is— oh!"

The curtains around the carriage window flapped wildly. An angry ball of feathers shot in through them and collided with Fred's chest. "Hoy! There you are!"

Before Corvinalias could say anything more, Fred swept him up in his hands and pushed his head under one of his wings. "Why, would you look at this! It's a magpie! So many stories about what good luck they are."

"I'd often heard the opposite," said Dame Elsebet doubtfully, but Fred continued: "...yes, how lucky it is for people to randomly come across a magpie."

Corvinalias caught on: during their travels, he had often helped Fred out by playing the part of his shill. He yanked his head free, shook it and began preening his crest back into place with one foot. "Good lady and gentleman, I am looking for my pet, who slipped away from me without so much as a word, the boilsore." Addressing himself solely to Fred, he continued: "You haven't seen my pet, have you? Took off while I was trying to find us some food... selfish mumping vagabond about your size..." Fred gave him a little glare to say he was selling it too hard.

Dame Elsebet hadn't taken her eyes off the window. She was holding the curtain back, searching for something. "I hope you're right about the luck, Malfred. We'll be needing it. You see, I have ulterior motives." She let the curtain fall back and wrung her hands together, looking away from him in embarrassment. "I brought you out here to help me do magic."

"Hocka, bocka, dominaka!" yelled Corvinalias. "I've conjured a magic bird. What fun!" He bounced from wall to wall, continuing in the guttural growl of another one of Fred's characters: "Is this black sorcery? Is it foul witchery from the deeps of all deepest hells? O No, ladies and gentlemen! It's only..." and again he changed characters, to the sassy patter of a fairground mountebank: "...health, my good friends! Health in a bottle, healing that's appealing! Got a scrape, lady? Got a scratch? Maybe your sweetheart gave you—"

"Shut up, bird!" snapped Fred. But he was too late. Dame Elsebet's face was red. Her mouth was a hard line, and the wrinkles around her eyes unsmiling. A lump rippled among the cords of her throat.

"I realize I am no Prophessor. I'm only an old woman, of the old ways and the old days. I mean, I used to, to, breach the lairs of firewyrms and slay them and bring back their heads, the way young damsels will do. That's all. I'm not learned, like Doktor Lively— he is the one who discovered that firewyrm saliva can be manufactured in a workshop, by the way— but never mind that. Brother Malfred, I need you for a simple reason: you can read. You can read a *spell*."

She glared at Fred, daring him to mock her, and pulled a scrap of paper from a pocket in her sleeve.

"Last night I did more than just pray. I took this from Doktor Lively's desk. I know many would call it ridiculous to suggest that a holy man touch magic— but Doktor Lively is a holy man too, and yet he is a great magician. He knows a spell, brother Malfred, that can heal any wound, no matter how dire." She raised her chin. "I see you don't believe me. But it's true, I swear it on the Heart of Stone itself. By the time most Doktors of Healing can staunch a mortal wound, clean it and paint it with herbs— it's too late. But if Doktor Lively utters his spell, why, the wound closes before your very eyes! Once an engineer cut his fingers off, repairing a saw. Well, we found them, strapped them in place with a bit of linen, Doktor Lively cast his spell and within minutes the gentleman's fingers were grown back on, tight as could be. If only we'd put them in the right order..." She shook her head. "But back to our present calamity. The Doktor was prepared for an emergency: he told me that if something—anything— were to go wrong, Lorenz should help me cast this protective spell." She held up the fold of paper. "Yet I dare not ask my precious only brother, who all but saved my life, to help me do such a hazardous thing. And so I have brought you."

Ah, thought Fred. So Lorenz is... wait, *hazardous thing*? He looked around for means of escape, but knew it was futile. He could hear the scraping and thumping of an archer's boots on the floorboards of the driver's seat.

To tamper with this woman's business is a crime. Endangerment of the realm, tantamount to treason. But can I really be a traitor, *per se*, if I'm not even a citizen of her country? Maybe she'll see reason and let me go... sure she will. Because old women who believe in spells are so reasonable.

The carriage jolted to a halt so abrupt that Fred nearly flew across into Dame Elsebet's lap. They had arrived in a gigantic valley where the earth slowly curved up around them, with the mountains of Yondstone away northward. In this valley, the sun flashed upon massive fins of salmon-pink limestone, standing upright among hundreds of odd pools and truncated creeks. The shadows between them were purple and cold; the ground was all of stone, worn into hoops and loops and bridges like steepled fingers. Everywhere, Fred could hear the lap and trickle of water. But there was another sound there too— so big, so deep, so low that it was no sound at all.

The horses capered at the edge of fear, held back only by their training and by the efforts of the archers to soothe them. The archer at the box reined them in and they walked, very slowly; abruptly, in a jingle of harness, the horses stopped dead and began pushing the carriage backward.

"Medame, we can't get 'em any closer," reported the archer who had dismounted from the near-side leader. She opened the door for Dame Elsebet. "You understand."

"Stay close to me, brother Malfred. Bird. Diannia." The archer holding the door nodded, but did not speak. No one spoke. Dame Elsebet alighted from the carriage, and Fred followed.

The moment the sole of his bare dirty foot touched the ground, he wanted to snatch it back. He wanted to jump in the carriage and get the smoking hollow hells out of this place. Because the ground was humming. Furiously. The sound that was no sound came up through his bones, and his heart was humming too, vibrating, dancing against its will to the note of a pipe as big as the world.

Among the strange pools and ponds they crept. There were stretches of stream where water showed itself through the stones, ran wildly for some distance, and then seeped away. There were waterfalls in every configuration. There were spouting jets and bubbling bowls. Still Dame Elsebet, Fred, Corvinalias and the archer went onward. The humming grew louder, louder, deafening, even though it never touched their ears: they could still hear the shrieks of eagles passing overhead, the play of the wind in the sparse bushes that grew here and there amid the pools. Dame Elsebet stopped walking and pointed at an empty place ahead of them.

There was nothing there but oh my great good oh.

There was a deep long cleft.

Shooting from a hole in the side of the cleft was water.

The water was a roaring jet broad as a barn door, straight as a mast, white as a bar of steel forgotten in the forge. On the cleft ran, arrow-straight, deeper, narrower, tighter— from both sides continually pouring jet after jet, each fiercer than the last, the torrents combining, magnifying, intensifying, all of them finally merging to form a single ray of inconceivable force, imprisoned within a limestone slot: the tail of a comet on earth.

Fred scrambled away from it so fast he fell back and started crab-walking on his hands. Dame Elsebet nodded. "People often react that way, the first time they see the Leet of the Heart."

"Leet. Leet." Fred dimly recognized the word. The ground under his hands was humming too. He leaped to his feet in horror and raced back to the carriage, where he found the humming wasn't so bad if he climbed up the side and cringed on the roof.

Leet. His brain took a break from its yammering to show him a pale image of the water mill back on the Isle of Gold. The little canal that collected water for the mill wheel, that was a leet. He laughed out loud, imagining the Leet of the Heart blasting away the wheel, the mill, or perhaps the entire Isle. What a blessing *that* would be.

Dame Elsebet joined him at the carriage, handed him up that little scrap of paper, and began telling him that the spell Doktor Lively had been working on would allow her to dive safely into the Leet of the Heart and bring back a stone of protection, which stone would embolden the bearer, cause villains to fall back in disarray, and smooth obstacles large and small.

"Back up, back up. This spell will allow you to get a what now?"

"A stone of protection. By allowing me to dive safely into the Leet of the Heart." Dame Elsebet stood away from the carriage and took off her shoes. She began untying her sash.

"Are you crazy?" yelped Fred, and she stopped as if he had hit her. A sick feeling swept over him. Frantically he pushed the feeling away.

"I am not crazy, sir. I *was*, once, I will grant that. But now I am only doing what I can. Ye Gods made us the way we are, sir, as you well know: the father reaches out to discover, the mother stands fast to defend. So while you gentlemen enjoy your pens and books and abacuses, the hand of a lady is shaped only to hold a weapon or a child. So be it. If that is all I have, that is what I give. And I cannot read this spell, sir, so I require your assistance. *I require it.*"

At Dame Elsebet's last words, the archer reached to her hip and drew out a broad-headed arrow.

"Let me see." Fred heard himself talking. He saw his hands take the paper. He watched them unfolding it and then he was laughing again, bitterly. This is ridiculous. This is hilarious. And why not? After all, I'm a fool...

"You mock me, sir?" Now he could hear it, unmistakably. The wound of madness, ready to reopen.

"Oh, no no no no. No, I do not. No. It's just..."

Just that this is my death warrant, Fred wanted to exclaim. It's gibberish. *Barking with zeal, the vixen jumped quickly on her foe. We have just quoted on nine dozen boxes of gray lamp wicks. My grandfather picks up valuable quartz and onyx jewels.* He'd read phrases like these before: back at the monastery the boys had copied them, over and over. They were pangrams— sentences that contained every letter of the alphabet. What you grabbed from that desk wasn't a spell at all, lady. It was a penmanship lesson. Guess you'll be chopping off my head, then! This trash here is about as magic as...

He stopped himself. It was as magic as he needed it to be.

At one time, a travelling conjuror who was getting very, very old had bequeathed to Fred the secret of his powers.

"Listen up, kid," the rheumy ancient fellow with the brightly dyed long mustache had told him as he stood in front of the Palace unpacking boxes of golden orbs, brazen monkeys and silken streamers. "There's only one thing about this business ya gotta know— all the rest of it is tecknick. Here's the fillarsaphy, kid." He'd paused for a coughing attack while young Fred, newly arrived at court and burning with ambition to prove himself, hung on his every word. "Misdireck 'em. You've heard that before, right?" Fred had nodded, staring at the old conjuror's hands as if they might do a trick spontaneously. "Well, misdireckin' means more than ya think. Marks are leery, kid. They're on to ya. They're not blind— but they've all got one blind *spot*. Who do they think will never trick 'em? Their own selves."

The old conjuror had nearly bent double with his next fit of coughing; Fred hid behind a brass-cornered trunk until it was safe and the fellow resumed: "When ya gotta force somethin' on a mark, kid, give 'em the eye heff see. That's writin', kid. Bet you never heard of no eye heff see." Fred nodded again, without saying that yes, he knew I, F, and C intimately, along with all the other letters. "Eye stands for Illusion. Heff stands for Free. See stands for Choice. Get it, kid? Ya give 'em a free choice. Ya let 'em think it was their idea. But that's just an illusion, 'cause you're the one runnin' the show."

Fred had to sell this, and hard. So he held the scrap of paper at arm's length, feigning the most extreme excitement.

"Medame, Medame! The gods truly did send me to you this day. I laugh only in my joy, that you did not attempt this alone. You would never have succeeded, you see." He leaned down from the carriage roof, making vast sad eyes of wisdom, and attempted to press his hand sagely against Dame Elsebet's shoulder. Instead he toppled off the roof in front of her but thank his god for all the long years of training that let him turn the fall into a tumble, a roll, a clever spring. Corvinalias whistled in admiration, so he knew it was really a good one. "Even if someone had read it to you, and you had memorized it, you would never have been able to cast this subtle, powerful, most impressive spell, for it is a cantrip." He leaned conspiratorially close to her. "Do you know what a cantrip is?"

"No."

"Good. I mean, very well. A cantrip, your High Honor, is a spell that may not be spoken. Rather, it must be written in the air." Again he leaned closer. "And furthermore, it says here—" Fred scanned his finger along the nonsense with great authority, murmuring until he reached the pertinent phrase— "it says 'the practitioner'— that would be me— 'the practitioner must fetch the stone of protection with his own hands; this cantrip applies to him and none other. The practitioner may also wish to inform interested parties that this cantrip has been known to fail, should the practitioner be watched as he executes it'."

"Great God protect us! Then of course I won't watch you! I won't let Diannia or Arremisa watch you, either. Ladies!" she snapped at the archers. "Leave us!"

Before the final coughing fit that sent him to the King's infirmary, never to return, the old conjuror had given Fred one further piece of wisdom. "Details, kid. The difference between a mark who says he saw a good trick and a mark who swears he saw his god's truth is usually one last detail."

So Fred let his workaday face set up shop as an anxious, pleading face and moaned, "But...unless you watch me, how will you know I really did it? How will you know I'm not tricking you? That I'm not....a traitor?"

He motioned, just one finger, to his shill. On cue, Corvinalias fluttered onto Dame Elsebet's shoulder. Her hand reached idly up and he stepped onto it.

"Brother Malfred," she said. "I just had an idea. Would the cantrip still work if the witness were an animal?"

CHAPTER 15

WHEN THEY WERE ONCE AGAIN back in the carriage, Fred sat with his arms folded, shivering slightly and holding back a grin of the most complacent pride. Corvinalias perched on Dame Elsebet's knee, giving her a long and detailed account of the vivid rainbow spangles that had followed Brother Malfred's magical index finger when he wrote the cantrip in the air, and of his daring plunge into the Leet of the Heart to bring back the chip of limestone she now held so reverentially before her.

In fact Fred had simply grabbed the first chunk of rock he dared to reach down and touch. He'd been halfway back to the carriage when Corvinalias had advised him to go back and at least roll in a puddle.

"Are you trying to sell this or not? You're supposed to have dived into a... a... what the three-ply hell is this awful Leet even supposed to *be*?"

"I don't know and I don't care. There. Am I wet enough now?"

"You look like a gutter bug! It's perfect."

UP, UP THE BLUFF AND away from the Leet of the Heart the power carriage flew. The booster mechanism had kicked in with a vengeance; the horses were hard pressed to keep up with the whirring machine behind them. Ticking rhythmically, the carriage pulled itself at an unflagging pace, snaking ever higher on a steep, narrow track whose zigzags would have made a mountain goat uneasy. At every turn, the archers shouted to one another: the one at the box pulling on a lever that disengaged the power, the one riding post bidding the animals to slow down and take care. If Fred had had the smallest notion of how close the wheels were to the edge of the track, he would have jumped out the window and taken his chances, regardless of the sheepskin blade case on the seat beside Dame Elsebet and the wool-wrapped lacquered wooden staff strapped to the roof.

At last they emerged through a stand of narrow white trees with leaves that flashed and clattered like coins. Here Dame Elsebet leaned out the window and in a commanding voice she said "Whoa."

A stand of trees had been cut down to form an overlook, which was guarded by a low fence: simple stakes driven into the ground and joined by ropes. The ropes sagged under a thick pelt of ribbons, fabric strips, twine and wire and bits of chain. Dame Elsebet threw open the carriage door and pointed past them.

"Brother Malfred, you wanted to know the purpose of the Leet. Look: that is the mill wheel it drives. We call it the Heart of Stone."

Below them stretched the strange valley they had just left, with all its ponds and pools and pink limestone monoliths. Even from such a distance, Fred could distinguish the Leet: a perfectly straight white streak aimed directly toward the largest stone of them all.

This one towered over the others, standing apart from them, completely encircled by a small city of wood, metal and stone buildings arrayed there as densely as the bits of cord that smothered the fence. From the buildings radiated countless beams: beams of wood, made from the trunks of great trees, or from heavily painted iron. Or else there were canals, or cables stretched taut; these led to further rings of buildings, and onward to yet others; eventually the stoutest beams led down into holes in the earth, just as the beam of the capstan had entered the carriage. Corvinalias flicked his tail in bafflement. Fred shaded his eyes. Why all the construction? And then he saw it.

The shadow of a single stunted tree, small and wind-smoothed and ancient, growing in a crack some distance up the stone's lofty face, changed its angle. Fred glanced at the sun. The sun was still. But when he looked back upon the stone, his mind opened up and let the plain truth in: the stone was turning.

Slowly, ever so slowly, the shadows between the crevasses and striations on its huge high face were melting from shape to shape. As fluid as clouds, as inexorable as the tide. Dame Elsebet cleared her throat a little.

"Engineers work there, you see." And Fred saw. There were men in that city— not too many, but they were there: moving between the buildings, busy tending the beams, sending motive force to countless machines and onward to places unseen. Within him, some old and respectful voice said: *this is no slave. The earth gives a gift.*

"The Heart of Stone is why my people have all the things they do. It does the hardest work of life for them, so their spirits might have room to aim higher. They've tied those ribbons on the fence to thank the Heart— even written a song."

Her voice was bad, if Fred was being honest. It was rough and cracked and didn't hit the notes the way he could have hit them. But somehow, that made it better when she sang:

> " *'Heart of Stone, Heart of Stone,*
> *lend us your endless power.*
> *Long may your fierce blood flow.*
> *Ever giving, ever turning Heart of Stone.*
> *Fair may our country grow.'*

"Please do excuse me, Malfred. That always makes me cry. But. We didn't come here to stand staring— we must hurry to Coastwall. I mean to ask my cousins the de Brewels for help finding Doktor Lively: he alone can save the good works of my people from destruction."

CHAPTER 16

THE CARRIAGE CAME DOWN FROM the bluffs at a tearing pace and pulled up to a boathouse on the bank of the Greater Good River, a tributary of the Whellen. There another capstan was busy winding up the mechanism of a long, elegant rowing barge. Eight brawny oarmaids helped their mistress and her companions aboard, cast the craft loose, and began pulling the sweeps; but just like the horses, they had unseen help. Under the barge rotated a bronze screw that formed a ninth, and tireless, oar.

Fred paced and fidgeted under the awning of the cabin, watching as boulders of limestone, great waxy fir trees and meadows full of redflowers swept by. Soon they were flying past stony fields planted with herbs; then lush fields planted with crops; then towns bustling with people who gathered not only around public pumps and fountains, but around more of those capstans. Every town in the Whellen Country had them, big squat cylinders perforated with holes, into which people plugged all kinds of household machinery: Fred recognized coffee grinders, eggbeaters, spindles, drills— tools he's only ever seen powered by sweat.

Shortly before sunset they passed the winch ferry at Good Market. One of the oarmaids disengaged the screw and blew a long, loud bugle to announce their coming. As the maids guided the barge carefully past the ferry's cable, Fred found himself face to face with the crowd in one of the other boats. They were close enough for him to make a jump for it— maybe. But he took a moment too long imagining the consequences if he failed, and then the moment was gone.

Night drew in. Now they were in the patchwork of fiefdoms encircling the Brewel Country. No wyrmlight lamps brightened the gloom; instead there were only lumpen villages of fishers and farmers, the glint of an occasional lantern, the clank of a distant lonely cattle bell and everywhere a mucky, earthy stink. In the cabin, Dame Elsebet sat cross-legged before a low table. Her voice was small and tired when she asked, "Won't you have tea? In just a few more turns of the sandglass, we'll find ourselves very busy."

Fred did not reply.

"Come on, holy fella," Corvinalias burbled, hopping down from the awning onto his pet's shoulder. "Time for a little tea and meditation before things take off."

"You know very well what I don't want taken off," growled Fred, swatting at Corvinalias. The magpie squeaked, dodged, and fluttered to the table, there to walk among the teapot, the kettle, a small brazier and two perfect, simple cylindrical glasses. He turned his head to one side and stared into a lacquered box.

"Hmmm. Oola tips. Nice."

For a moment Dame Elsebet brightened up. "Birds drink tea?"

"I don't know," replied Corvinalias. "Magpies do, though. My father used to send for oola tips from— I believe you call that city 'Castra Mar'."

Dame Elsebet had been reaching out for the lacquered box, but her hand stopped in midair. "You are acquainted with the Isle of Gold?"

Corvinalias bent back to dip his beak into the preening oil at the root of his tail. He could not keep a touch of pride out of his voice as he smoothed his feathers. "Pretty well," he said. "I'm Corvinalias Elsternom e Rokonoma the Fourth— named for my uncle, Corvinalias the Third." When the name provoked no response in Dame Elsebet, Fred took notice and sighed inwardly. *Here it comes*, he thought.

"I mean, a *lot* would have to happen for me to become king. Uncle Cory would have to fall out of a tree, ha ha. And then a whole big long string of my other relatives too, before *I* could ever wrap my fingers around the throne." He coughed mildly and examined his reflection in one of the glasses. "Instead I've decided to go on adventures. It beats lying around at home drinking tea and scratching epic poetry."

Fred watched Dame Elsebet bow her head before Corvinalias. When he did it, it was a joke. But somehow this seemed very real, and very sad. "My title ends with me and my brother," she said, tracing figures on the tabletop with a drop of tea. "That is, unless the King takes my bribe." She smirked then, a cynical and bitter expression that looked all wrong on her kind, weathered face.

"Bribe?" peeped Corvinalias, raising his crest. "Shinies?"

"If you mean gold, Doktor Lively is more valuable by far. I can hardly bear to lose him. But you see, I will stop at nothing. Even though my ancestors had no intention whatsoever of starting that frightful war, I am perfectly willing to pretend they did, and to offer up my greatest treasure by way of apology. I will do whatever it takes to secure the King's forgiveness."

All of a sudden the sick feeling that had come over Fred earlier was back. Back with bells on. He knew there was nothing in the whole weeping world he wanted less than to ever again think about what had happened back on the Isle— he'd told Corvinalias rather he'd rather *rot in the deepest dankest hole of hell*. But those were just words. He hadn't thought the feeling would be this strong. His heart took some kind of diagonal step so its beating became scrambled, and the mutton sandwiches bulged up against the gateway to his throat.

Dame Elsebet lifted one of the glasses and stared into it. "But now this terrible message. 'Send Help'. Why? What's gone wrong?" Her glove creaked as she squeezed the glass. "I so desperately wanted to escort Doktor Lively myself. But he pointed out, quite rightly, that my presence would have ruined everything... yet now it's come to that. I cannot stay behind the scenes any longer." She turned to the queasy

Fred with a painfully wrought smile. "Thank Ye Gods for your help. You will be right by my side, brother Malfred. Together we'll find the Doktor, take him to the Isle of Gold, and kneel before the throne."

Her eyes went wide with alarm as she saw Fred turn and dash out into the night, up the lamplit bows of the craft, past the rowers. When she heard him start heaving she sprang to her feet, dropped the glass and ran out to him.

CHAPTER 17

Alvert was no stranger to rough conditions, having grown up in a land where falling into a crevasse or getting attacked by an eagle was a daily possibility. He didn't need coddling. But this new job— he hated it.

Oh, he knew he should be grateful to have a job at all. His Ma would have jumped up and cracked him right in the forehead wi' her shoe if she had heard of him not being grateful to the girl wi' the coily hair, who had barged right up to him as he'd sat a-weepin' in front of the major-domo's office at Whellengood. Barged up to him, seen his Private Delivery Operators' Guild contract wi' the great big ugly crossmark drawn through it, took that and tore it in half and told him to stand up straight, get on the march, she'd lost two internal couriers that day and besides, if he didn't come wi' her he was welcome to starve. Oh, he were right grateful for that, nobody get him wrong, and the swat she give his bottom didn't hurt that much at all. Ma had swatted much harder, when he deserved it.

But internal courier work was *hard*. It was like being bled to death by gnats. Some new chore every time you turned around— toting parcels back and forth from one wagon to the next — strange messages to remember like "break bulk on 22, consolidate 55, 101, 83"— all the while a-movin' down the road. No, all in all Alvert didn't think it was wrong or ungrateful simply to observe that it were a proper red-rimmed boil, this job.

But at long last, the sun lumbered down out of the sky. The horns blew, the bells clanged, the drums beat. The fleet drew to a halt three miles from a town known as Big Fair, and in the light of a campfire Alvert was confronted with more beef than he'd ever seen in his life. The teamsters around him demolished their mountains of charred, slippery slabs as if they were nothing. After giving his meal a spirited attempt, he had become staggeringly sleepy. He asked around about bunks and got nowhere, for the teamsters seemed to be more interested in throwing dice and dancing to a fiddle than in sleeping; so he had crawled painfully under a wagon, wishing the meat that clogged his guts could decide whether it was going to stay or go.

There were dogs under the wagon. Bugs, too. And bits of torn rope, broken crockery and rusted ox shoes. Alvert smoothed the lumpy earth, picked a few bent nails out of it and flicked them away before he tried lying down again. He had just managed to settle his bellyful of steak, fold his limbs into a bundle and close his eyes when some of the dogs around him shifted and whined. Feet crunched by the wagonside. A teamster's upside-down face appeared.

"Hoy, tallboy. Boss needs something. Your turn to go."

He stumbled through the camp, looking for Ata Maroo's private wagon. It sat apart from the rest of the fleet, protected by a pair of highcats that eyed him like sentinels, lashing their long spotted tails. The wagon resembled one of the ships he'd seen in Coastwall harbor: a gray hull under taut curves of canvas, rocking slightly in the sea of night. Alvert shambled to its high wooden side, where the steps were folded up, and knocked.

A ripple of male laughter came from within, but no reply.

Alvert felt around the side of the wagon for a bit. It wasn't clear at all how this here what's-it let loose o' the cart, and he had never been much of a one for machines or gadgets of any sort. From inside the wagon he heard more laughter, and the jingling of something made from glass. The latch of the steps abruptly let go and they fell into position, scraping down the whole length of his shin; for a while he stood screaming on the inside, and after the fiery crush of pain had died away he mounted the stairs and entered an arched, candlelit room.

There— under a huge embroidered quilt, among a wealth of embroidered pillows, in a gigantic rosewood bed— lay Ata Maroo. And beside her was a man: thick and handsome, clear as day a rich man.

The man laughed again and tipped the contents of a little sparkling cup into his mouth. He drew closer to Ata Maroo, to kiss her, but she turned her head to one side so that the rich man only kissed her golden cheek. Her eyes were as closed as fists.

"Keep drinking, make fool you self," she growled. "I invite you because I had bad day, not for—" but when she opened her eyes to see Alvert in the doorway, she yanked the quilt up high around her neck. "Aiee! Nadima hire *you?*"

The man surfaced from the pillows, holding an empty bottle whose faceted sides flashed as if it had been cut from a single giant diamond. "Is the courier bothering you, my treasure?" murmured the rich man. "Kick him down the stairs. I'll buy you a new one."

Ata Maroo snatched the bottle away from him and pushed her hand into his face, not unkindly. He tipped backward as if dead and laughed again, muffled in the sea of pillows. "No. I buy *you* more of this. Again. You want anything else?"

"No, my gem, my brilliant one. Only its fiery sweetness can compare with thine."

Ata Maroo sighed. "All right. You sweet tongue get you out of trouble." Before the man could enlarge upon this remark, she held the bottle out to Alvert, although she held her eyes away. "Stupid man, ah. You go to Big Fair and find shop call Copper Coil, tell owner I want more of this, put it on my bill." Then she bent down again, back to her lover sunk among the pillows.

The bottle was heavy crystal and Alvert was overcome with a furious desire to crush the rich man's forehead with it. It was a desire completely unexpected, wordless and wild, deep in his bowels like something alive. He fought his own hands to keep them from raising the bottle more than an inch or two, fought his legs to make 'em step down out o' the wagon and out onto the road.

For the first mile he didn't think. For the next mile he didn't shout. Finally, as he loped into the town of Big Fair feeling absolutely disembodied, he threw his head up toward the dark new moon and let loose with a torrent of every curseword he'd ever heard his Ma say, plus all the others he'd learned since then. The cursing felt good so he repeated it, with the satisfying addition of imagining he shouted it all into the rich man's face while Ata Maroo listened in delight. After a few iterations of this, he experimented with the thought of her tipping *him* into the pillows instead of the rich man, but this was too strange and embarrassing; his mind squirmed away from it, yet he couldn't stop poking at the thought, as if it were a scab or sore too painful to leave alone. Alvert was fully aware that none o' this made any sense, that he had no more right to think these things than he had to grab a star out o' the sky, but he was powerless to stop it. It was like watching an avalanche.

He was relieved to arrive at a shop with a sign made from a coil of copper tubing over its door.

"I'm just closing, good fellow," said the owner, who was moving about the shop with a candle snuffer. He gave a decisive nod, as if the matter were settled. But it was not settled. Alvert raised the crystal bottle and shook it menacingly.

"Medame sent me for more o' this. This exact drink. It's got to be this one, she's made her choice, what else did you expect!"

"Ah. Well then, I'll just stay open a few moments longer... "

Alvert crowded closer to the fellow. "Medame doesn't want to wait. She wants it right now, to share wi' her— her— flux-pumpin' bastard!"

"Oh. I see. Well, I can certainly hurry to..."

By now Alvert was nearly apoplectic. "She wants what she wants, because she's a fine powerful learned lady, and you're no one to her, just some clotty clump who ran into her bull— so be quick about it!"

In terror of the foul-mouthed, scrawny madman towering over him, the fellow darted away to a wall stacked high with casks. He sniffed the bottle's cork and quickly found the right cordial; he filled it and returned it with shaking hands.

"Bill it to me mistress!" roared Alvert, brandishing his left fist in the fellow's face. He realized too late that there was no seal-ring on his finger to prove the Ox-Train Queen employed him; but still it felt good to brandish a fist, and so he held it out for a few seconds longer before turning and leaping out the door.

On the return run, plagued by cringeworthy thoughts, he found himself breathing much harder than was wise. He stopped on the roadside and took a closer look at the crystal bottle.

Linkapaa. That's what it was in there, and that's what had been in the tea last night; it had tasted good, that was the trouble, so good he hadn't recognized it.

Back in his mountain village, no one sold alcohol— folks made their own, turning plums and such into *linkapaa*, a concoction that stung your throat and scoured your tongue, but was also good for sterilizing milk crocks, rubbing on wounds and starting fires. Everyone had heard tell about youngsters who drank the linkapaa they were supposed to be wiping down the cheese-hoops with, and oldsters who took a spoonful of linkapaa before bed and a cupful of linkapaa after the spoon;

sometimes such stories ended funny, sometimes sad. But linkapaa always made *something* happen.

Alvert wished something would happen to him. Right now. Anything at all, anything but to stand on the roadside feeling those strange overpowering gusts of unventable rage. He pulled the cork out of the bottle, sickened and excited by his sudden vision of the bottle's mouth as *hers*. He pressed it to his lips, parted them a little, and in rushed her coveted kiss.

It was sweet, like honey from a hive in the white birch forest, and had just as fierce a sting.

He did it again. And again. He discovered that it was entirely possible to gulp from the bottle and run at the same time. And so down the road he went.

Wouldn't the joke be on *him*, that rich blister back in the wagon, when Alvert showed up wi' nothin' in the bottle at all? And if he complained, wouldn't it be funny if Alvert beat the crusty reeking scabs off o' him? And wouldn't it be fine if the story ended with the Ox-Train Queen taking him— Alvert, now, not the rich blister— taking *him* in her golden arms and...

Whether it was from dizziness, or breathing wrong, or the weird feelings accumulating low in his belly, Alvert was finding it difficult to run. So he just trotted. And soon he couldn't trot, so he just walked. And soon enough he could hardly do that, which was all right because the moon was high over his head, the roadside was soft under his knees, and there was no more *linkapaa*.

CHAPTER 18

THE LATE-AFTERNOON SUN ON COASTWALL Harbor was blinding— a scorching color, far beyond white. The water was as crowded as the markets onshore, and ships' owners and their crews all seethed with impatience: the authorities had announced a ban on travel. Valuable cargo sat waiting, as time and money ticked away; passengers were distressed at the ruin of their plans; it was infuriating. But Dame Irona and Donn Felip wanted it thus, and what the de Brewels wanted, Coastwall did.

At a mooring floated a small, elderly round carrevelle upon whose stern was carved the figure of a little dog shaking an alarmingly oversized rat. Most people knew the vessel was called the *Terrier*, but there were always those who misunderstood and instead called it the *Big Rat*. The crew didn't really mind— in fact, *Big Rat* seemed to suit them better. They did transport legitimate goods, when anyone wanted it done, but the Terriers' special skill lay in finding creative ways to insinuate stolen items into the cargo. The crew plied this trade right under the owner's nose; he was an uncommonly dim old fellow, and had never asked for one brass penny, which proved he didn't know a thing.

"Hoy, anyone aboard not feeling well?" one of the Terriers called out, turning back from a good long look over the side. The rest of the crew grunted, snorted, or shook their heads. The sailor who'd spoken spat a gob into the harbor and with a sneer in her voice she addressed someone down at the waterline.

"You must have the wrong barky, Dok. Everyone here's fighting fit."

Down in the little boat, a plague healer tipped back his broad hat and appeared to glare. Of course this was only an impression; the healer's face was completely invisible behind his mask and goggles, and he said nothing. But he seemed determined to come aboard.

The plague healer passed his cane to the enormous servant rowing the boat, and bid her knock on the Terrier's side with it. Above them, the sailor set her jaw and yelled, "All right! All right! Keep your louse-pickin' britches on. I'll get the skipper."

The Terrier's captain was a man, a hardy and crafty-looking man who flattered himself that he was clever: if not for circumstances, he might have had education, might have owned a ship rather than merely commanding one. And so out of respect for learning, the captain ordered a rope sent down. The plague healer and his enormous servant scrambled up.

"Well, Doktor," the captain began. "I think you'll find that..."

But instead of replying, as one learned gentleman to another, the plague healer began an unhurried stroll about the deck, just as bold as you please, craning his masked head into all the places nobody ever ought to look.

The captain was baffled. Certainly, men of wisdom could be eccentric and spare with words. But surely the gentleman would be more interested in examining the sailors' tongues and toes and armpits than gawking about the ship like a deep-damned customhouse pig.

"We've got no illness here, Doktor. Oh, a couple of the hands may have had bad maidenroot foisted on them and will have to whelp a brat or so, given a few months. But nothing in *your* line."

Now the healer's searches had become shockingly intrusive: he had discovered many of the hiding places the captain prided himself on. And still he hadn't spoken— gave off, in fact, a strange aura that made others loath to speak. The captain stepped in front of his lumpy, ovoid figure.

"Tell me who you are and what you want aboard my ship."

"Neh! This barque ain' yours, me gentleman. It's mine. I bought it."

"What?"

"Bought it, and bought all a *you*."

"Well, I suppose there's no law against a healer dabbling in another line of business. You know, if things had been different I might have been an owner, too. I can read figures just as well as anyone. But listen, Mesir: the old Terrier's hold is none too big and we don't ship much cargo. If you're imagining you can become a big fellow in the merchant line, with only..."

"Hush it shut, me gentleman. I know jez what this benny little tub can haul. Like what went inside a certain hollow spar las' week. I ain' got to say more, neh?"

"Well now, if *you* aren't well informed! So you want a cut of our side business, eh? Just how much do you expect me to give you?"

The enormous servant had been looking at the horizon, but now her head spun toward the captain, upon whom it was dawning that the plague healer's voice— a harsh and gritty tenor— was strangely like the voice of a crone. A chill ran up his back. Suddenly he knew who was behind the goggles and the mask: "Granny" Almantree, whose withered hands kept a stranglehold on the world of stolen goods, smuggled goods, secret corpses, vanished persons. The kind of thing he'd just said might get him packed in a cask and shipped to the bottom of the sea. Before the captain could repair his words, the healer gave a wheezing chuckle and pulled one corner of the goggles aside. The sharp, dirty-green eye revealed there looked as if it had never blinked and never would.

"Tha gez me nothing, me wight. It's *I* decide what to gi' *thee*. Today I let ye mouth off to Granny— jez this once."

The captain swallowed hard but didn't speak. Granny Almantree carried on: "It's fair small bits thaz been hauling till now, me mouthy wight. But this barque has a benny quick way about goin' to the Herb Isles, and that caught me weeper. I know yez waitin' to load cargo. Load it then, keep on. But the minute it's aboard, y' cut and run for the Herbs. Those are me orders. Understand 'em?"

Before she took the rope and climbed back down into her boat, she pointed at the enormous servant. "I'm leavin' me extra pair a weepers behind. She ain' never slept a wink in 'er life an' she's strong as ox, sly as fox. Bet tha dezen even know she's got at least ten weapons on 'er. Don't try and learn where."

"But the blockade!" cried the Captain after his new owner. "All ships are forbidden to leave port. How can we—"

"Thick hot weeping sores on the blockade," growled Granny Almantree. "When I sez go, thaz gone."

The Captain seemed unable to control his speech. As if by itself his tongue began to form a sentence: "But what is it we're—"

The enormous servant stepped forward and with a single soft shake of her head she reached out to cover the Captain's mouth. "Do me a favor and don't pry, huh? Whatever it is, it's probably aboard already, and that's more than you oughta know. I sure would hate to hafta fling your head over the port side and the rest of you over starboard." She stretched lazily, broad slabs of flesh rippling, and gazed down at the captain, who seemed to have shrunk quite dramatically. The hot sun burned on the deck, and the Terrier's crew— who couldn't have helped overhearing everything— drooped like melting wax. The enormous servant folded her arms and half-closed her eyes. "Go on about your work," she said. "Forget I'm even here."

CHAPTER 19

Dame Irona de Brewel was nearly ready for bed. The maid who buffed and anointed her forehead traded friendly little jokes with the ones who cared for her cheeks, nose and chin; the tea she paused to sip through a sweet rye straw amplified the pleasant flavor of the paste with which her teeth had been cleansed; and her nightgown was in readiness, hanging on the dress form in its customary place so the delicate waft of incense could permeate its carefully pressed folds. In short, a perfectly ordinary evening.

Dame Irona's maids dressed her and unrolled a velvet runner before her so she could stroll across the room barefoot. The Domina maintained that spending time each day barefoot was of vast importance; the sense of texture must not be neglected, as it was the basis for all true experience.

She approached the bed platform and strode up its upholstered steps three at a time. In summer the platform was not heated; instead the attendants beside it plied their palm fronds busily, stirring up a comfortable breeze. For a few moments Dame Irona crawled about the expansive structure on hands and knees, finally choosing one particularly dark and cozy spot from the mosaic of mattresses and coverlets spread there.

"Are you finished listening to that music, darling?" she yawned to Donn Felip. "You know I can't sleep if it's playing."

"Of course." Donn Felip rose from his pillow and gestured to the orchestra; they picked up their instruments, bowed and filed out of the room. All was peace.

But after a few minutes, Donn Felip spoke up. "Do you know, Rona, I think it's quite odd that Elsie's deputation still isn't here."

"Wha? Mmmm?"

"Cousin Elsie's people— that healer gentleman and his escort party. They were supposed to come here, stay the night, then board some ship or other. *I* haven't seen them. Have you?"

"Well... no. But my maids did give a very amusing account of someone who stayed in the servants' dorm recently. They said 'he looked like a miser's greyhound, swore like a sailor's parrot, and smashed the doorframe all to flinders with his great big shaven head'! Isn't that just pure poetry, darling?"

"Indeed. But back to the original question— why have we not seen these people? It's baffling. Tomorrow, I'll send a message to Whellengood."

Dame Irona lay watching the palm fronds flap overhead, but with a squeal she jerked bolt upright. It was enough to send a ripple through the mattresses and coverlets, and to make Donn Felip grunt.

"Felip!" She cried. "I just had the most frightful thought! What if that cursing parrot fellow was the one who stole the notes?"

"Impossible. Guests' servants are watched like... like a navigator watches the stars."

"But if we haven't had any guests, then who smuggled in this servant?" Her tone was triumphant.

"Sweetheart. Of course we've had guests. Why, plenty of them are here right now— Petey and Kiki's friends. The Marchess de Ponto's half-sister. That philosophic Doktor with the funny hair. I keep urging you to pop in for supper and meet them."

"Oh! That doesn't make me feel any better at all! Any one of them could be a villain with a cunning plan!"

"My dear. You *have* been commissioning too many theatricals."

"Art simply holds the mirror to life, Felip, you know that. Oh, it's all so obvious now! What if one morning we wake up murdered, darling?"

"Now, that is quite enough. You are simply frightening yourself with nonsense." Donn Felip's words were decisive, but his tone did not reassure Dame Irona.

"I'm going to call the Grand Constable," she said, and seized a thick, decoratively twisted silken cord which hung from the ceiling. She gave it a sharp tug.

In a tower high above Brewel Hall, a small bell rang. Yawning flamboyantly, a signal operator lit a particular lantern, set it on the windowsill and opened its louvers.

Far across the Denna, an officer who sat watching the tower jolted in his seat and hurried to scribble a barely legible note upon a card.

This card, inside a sealed case, went into a message bag around a night flyer's neck, and that flyer rushed through the sleeping city, hurdling the drunks who lay across her path and zigzagging around street brats who knew better than to touch a bag with a seahorse upon it. When the flyer reached a certain doorway, she stooped down so the bleary-eyed fellow who greeted her could take the bag.

In his dream, the Grand Constable was firmly seated upon a cloud; he was about to direct his fluffy mount to leap over the horizon when something tapped most obtrusively on his shoulder.

"I do beg your pardon, Mesir," said his manservant. "But the de Brewels are requesting your presence. Shall I send for a chair?"

CHAPTER 20

ALVERT REALLY HAD NO IDEA where he was. He'd spent the night on the roadside, awakening at intervals to walk in some direction or other, with his head spinning; after a few of these walks he had become enmeshed in the outlying lanes of a town called Silver Bit, which had funneled him into the maze of the town proper. As he stumbled along trying to orient himself, he found that some clay-brained oik had left a big stack o' something in the middle of the road, right where an honest flyer might trip over it; and after having done so, he found no motivation to get up again. The Ox-Train Queen would surely sack him for drinking up her beautiful bottle, so there seemed to be no reason why he shouldn't just lie there in the wagon ruts and die.

A town officer soon noticed him. The officer helped him get up and took him to a dorm with an iron door like the cage o' some fancy bird.

"Hoy, fellow. Lost your bag?"

There appeared to be two or three officers in front of Alvert, all exactly alike. He addressed the one in the middle, the least blurry one. "Nay. Lost me mistress."

"Who is your mistress? Where is she?"

"The Ox-Train Queen. She's on the Trade Road— I ain't sure where. But she's in her wagon...kissing... " the ugly memory flooded in and Alvert had to do something about it. With a choking growl, he hurled the crystal bottle against the log wall of the cell. Instead of smashing into a satisfying galaxy of diamond-bright deadly shards it glanced off and rolled under a bench, coming to rest beside a dented tin chamber pot.

"You've had far too much of that. You'll be staying here till it's dried out of you, fellow."

"The scabby-flapped boils I will! I've got to get back! She sent me to get her some more..." the empty bottle reproached him from its hiding place. He slumped against the bars, oozed down to the floor and was silent.

"Finished? Very well. Hear you now, that a charge of disturbance has been brought against you by an officer of the municipality of Silver Bit..."

Alvert had never been a disturbance before. It was more of a thing his Ma did, and by all accounts she had a certain flair for it; but he didn't want to follow her example. All he wanted was... what, exactly?

"...if you are unable to pay said fine, you will remain immured till the next available audience before the magistrate; alternatively, a guardian taking custody of you may swear..."

Aiee! Nadima hire you?

Ata Maroo's voice suddenly spoke from inside Alvert's head. It was startling, sounding just as if she were really there, and with a flutter in his midriff he willed it to happen again. It was fainter this time, but he could just make it out: *You?*

So he was a *you*. So she'd noticed him, recognized him. Just knowing that Ata Maroo had thought about him— even for a fraction of a moment— sent his chest into a minor spasm.

The officer was looking at him a bit oddly, but Alvert didn't notice. He didn't notice much of anything. He only put his head against the gouged and dented wall of the cell and let that strange hopeful feeling wash over him again and again. Listening, longing.

You?

Me Mistress.

CHAPTER 21

THE OARMAIDS MOVED AS IF they were part of the machine. Periodically a soft note would chime from the housing that ran down the power barge's long graceful spine, but the sound of it disappeared before ever it reached the dark distant banks of the Denna. The only noise the rowers made were the huff of breathing, the creak of oars and the gentle rasp of seats sliding fore and aft. Again, again, again the long oars' blades clawed into water that stretched wide around them, and the screw-shaped oar under the craft whispered on and on.

They flashed past sleeping vessels by the dozen, by the hundred. Among them, a few lanterns were just beginning to glow.

Fred lay on the deck like a dead man, his head hanging over the bow, seeing nothing. The spray that flew from the craft's gold-leafed cutwater spattered his face and hair. He felt Dame Elsebet's footsteps, approaching softly on the deck, and the eddy of warm night air from the sweep of her sleeve. He knew she was reaching out to him, but when her hand touched his back he still twitched.

He heard her sit, felt the breeze shift. A fish stared up at him.

So she's bound for the Isle, he thought. Good for her—I'm not. I'll just slip down into this big muddy river, I'll swim for it, it's night, they won't see me... the fish in front of him vanished between a massive pair of jaws. Fred sat up in fright and Dame Elsebet laughed, but not cruelly.

"Are you feeling any better?"

"Lots." After a while he added, "Thanks."

She pointed downriver. "We're almost there. I can see Brewel Hall."

A massive white shape clung to the eastern bank, somehow alive, its upper edge rippling in many colors like sunlight on water. Some kind of chalk cliff? Covered with birds? Then Fred recognized the shape as a building, and the ripples as flags— signal flags, hoisted high on a forest of masts and yards sprouting from the roof. The building grew and grew, a massive eminence as white as ivory, its towering walls gleaming with flash after flash of brilliance, bathed in the light of great lens-lanterns.

Fred wiped his face with the heel of his hand and yawned. "That's the de Brewels' palace?"

"No, just their boathouse."

As the barge drew up to a golden teak dock Fred tilted his head back for a look. The ivory-tiled walls were not flat; instead they were dimensional, forming murals of waves and merfolk and seahorses. A mermaid as tall as a rooftop drove her team with a lash made from the arm of a fearsome kraken; beside her a merman with a beard of enormous waves raised an astrolabe toward thousands of stars, each wrought from a lump of pure gold. When he and Dame Elsebet stepped out onto the dock, a servant rushed up to wrap them in fine, clean sea-green linen cloaks and, chattering friendly inconsequential babble, led them to a sedan chair. Its frame was painted in the same sea green, and the coat of arms upon its curtains was a seahorse wearing a draft collar under the words "Ours To Command".

The chairmaids carried them through a boat yard where a fleet of beautiful pleasure craft stood in various stages of repair, then along a walkway of crushed oyster shells, through a series of bronze gates adorned with the de Brewel seahorse, across a courtyard filled with fountains, up a magnificent but very shallow sea-green marble staircase that went on and on and on, past a conservatory filled with miniature blueneedle trees and finally to Brewel Hall itself, which made the stuff Fred had seen up until then look modest.

Two pairs of footmaids helped them out of the chair, drew open the bronze entry doors and showed them into a receiving hall with a big, deep sea-green leather sofa at its center. Dame Elsebet did not sit. She pulled a large fan from her sleeve and swatted it rapidly back and forth, pacing, while Fred gazed up at a ceiling encrusted with an undersea cavern's worth of plaster shells, starfish and corals.

When the de Brewels' major-domo came rushing in, tweaking his hastily donned robe and barely stifling a yawn, Dame Elsebet stopped in mid-fan and spoke first.

"Rhonso. Please, please tell cousin Felip I must see him immediately. It's extremely—"

"Your High Honor! Such a pleasant surprise. We were expecting a deputation from you a few days ago, and—"

"You *were* expecting? You mean they never—"

"Donn Felip will certainly wish to speak to you about it first thing in the—"

"But Rhonso! You really must go back to your master and tell him—"

"Alas, my hands are tied. Donn Felip and Dame Irona have left the very strictest instructions that they are not to be disturbed until the hour of the morning levee. I am sure you understand, Medame."

"Pocks on cousin Felip's strict instructions!" snapped Dame Elsebet, whipping the fan shut. But it was no use. Rhonso was all smiles and courtesy, but afflicted with a sudden obdurate deafness. He summoned a whole new round of servants to take the guests and their nonexistent luggage on a long, long trek over velvet runners, woolen carpets and inlays of rare wood to a pair of rooms, where Fred groaned as he peered beyond his pecky cypress door into a chamber that positively writhed with decorations wrought in silk, satin, suede, lace, tapestry, skins, feathers, marble, porphyry, bronze, gilt, crystals, mirrors, and Ye Gods only knew what else. The bed alone looked as though its curtains would instantly smother him.

"Malfred? I see your... your difficulty. Shall I come stay in the servant's room of your suite?"

I can't escape if you're right there. "Don't! It's... my vows, you see. You're a, a, lady and I'm a monk and that's just a great big no-no." Fred darted in and slammed the door behind him.

He moved fast, holding his breath as he ran under the saggy ceiling, every bit as heavy with plaster encrustations as the one he'd seen earlier. Past the side door to the servants' room. Past the side door to the privy. Past a side door to other side doors. Past the bloated deathtrap of a bed. There! Behind a sea-green scented candle were the windows, panes of iridescent stained glass shaped like fish scales. He reached out— the window latch was far away and still receding— the walls behind him were expanding— Fred flung the window open and somersaulted through.

He landed several feet below, in a bed of intensely fragrant night-blooming flowers. All around him stretched a garden, every bit as unrelenting in its magnificence as the rest of Brewel Hall. But at least, thought Fred as he picked his way along a gravel walk, it's outside.

As his eyes accustomed themselves to darkness, he began to get the lay of the place. He walked around several pools with strange outlines, up and down slopes sculpted in what seemed to be particular but unexplainable shapes, many changes of soil and footing, and quite a few gazebos of different sizes. Night-cricks creaked, flashbugs twinkled. But if there was a gate to this garden, he couldn't find it, and a crapulous, jaded feeling of sleeplessness began corroding the edge of his senses. He sat heavily down in one of the gazebos and his eyelids drooped.

Close beside him, something snarled. Hot breath blew on the back of his neck.

A brief image of one of Dame Elsebet's monsters burned before his inner eye, but before he could die of fright Fred found a highcat sitting beside him, butting its spotted head against his. The snarling was only purring; in the gloom he could make out the dark stripes running from the creature's jaw up to eyes closed in bliss.

"Watch this, watch this," cackled Corvinalias, fluttering down from the roof of the gazebo to hook his claws into the embroidered ribbon tied around the highcat's neck. He bent to its ear, whispered something, and instantly the beast sprang from the gazebo out into the vast de Brewel garden, a black-and-golden blur, the long long rudder of its white-tipped tail streaming out behind it as it sped faster and faster. Corvinalias rode along shrieking with glee and when the highcat had reached maximum speed the magpie launched himself up into the air so hard Fred saw his white markings trace a gigantic backward loop around the meager crescent moon. He landed on his back in the grass, giggling drunkenly. The highcat trotted to its new friend and lay down.

"You see that? Fred! Did you see that? Yuss.Yuss! Who's a cute big terrifying *cat*, Fred, I tamed a cat! *This* is an adventure!"

"Hurray for you," growled Fred, although Corvinalias was so busy pecking at the highcat's tail and getting lightly swatted for it that he wouldn't care if he heard or not. Fred lay down in the gazebo. A stone gazebo, he thought. Kind of a grotto, maybe. Then, with no warning or preparation, his eyes fell shut and he began to dream.

CHAPTER 22

His High Honor Felip, the Seigneur de Brewel, was the son of Dame Elsebet's cousin Onri de Brewel and sometimes, when the light was just so and he was in a certain kind of a mood, there was a resemblance between him and Dame Elsebet— mostly in the area of the right eyebrow.

Donn Felip's eyebrows got their toughest workout in the mornings, when four times a week he held a levee. By the morning bell he would be shaved, dressed and ready for action: in the antechamber of his apartment he would receive a positive flood of courtiers, emissaries and plain citizens, each with a request of some kind— favor, advice, permission. Bowing they would come, or curtseying, and once a petitioner had even groveled, which had alarmed Donn Felip greatly since he considered groveling a painful relic of unenlightened times. He would listen carefully to each supplicant in turn, with his eyebrows rising in astonishment or knitting in deep abstraction or perhaps slanting in puckish asymmetry, depending on what he heard and what he was planning to do about it.

Today the crowd was large and Donn Felip's eyebrows were exhausted before he heard the first word. He had not slept much, for his wife had been in earnest with her ringing of the signal bell. The Grand Constable had been with them for much of the night, perched uncomfortably on a little teak footstool and listening as Dame Irona expounded on all her fears. Of course Dame Irona's maids were there too, and one of them had a nervous habit of sniffling, begging pardon, and then clearing her throat, which made her sniffle again.

The major-domo approached Donn Felip's comfortable desk and chair with a list written on sea-green paper. "Good morning, your High Honor. After this business I beg to inform you of a most—"

"After, Rhonso, after. Let us begin. Good lady, I see here you have a complaint about your neighbor's flying her falcon at your ... Rhonso, what is this word? Your plainhand is atrocious."

"Sow, Mesir."

"*Son!*" cried the angry woman.

This was going to be a long levee.

All at once the chamber resounded to the doleful groan of a bassoon. A gilded door at the back of the room swung open.

The crowd fell silent as Dame Irona de Brewel strode into their midst, head cast downward, arms outstretched, wordlessly pushing them back to clear a space for herself. She was clad in a simple smock and pantaloons of white linen, and her bare feet swished upon the floor.

Four little servant girls came forth, each bearing a wooden frame. They encircled their mistress with these, forming a box; slowly the box rotated and within it, Dame Irona took a series of tranquil poses. But a fifth little girl— dressed in shadowy gray— leaped through one of the frames and into the box. The bassoon squealed. Dame Irona's body contorted in spasms of stylized terror.

Other instruments joined the wail of the music, all keening and questioning, while the girl in gray clawed into her pockets and from them began hurling handfuls of powdered dye, in many filthy colors, onto Dame Irona's white linen body.

The scene turned ugly. Dame Irona's steps drummed out a desperate pattern. Then yet another dancer stepped in: she wore a thick gray false mustachio and a uniform with golden seahorses upon its shoulders. Around and about she searched the box. With commanding gestures she ordered it taken apart and re-formed, desired the dancers to assume various unnatural positions as Dame Irona cringed piteously in one corner of the imaginary space. The dance rose to a maddening crescendo; the gray intruder clashed with the one in uniform; imperceptibly the whole tableau had been moving backward until it reached the rearmost wall of the chamber where a great rectangle stood propped up and covered with a massive gray curtain. There, with a heart-stopping boom of kettledrums and a grief-stricken scream of trumpets, the dancers all vanished behind the rectangle and the curtain fell away to reveal a huge mirror. The dumbstruck viewers were left staring back at themselves in impotent silence.

Shaking his head in defeat, Donn Felip rose from his chair.

"Well, there it is," he said. "I can't imagine how my wife could possibly have made it any clearer: security takes precedence. This levee must be postponed indefinitely."

It took a long time for the crowd to flow out of the chamber. When they had gone, there remained only Felip de Brewel, his major-domo, and—

"Why, Elsie! We were just talking about you the other night! Did your vassals enjoy the Accession Day feast? When can we expect your healer gentleman?"

Dame Elsebet stepped forward and poured forth a story that put Donn Felip's eyebrows through a trying obstacle course indeed.

CHAPTER 23

JUST A FEW HOURS IN that stone gazebo brought Fred more dreams that he'd had in months. Years. He saw people he'd forgotten, tasted strange flavors, heard noises loud and low and pliable and translucent, flew voluminously, cringed in fear of things long done and exulted in angular undescriptions. Something was busily grinding away his face with a warm rasp when he awoke, startled.

The highcat was licking him. Behind him a woman was saying:

"Why, cousin Elsie, darling! How extremely kind of you to bring Kestrella such a wonderful birthday present. She will enjoy him immensely, I am sure."

"Brother Malfred is not a garden hermit. He is my helpmate on a quest. I sent Kestrella's present last month— the little runabout carriage and the two buckskin ponies..."

"Oh, yes! The carriage! Please forgive me, Elsie, I am so terribly deranged by this, this, oozing boilsore of a scabby burglary incident. Excuse my language."

Fred rolled over. His vision framed Dame Elsebet's legs— in freshly pressed silk breeches and eelskin shoes— and a pair of large, well manicured bare feet. One of the feet stepped onto the deck of the stone gazebo and Fred followed its leg up, up until he was looking at a graceful strongly-built lady, covered in white linen clothing that was dirty as all hell's hollows.

"What flower bed did *you* fall into?" His voice was deep with dreaming.

The lady turned to look over her shoulder. "Felip!" she sang out. "Have you ordered bruncheon? Make sure they bring something for the cat— he was out all night and looks positively worn." She kneeled on the gazebo stairs and Fred saw that the blotches of dirt on her white linen smock— a smock very much like his own— were each a pure, solid color. *Fake*, said his brain, and then turned lazily back to enjoying how good it felt to not have a town officer chasing him out of a doorway, or a farmer chasing him out of a haystack, or another vagabond chasing him away from some prime spot under a bridge.

"Good sir," said the lady. "Brother Balfred. Wise dweller in the grove primeval. Prophesy something for me, could you?"

"He doesn't prophesy, Irona. He casts *spells*."

"Do you know who would love a spell? Petir. He is home from University, as a matter of fact. He really should come chat with your Brother Balfred."

"Malfred, Irona. And I told you, we haven't got time to chat. We are on a *quest*! To discover what ill has befallen Doktor Lively!"

"Ah. And who is Doktor Lively again?"

Dame Elsebet yanked her fan furiously from one sleeve and flailed the air around her into a blur.

Refreshment was served in a giant canvas pavilion in the garden, cooled by servants fanning palm fronds. On the long trestle table lay tidbits of every description, stacks and stacks of porcelain rimmed in sea-green glaze, glasses etched with the de Brewel seahorse and serving implements with tortoiseshell handles. Under the table, the highcat munched noisily on a fish. "I am so sorry to receive you in this crude way, Elsie," apologized Dame Irona.

A rough trundling sound announced the arrival of young Petir de Brewel. The Seigneurin de Brewel was an admirably sound copy of Donn Felip, rendered in a lank adolescent form, wearing a robe embroidered with the emblem of Mitsa-Konig University and pulling a wagon full of books. The moment he sat down, his hand was in a fruit basket; he applied his downy creaseless face vigorously to a peach that quite resembled it.

"Petey! That is no way to act around guests. What have you got there?"

"Scrolls, codices, grimoires, metacompiliations and a few incunabula." Petir noticed Fred and Dame Elsebet. "Oh! Hello, Medame Elsie. Hello, Mesir monk." He put his hands together and bowed his head to Fred. "Homm Mahdi Bah-mei Yomm."

"Uh, hommity yommity."

Petir's face seemed to consider its options for a few moments. At length it broke into a grin. "Well jested, good brother! Ha, ha! Everyone tells me I'm too serious."

Donn Felip, near the end of the table, leaned past a stack of butter cakes and said to his son: "Brother Malfred is here to aid Elsie. He can cast spells! Perhaps he can help you study." He turned to Fred and with a flush of fatherly pride explained, "Petir is studying Applied Esoterics, with a particular concentration in occult philology. Just like his old man!" He reached out across the table and ran through an elaborate series of mudras with his son.

"Oh, the gentlemen, with their scholarly ways," sighed Dame Irona indulgently, waving a stalk of stringherb dipped in goat cheese, from which she had taken only the very tiniest bite. "I've tried and tried to understand them, but it's no use. Give me a harp or a harpoon. The idea of reading a book, that is as alien to me as a man going hu... Oh!" Donn Felip didn't have to stop her. Dame Irona stopped herself, turning bright red and deliberately upsetting a tall sea-green vase. She stole a glance at Dame Elsebet, who seemed not to have heard— indeed she seemed not to be paying attention to the conversation at all— and the de Brewels exchanged glances of relief.

Donn Felip stood up and dusted a few crumbs from his sleeve. "Petir. What do you say we show Brother Malfred the library? I'm sure he would be most impressed with our new acquisitions. And aren't your friends around here somewhere?"

"About them. They're really kind of a drag, Da, if you want to know the truth. All they ever do is ask where Kiki is."

Dame Irona was glad to plunge into discussion of her daughter. "Yes! Where *is* she? If I have said to her once, I've said it a thousand times—and that is no exaggeration, Elsie dear, I must say it ten times a day—once she turns eighteen she will need to start behaving like a lady. Well, starting the day after tomorrow, she will *not* ignore guests! Petey, when you find your sister, tell her I would like a word."

Dame Elsebet sat glaring out at the garden, fanning her fan despite the breeze from the servants' palm fronds waving all around the table. When their bruncheon finally, *finally* seemed to be at an end, the party of de Brewels, guests, servants, and the cat flowed languidly through the enormous garden as Dame Irona explained its layout, freshly designed in the last few seasons as a replica of the Kingdom. "You see? That collection of stone benches over there are your mountains, Elsie, and the pink waterwheel with its little stream is your Heart. The path we've been walking on is the Denna, and it turns into this blue and brown tiled plaza, here, which is the Great Estuary. Look: a miniature of our house. Ah, our dear little home! And that flower bed—" she indicated the one Fred had fallen into— "is supposed to be the city of Oldmarsh. Do you see the miniature of Micalossa's Theater in the center? The woman who sculpted it is almost ninety-nine years old! She remembers when Oldmarsh was just a, a... what is the word? A marsh. Oh, but let's go indoors." Dame Irona shaded her eyes. "The sun is simply brutal."

SLOWLY, SLOWLY THEY WOUND THROUGH the interior of Brewel Hall, one space after the next stuffed with ostentation such as Fred had not seen even back at the Royal Palace itself. Every time Dame Elsebet attempted to raise the subject of her healer and the possibility that she might need to borrow the Grand Constable, the de Brewels managed to elide the conversation onto some other track. Eventually, after two or three lengthy pauses for further refreshment along the way, they reached the library, where a dusky afternoon light glowed down upon row after row of bookcases. Donn Felip brought his hands together with great satisfaction and said:

"So, brother Malfred— you share my enthusiasm for mystical practices! Of course, men of erudition are working day and night to unravel the actual mechanisms at work in so-called magic phenomena, but I confess to a deep love for scholars' older attitudes. Don't you?"

"You bet I do. I really love those old attitudes. Like, like..." Fred rummaged madly through his youthful memories of copying books and came up with a few scraps. "Like the Prophessor who, uh, posited that the whole world was a shadow—" to Fred's extreme relief, Donn Felip finished for him: "—'cast unawares by the doer of the ineffable'."

"Yes! The ineffable! I've often thought that it isn't enough to just *eff* a thing, you know? You have to...to..."

"Apprehend it ontologically," Petir chimed in."How true. But I imagine, brother Malfred, you've also studied the moderns?"

"Well, ha, that depends on what you mean by modern."

"Such as Doktor Fu, Grandmaster Bharr..."

"Alas, not in person. Doktor Fu, in particular, has been most unwell."

Petir fell silent; after a few false starts his face generated another smile and he laughed aloud. "Ha ha ha! Oh, brother Malfred, your humor is almost too dry. For a moment I thought you were serious." The smile vanished. "But no doubt you've visited his grave."

Donn Felip sidled over to Petir and assumed an off-balance posture. "Petir. Show brother Malfred some of those asymmetric maneuvers. Petir and one of his Prophessors are engaged in the very first in-depth study of the Spiral-Striding Fakirs of Pharendolia! How was it you showed me they transmit semiotic content, Petir? With a... and a..." Father and son began a lurching counterclockwise progression under the library's great chandelier, pausing every so often to whoop and point at the floor.

Fred, now rapidly feeling out of his depth, had no reply and turned instead to Dame Irona, ready to make some comment she would find witty. But her head was craned toward someone behind him and before he could say anything, witty or not, she burst out:

"*There* you are, young miss! We have been wondering when you'd remember you have a family. Look, cousin Elsebet is here and she's brought a friend."

"A helpmate," growled Dame Elsebet, "for my quest, which I repeat is extremely—"

Dame Irona did not pause. She reached out, made a grab, and pulled her daughter decisively to her side. "Kiki, be a lady and introduce yourself."

"Oh but Mumsy dear," said the Dominelle de Brewel with the languid sarcasm only the young can muster. "I'm not a *lady*. I'm still a *child*, didn't you know? That's why I can't drive my carriage outside the garden or use mordant etch or let Lady Fauchard sharpen my broadspear."

"That— is— enough! We will speak of this later." With her teeth clenched Dame Irona made an introductory gesture. "Brother Malfred. Allow me to present our daughter, Kestrella."

Kestrella de Brewel wasn't as tall as her mother, or as hale and broad-shouldered, but somehow neither of these faults made her seem unfeminine; instead, she had the look of a small and beautiful deadly creature, lazily biding its time before it struck. She held her hand out to Fred and, unable to stop himself, he seized it and blurted:

> *"My fingers halt upon the strings.*
> *I dare not move them, for I know*
> *not what your taste in music is—*
> *how strike the harp? How ply the bow?*
> *O fain would I play notes of brass,*
> *or bars of silver, lines of gold,*
> *if only you would play the dancer,*
> *bidding me behold."*

Kestrella's feral amber eyes grew wide. She did not release his hand. "You made that up? Just now? For me?"

"Yes." Really, Fred had written it to win a jug of Lorroso in a contest with the old court composer.

She stared deeply into him. "You're very smart." And she twisted Fred's hand in a way that hurt, but hinted that she wanted to hurt him again later, in a more appealingly specific manner, somewhere in private.

"Mumsy! May I show Mesir Malfred my special place in the Spiral Garden? He'd like it, I'm sure. How the entrance goes around counter-clockwise— like Petey's striding fuckers."

"*Fakirs*, darling."

"Whatever, Mumsy. May I?" She let Fred's hand go; never had he felt so alone. But she beckoned with one finger over her shoulder and there was nothing, nothing at all he could do but follow.

CHAPTER 24

Morning had brought Alvert the stench of the empty bottle, lying on the floor of the cell near his face. He'd seized the nearby chamber pot and drooled a modest quantity of bile into it, then crawled onto the bench because it looked marginally more comfortable than the cell's plank floor. His brains pulsated. That damned linkapaa was a throbbing hot cyst of a thing.

But if he thought he couldn't feel any worse, he was wrong: at that moment, shouts filled the hallway outside the cell and an official voice floated above them, saying: "Hear you now, that a charge of severely aggravated disturbance has been brought against each of you by an officer of the municipality of Silver Bit. Due to the pernicious nature of the offense, the magistrate orders that each of you shall remain immured until the next available audience..."

Alvert covered his ears and moaned. The noise grew closer, louder, more painful. Within moments, its source appeared: two men, kept from attacking one another only by the bailiffs twisting their arms behind their backs. The pungent creativity with which they cursed one another impressed even Alvert, who had heard his first profanities in the womb.

He nearly fell off the bench in surprise when he recognized one of them.

It was the rich man from Ata Maroo's bed. Him, all right, wi' all them curls done up in 'is beard, an' them dark thick eyebrows wi' exactly the perfect spot between 'em, where Alvert still craved to smash the crystal bottle. He reached over the edge of the bench and scrabbled one arm frantically about, trying to find it, and something about the motion dislodged another one of his meager, infrequent memories.

It was of the one and only time he'd ever fought: during a duel, Yondstone style— that is to say wrestling, on a square woollen pad staked down to the hard alpine soil, with the loser to be shunned out of the village like a mange-ridden cur. Alvert wasn't even supposed to be involved— the duel had been between his Ma and some big ginger wench, over a man they'd both led behind the same haystack on different nights— but some overexcited spectator had pushed him right into the midst of the action. Back then, he'd fought only for self-preservation; now, Alvert felt driven to it by hate.

But who was the second man? This one was clean-shaven and had thick, wavy nut-brown hair. Otherwise he looked to be of the same species as the first. Alvert barely glanced at him, for he bore the second man no grudge— or so he thought. A few moments of listening to them revealed the horrific truth: this one needed hating, too.

The two of them were rivals for the affection of the Ox-Train Queen. Despite the burden it put on his throbbing brain, Alvert pieced the story together: apparently the second man, riding past the wagon camp in a sedan chair, had seen the first man exiting Ata Maroo's wagon. Upon hearing a sharp word from the sedan chair, the first man had taken off in whatever parody of running a rich well-fed fellow can manage, pursued by whatever variation on chasing four bearers and a silk chair can devise. Caught at bay in a ditch, the first man had jumped into the chair and begun clawing at its occupant; the ensuing brawl had attracted much attention and, ultimately, the law.

The bailiffs forced the rivals into the cell, levered them down and shackled them to opposing walls. Much to Alvert's dismay, one of the bailiffs took the empty crystal bottle with her as she left, locking the cell behind her.

From their shackles the rivals glared at one another, and at the scrawny thing on the bench between them.

"Hoy. Horse face. I've seen *you* before." The bearded man addressed this to Alvert; but upon hearing it, the sedan-chair man snorted.

"Go ahead, insult some strange wight while he's roaming around free and you're chained to a wall. You really are as dumb as cat-shit soap."

"Come over here and say that!"

"Ye Gods, listen to yourself, idiot."

The bearded man turned to Alvert and in the tone of someone who is used to getting his way said, "You're a courier. How about you deliver something for me? Hop up, fellow, and fetch that boilsore over there a sharp pop in the ear."

Alvert dearly wanted to pop them both. He pushed himself up from the bench. The room was rocking. He willed it to be still, or at least still enough to let him sway to his feet, his head sloshing like a half-filled milk crock being hoisted up to a goatherd in his vantage tower. Just as he managed to stand upright, the sedan-chair man snorted again.

"Hoy. Stretch. That scabflap over there thinks you work for free! Listen, *I'll* give you a brass penny to go kick him in the beans."

This sounded like a job Alvert could take pride in. Lurching over to the bearded man, he raised one foot, gauged the angle, pump-faked the first kick and landed the second one with no difficulty. While the fellow gagged and gurgled, and his rival laughed maniacally, Alvert waited for the inevitable counter-offer.

"I'll give you three..." wheezed the bearded man, "to poke... *him*... in the eye."

Alvert considered it and asked for six; they agreed on four, plus an option to poke the fellow's other eye for one penny extra, if it happened to be convenient. Alvert was just setting up for business when the officer returned.

"Which of you is an associate of..." he checked his notes. "Medame Ata Maroo?"

All three of them spoke up at the same time. The officer scowled and retreated.

Alvert seized the brief silence. "Cowards, that's what *you* are," he declared. A thrill of fear raced up his spine: no good ever came o' tellin' off a rich man. But upon second thought, he wasn't afraid. They really *were* cowards. "You rip each other's togs like brats— you sit there a-whinin'— you ask me to send bleedin' *messages*— but if either o' you really loved Medame, you'd a stood up straight and said 'Right. It's come down to this: you and me, on the mat, at break o' dawn!' "

After this mildly poetic outburst, the men eyed him. Finally the first one spoke to the second. "Do you know, I think we've got a little admirer here."

"I believe you're right. But what did he mean, 'on the mat'?"

"Oh, that's how those Yondies settle it, you know. Throw a blanket on the ground and grab at each other like drowning apes having a pleptic seizure." And the two men roared with laughter, suddenly the best of friends, staring all the while at Alvert as if he were something they'd bought a ticket to see. He felt his face warming to a shameful red just as the officer returned, accompanied by that coily-haired woman who'd hired him.

She knew the rich men on sight.

"So," she smirked. "You two blisters have finally crossed paths! About time. Back in the fleet we've had a little pool going on how long it would take The Dolphin to meet The Sea Otter." At their looks of puzzlement Nadima tossed her head. "You didn't know? Those are her nicknames for you." Now she pointed toward the bench. "That's the one I want, officer. It's your lucky day, Spindly— Medame wants you back. Only her god knows why."

CHAPTER 25

As Kestrella led him away, Fred caught a glimpse of Dame Elsebet's face: shock, distress. But what could he do about it? He was at the mercy of the Dominelle de Brewel.

"This way," murmured Kestrella as she strode along a few steps ahead of him.

She was not dressed in pantaloons and tunic. Instead she was wearing some radical modern fashion: a long, opulent, completely impractical gown made of aquamarine velvet that dragged the garden path as she walked. Every step she took caused a fresh, sinuous wave to tug from the crunching stone dust at her feet, up the soft heavy catenary of her skirt, to the waist of the gown— a tightly sewn accordion that crossed the small of her back in a horizontal bar so low it exposed the two divots flanking her spine. At every tug this bar parted ways with her skin ever so slightly, in a rhythm more compelling than the tide in the mouth of the Denna. And worse, Fred could see quite clearly that the only thing holding it all together was one single slender velvet tie, looped into a feeble bow, that looked as if it might, just might, be working itself loose. He hunched forward a bit and walked on, powerless to avert his eyes.

They left the path and walked on grass. Step after step, Kestrella de Brewel led him further into the midst of a quiet, empty lawn set with hexagonal glass jewels. Fred pulled the smudgy folds of his smock forward, wringing his hands in them and trying to remember some prayers. He realized Kestrella had stopped walking when he crashed into her.

"La, Mesir Malfred, you are not paying attention to me," she said over her shoulder. "The Spiral Garden starts right here, and in the middle of it is my special place." They stood upon the lip of a grassy crater;

around its walls a grass walkway sank downward, downward in a great curving ramp. "Of course this really isn't a spiral at all. It's a helix, if you want to be technical about it. But *I* can't be technical— I'm going to be a lady, you know, and ladies only understand lady things. Like feasts. And tourneys. And balls."

At the uttermost depth of the helix, a verdant hush hid a recessed green door. Kestrella grasped the latch, lowered the dense line of her eyelashes and without a trace of timidity said: "I hope you won't mind if I add you to my collection? I promise you won't need to keep it up for terribly long."

Fred's heart rammed against his throat so hard he thought he might choke on it. In a blank haze he stepped through the door behind the Dominelle.

It was an art studio. All around the chamber's octagonal walls hung charcoal portraits; some were childishly fussy, but others were executed with a vision far more mature and confident. The jewels in the lawn had been skylights— long prisms that stretched up through the earth to admit a glow of sun to this hidden sanctuary, where a neatly prepared board sat upon an easel before a divan.

Kestrella led Fred to this divan and helped him recline in its upholstered embrace. His legs quaked as she guided them into position. She took one of his hands and set it on top of his knee, palm up, and into it he felt her press the ripe, smooth skin of a pomegranate.

"There, Mesir," she said, hurrying to her easel. "As I say, you won't need to keep up this pose for very long. The friends I've added to my portrait collection all tell me that staying motionless is a chore."

A small sigh escaped Fred. He didn't know if he was disappointed or relieved. "Ah! A portrait. A pose. Obviously. Right! Should I be doing anything? A counter-posto, a ki-arrow-scoorio, some kind of, of..."

"Hush." Kestrella put one finger to the cushion of her lips. "This is my special place. Here I can be an artist, not a lady." She took up a stick of charcoal and her hand, arm, shoulder— indeed her whole right side— began to sway and dance. "Here, I can examine your form... lay your structure bare... completely penetrate your essence."

"All right, but be gentle."

Kestrella raised her voice. "Teesha. Please bring me my earth-toned chalks. And set up the viewing mirror."

"Right away, Medamselle." A studio assistant emerged from an adjoining workroom with the materials. The mirror she set up behind Kestrella allowed Fred to watch over her shoulder as she drew.

Smoky charcoal lines trailed after her every gesture, establishing the axes of his figure and the surface upon which it lay. Then her movements became shorter, sharper, more focused. Fred stared, fascinated, as she built up the planes of his chest and abdomen, taking her time, stopping every so often to erase misdrawn strokes with her fingertips, smoothing them slowly away, thinking. His arms emerged; the position of his head came into focus; very delicately she laid down a single long, wandering line that Fred realized with alarm was the inseam of his breeches, leading upward, upward... and then she moved on, heartlessly, to his knee.

She drew the shadows, captured in the folds of his smock. She drew the light, playing upon his hair and the stubble of his cheek. She drew the smooth lushness of the pomegranate and the rough resignation of the mud on his feet. She drew everything but his face.

Kestrella's gaze was steady, her hand poised, but she made no move. She looked at Fred, and looked, and looked. Her brows gave a flicker of frustration.

"Could you perhaps turn your head? A little to the— no, not that much." She erased what she'd drawn and started over. "How about if you lowered your chin... no, not like that. More to the—" again she erased and redrew. "Boils! Sorry, I meant pocks. I dropped my charcoal."

Kestrella picked the charcoal up, bit her lower lip, and scribbled in a face that looked nothing at all like Fred's.

"There!" she exclaimed, hanging the portrait on the wall with the others. "You're mine now, Mesir Malfred. I'll keep you here in my special place forever."

With those words an abrupt, blinding, brilliant ray of relief gushed into Fred's heart. Or rather, his neck. In this place, forever! Suddenly it seemed to him a very, very real possibility— now that he had met the de Brewels and they seemed to approve of him— that they actually *would* keep him for a garden hermit. Then Dame Elsebet wouldn't be able to cut off his head— or fail to.

"Forever," he sighed, letting the pomegranate roll from his fingers. "That's right. Keep me, my dear good Dominelle. Do it. Keep me forever."

CHAPTER 26

THE MAGISTRATE OF THE MUNICIPALITY of Silver Bit normally thought of people as sitting— or rather, cringing— before him. More specifically, before his desk. It was the desk that put the fear of Ye Gods into people: a big, tall, wide oak monstrosity, covered with carvings depicting justice being done in particularly nasty, old-fashioned ways. He liked to give them time to examine the carvings, while he drew a quill out of one of the drawers on his side of the desk, and a penknife out of another, taking care to rattle and scrape the drawers as much as possible, and to breathe heavily as he cut the tip of the quill into a pen that would make a big, flat, angry signature. Sometimes the people before his desk would cry. That always gave him a wicked thrill.

Only for some reason, now he felt as though *his* side of the desk might be the wrong one. The woman before him shook her big, long coils of bronze-colored hair and leaned forward across the desktop without taking the slightest peek at the carvings.

"Hoy, judge," she said. "What say we get creative with this fellow Dragonsson's fine?" and she set a crystal bottle decisively before him. The office filled with little dancing lights. "I'd pay you the silver coin, but I dropped it on the way here, so I'll just have to give you the birthday gift I was taking to my sweet old auntie."

The magistrate didn't believe it for a minute about any sweet old auntie, but he knew a Stewen crystal bottle when he saw one. "Deal," he said, grabbing it before she could change her mind. "A bailiff will bring out your man. Let this, mm, let this be a lesson to you."

"Oh, it has been."

The door of the Silver Bit station house nearly hit Alvert as he followed Nadima out. She made sure the silver coin Ata Maroo had given her for his fine was safely tucked into the toe of her shoe, and whistled for the ox she'd ridden. She put no pennies into the hand of the brat who led it to her; instead she sprang up onto the animal's back, gave it a decisive kick and left Alvert to follow.

The rest of the fleet had been on the move for hours. The long-haul wagons, and Ata Maroo's private rig, were headed back toward Coastwall and Nadima was supposed to catch up with them: she held her ox to a brisk trot that would have done many a riding horse proud. Alvert did his best to keep up, but after about an hour hunger, thirst, and a skinful of alcohol all took their toll. Entering the main square of a town known as Ringtrue, he went down like a sack of sod.

Then he was sitting up against the wheel of a vegetable barrow. A small knot of fellow flyers were clustered around him, patting his face and loosening the drawstring of his knitted pantaloons.

"Let him have some air, for pocks' sakes!"

"Naw mate, it's water he needs."

"Easy with that ox, Curly— it almost stepped on ya man, here."

Nadima gave a snort of annoyance and the flyers turned angrily upon her.

"Hoy, what kind a deep-damned shrew flogs a fella down the road instead a givin' im a lift on er ox?"

"Mumping termagant!"

"At least buy the boy some tea, ya heartless dragon!"

"All right! Ye *Gods*! I get it. My apologies. On your way, all of you. I'll look after him."

"Will ya? Take im to that inn on the square. Go on, so we can see ya! Buy im a whet. Get im cleaned up. Or we'll tell ya boss—that's right, everyone knows who owns them big brown oxes."

Nadima's eyes flashed with indignation but she did as she was told. She wrangled Alvert to his feet, frog-marched him to the inn, and sweet-talked an ox-groom into plying him with a hand pump and scrubbing him with a brush that looked like a hedgehog strapped to an axe handle. Then, as he shivered miserably, she dragged him to the front porch of the inn, pushed him into a chair, and set a mug of lukewarm water on the mosaic table in front of him.

While Nadima sat sipping a nice cool glass of rose-hip tea and biting a molasses bun, her wet, goose-pimpled, scratched-up charge slumped forward until the side of his face ground into the table. Nadima studied the slackness of his sunburned cheek and watched his colossal nose flare with each breath. Some flyer. But until she got him back to the fleet, this sorry wight was hers. There had to be a way to get some use out of him. But what? She chewed the bun and considered.

Ringtrue had a particularly clear, sharp-sounding town bell. When it rang to announce the crier's afternoon bulletin, Alvert cringed and moaned so miserably that Nadima tore off a chunk of the molasses bun and jammed it into his ear. The sticky plug of dough blocked the noise and he settled down. Nadima took a satisfied slurp of her tea and concentrated on the crier, who strode into position not far away.

"Hear now this summary of events on the afternoon of the Fifth Day, Month of the Peaches!" He lowered his scroll and spoke directly to the gathering audience. "Anyone here follow men's prize fighting? That's right! Those little fellows really can scrap, can't they? Well, listen up: 'Aficionados in every fief of the Brewel Country are expressing disappointment at the news that no challenger has been found to oppose men's fighting sensation Bulldog Pike.' " He lowered the scroll again and in a passionate whine he editorialized, "No challenger? What if there's no fight? Think of all that money we won't be able to bet!" The crowd around him began to warm up— and Nadima's attention glued itself to the words "money" and "bet".

The crier went on: "I mean, what are we supposed to do, just let the greatest male fighter of our time stand there in the middle of Micalossa's Theater, scratching his backside? Bleed that! If you've got a friend who don't mind a few knuckles to the head— a few boots to the shins—well, take him down to Oldmarsh. Pike's corner'll pay you a barrowful of gold!" The crowd laughed, but of course no one actually knew anybody stupid enough to go even one round with Bulldog Pike.

Nadima laid her hand on Alvert's clammy shoulder.

"Dragonsson," she murmured. "Come on, babe, sit up. Drink your tea." She put her glass into his hands and helped him raise it to his lips. He gulped it gratefully, and Nadima leaned in beside him, low and friendly.

"Listen, now, hon. I won't tell Ata Maroo how you lost her expensive bottle— that's between you and me. And I also won't mention all that stuff I overheard you telling her honey boys. I know you've got a thing for her. Shhh! It's all right! Half the men in the fleet do. They can't help it. She's impressive."

Alvert studied the table. ""Does she...ahh...love any of 'em back?"

"Who knows? But I'll tell you one thing. The good word about *you* has gotten around."

He couldn't have been more surprised at this. No good word about him had ever gotten around. "What kind o'... word?"

"Word that says you're a real highland scrapper, and if any wight dares to claim Medame, why, you'll see him on the mat. At dawn."

"An' so I will!" It was amazing how quickly this yokel lit up. Nadima had heard of shooting ducks in a box, but this was too easy.

"Well, down the road from here there's a fellow by the name of Bulldog Pike who says that Ata Maroo is his, all his. He specifically said, and I quote, 'that damned drunken flyer who run around last night, shouting the praises of the Ox-Train Queen— someone better tell that skinny lummox that she only has eyes for *me*'."

"Someone better tell me? Why don't he tell me himself? Coward! You just show 'im to me— I'll twist 'is arm! I'll pull 'is leg! I'll shove 'im through the mat so hard they'll have to climb down the hole to find 'im!"

Nadima patted Alvert's back. She wasn't about to say that the prize fighters of the Low Country didn't waste their time with Yondy bumpkin wrestling. They fought bare-knuckled, thick-booted, teeth-missing, ears-ragged brawls. Of course the crowd would explode with rage when the fight only lasted ten seconds. But by then, she'd be gone— wheeling gold down the road in a barrow.

CHAPTER 27

THE DE BREWELS HAD DECIDED to have some tea.

"It will settle my mind," declared Dame Irona. "I am still so agitated by this burglary, Elsie dear, I simply cannot tell you. It has been preying on my thoughts constantly, absolutely without cease."

"Even when we played three games of lawn bowls?" growled Dame Elsebet, poking around with her toe to make certain that her fan was still under the brocade floor cushion she sat upon. "And when we watched your cat play with his magpie friend— who, by the way, came here with *us*— for a solid hour? And when we critiqued every last one of Kestrella's drawings? And when..."

"Especially then, darling."

"I won't stand on etiquette any longer. *Where* is your Grand Constable, Irona? I wish to speak to him."

Dame Irona blinked. "I imagine he's at the Station House in the city."

"I thought you said he was here!"

Donn Felip sensed a storm brewing and spoke up. "Cousin Elsie. I get the feeling that you are not altogether at ease. While the brazier is boiling, why don't we discuss something pleasant? We've made plans for a wonderful tourney in celebration of Kestrella's birthday. Eighteen knights will—"

Dame Elsebet could no longer restrain herself. She pounded the low table with one fist; the exquisitely rustic teapot and the charmingly mismatched ancient cups and the elaborately simple implements of the ceremonial rite jumped. "Where are *my* knights?" she cried. "I sent you ten of them, where did they go? Did any of you so much as see Doktor Lively? Does no one want to help me find out what happened aboard the *Longwing*?"

Fred had been admiring his teacup; for the very first time, he'd found himself doing so in sober earnest. He really *did* find the cup beautiful. He really did find the flames of the charcoal brazier to be fascinating, the massive block of ice in its carved jade holder to be touching— solid, yet transitory, just like life itself, he thought. Why had he never seen this before? Oh, right. Because he'd spent the best years of his life watching the young King fail to properly light the brazier, fail to properly pour the tea, even once stab himself in the thigh trying to use the ice pick. Thank my god, thought Fred, I'll never have to think about him ever again. I'll just tell Dame Irona and Donn Felip that I'm staying. But then Dame Elsebet pounded on the table and interrupted these pleasant thoughts.

She was on her feet now, a grave breach of etiquette during the tea ceremony, and pulling her fan and shoes out from under her seat cushion. She was thrusting her feet angrily into the shoes, thrusting the fan angrily into her sleeve, taking Fred angrily by the arm. He opened his mouth to protest, but Dame Elsebet was quicker.

"We bid you good afternoon, Irona, Felip. Or good evening, whichever it is by now. I desire that you call for my rowing barge to be made ready immediately— Brother Malfred and I are going to handle this matter by ourselves."

The de Brewels all stared up at her with platter eyes. Donn Felip ventured, "But it can wait, surely? After all, the harbor blockade is still in force, so meanwhile you may as well stay a few days and enjoy Kestrella's b—"

A crowd of gentlemen burst into the room.

They were sweaty. They were irritated. They were dressed in the livery of the King.

"The face of His Highness demands to know what the poxboils is going on at your harbor!" This came from their leader, a stout pale-bearded man, scowling on the seeming verge of violence.

Fred knew him well. His name was Yanush Baekenfahd, and he was second deputy to the King's major-domo. Back at court, Fred had often lampooned him as a character named "Johnny Baconfat". It was during just such an imitation that he'd first made the young King laugh. Later, Fred had tried stunts such as stealing one of Johnny Baconfat's livery uniforms and pinching its folds from the inside so as to make the magpie embroidered on its chest seem to talk, or wearing his ruff collar as a tutu, or filling his boots with cheese; none of those had been as successful in entertaining the young King, but they had angered Baekenfahd greatly. Fred had done them again a few more times, just to grill his goat.

Now, he glared around the table and when he reached Fred there was a long, aching moment during which the former royal Fool prayed not to be recognized. And he wasn't. Long hair, an incipient beard, no hat and a seat in the de Brewels' own tearoom turned him into a stranger. Instead Baekenfahd aimed the blade of his attention at Donn Felip.

"Well, sir? Please explain why a royal deputation was not allowed to dock. Until the fourth— the *fourth* try, at which time the Face of the King— that's me, fellow! was forced to show his ring to the harbormaster. Show my ring! Like an illiterate servingman or a wench! With the banner of his Royal Highness flying above me! Explain this, I do beg."

"My dear Yanush..."

"It is the King to whom you are speaking."

"Ah... your Majesty... I abjectly beg your forgiveness. We have had a scare here— a crime committed in our very midst— and it has made us forget ourselves. No disrespect could possibly have been intended." Though the great block of ice was inches from Donn Felip, sweat showed upon his forehead, and he lowered his brow to the table; the rest of the de Brewels followed suit and so did Fred. From underneath, Fred heard Corvinalias and the highcat give two frightened squeals.

"Well.... humm...."

Fred knew these humming sounds. They meant Johnny Baconfat was satisfied, that his blunt aggression had served its purpose. Now he was sure to ask for some food. Wait for it.

"Humm... I will take a glass of that tea. And one of those pastries, there. And now I feel a curious desire to see your gallery of treasures. A curious desire indeed. I seem to have had it regularly for the last few years."

"Of... of course, your Majesty. Should we all—?"

"Yes. Let's all have a look at 'em."

They left the tearoom and walked— briskly this time, for the King's representative had no intention of enjoying Brewel Hall's comforts. Dame Elsebet exchanged a look with Fred, but he couldn't decipher what it meant. Was she looking down the gilded, polished, candlelit corridor, at the door? Motioning with her head? Squinting? Frowning? Beckoning? Was she leaving? Fred ignored her and walked on, though with every step he felt as though he were somehow in the wrong.

They reached a breathtaking display gallery, unlocked just for the occasion. The King's representative slowed his step before the gleaming hoard of treasures, bending to examine them. Dame Irona's lips trembled. So did Kestrella's. Mother and daughter gripped each other's hands.

He stopped in front of one of the cases. The other gentlemen in his retinue drew scrolls and pads and ink and pencils from their sleeves, ready to document the moment— except for four who turned out not to be men at all but knights in disguise. They didn't pull out any scrolls. Instead they pushed their robes discreetly aside to show swords, daggers.

"What a colorful stone that is," said Baekenfahd, tracing his thick pink finger along the glass. "What a pretty sculpture. Hmmm, that miniature looks so real. That necklace must weigh five pounds. Very fine things you've got here, Felip, very fine. But do you know which one is my *favorite*?"

Petir drew a deep manly breath and turned away; Donn Felip forged his pale bony face into a polite smile and said, "No, your Majesty. I really cannot guess."

"This pair of cans, here." Baekenfahd pointed. "Such simplicity. It's a shame, it really is, that back on the Isle of Gold, in the very palace of the monarch, there's nothing quite so fine. Open the case."

Huh, thought Fred. The de Brewels really don't seem to want anyone handling those cheap old pewter drinking cans. I wonder why they're even here with this other stuff? Maybe one of their ancestors' ashes are inside, or something.

Donn Felip fumbled the keys as he went to unlock the case. His hands shook so much he dropped them when he tried again. The keys bounced between the cases' low clawed feet and he had to crouch to find where they went; when he got hold of them he lost his balance and they went deeper under the case, so that he had to get on hands and knees to reach them.

That's where he was—down on his knees, reaching— when the fire bell went off.

CHAPTER 28

CORVINALIAS LATER MAINTAINED THAT HE had seen the blaze start, but that nobody wanted to listen to a magpie. "Do you people think we can't recognize *fire* when we see it?" he shouted into Fred's ear as they dodged through the crowds swarming out of every courtyard, garden, back lane and loading dock at Brewel Hall. "Don't you think someone might have listened to a fellow who said 'pardon me, that brazier is about to burn down your tearoom', even if he's got black and white feathers? But no! No one so much as—"

"Shut up! Where's Dame Elsebet? Did you see her when you were flapping around up there?"

The whole tearoom had gone up in flames— not surprisingly, as it was constructed mostly of oiled paper. But the breeze off the Denna was brisk at that time of evening, and there had most unfortunately been several wagonloads of fireworks stored downwind in preparation for the upcoming birthday party. When the alarm sounded, and the rockets began screaming and bursting, all of Brewel Hall's guests and servants had rushed madly out of doors— dozens of servants for every guest, it seemed, and hundreds more for no reason at all.

In the panic, Fred had lost the de Brewels. He dodged terrified serving wenches and clerks with bloodless faces and grooms leading fear-frenzied horses. The sudden jab of Corvinalias's claws into his shoulder had been the best thing he'd felt since being touched by Kestrella. With a pang Fred had wondered where she might be, but then— which surprised him greatly— he'd found himself asking after Dame Elsebet.

"Do you *hear* me, featherhead? Where is she?"

"I saw her at the boathouse. Why do you care?"

With a massive blaze and a column of soot rising from the Hall, the scene was madness. Fred could barely retrace his path to the great ivory-tiled building where they'd landed— so very, very long ago, it seemed to him. When he finally reached the boathouse, he was surrounded by servants busily launching every craft that would float in an effort to keep them safe from fire. Never mind that the actual flames were far away across the grounds; fear had spread much more quickly than danger, and between the swinging flare of lanterns and the frantic din, no one noticed a lean, leathery, white-haired woman pulling a little green rowing skiff across the gravel strand and into the river.

"There you are!" exclaimed Dame Elsebet when she noticed Fred. "I was beginning to think you weren't going to follow me. Do get in. This is our best opportunity." She stepped into the little skiff with one leg, kicked it away from the riverbank with the other, picked up an oar from inside and began poling the boat away into the Denna. "Hurry, brother Malfred, or you'll have to swim for it. That's the way! Oh, thank Ye Gods it's dark and nobody saw us."

Dame Elsebet snapped the oars into their locks, seized their handles and really began putting her back into it. The glow of the fire in the distance animated the shadows of her face, as if she were wearing a theatrical mask haunted by uneasy spirits. Corvinalias perched on the transom of the boat, looking back at Brewel Hall, and gave a long, long whistle.

There was quiet for a time. Only water sounds, muffled distant shouts, Corvinalias purring to try and soothe his Uman beings. Then Fred said, "Of course I was going to follow you."

"Hmm?" Dame Elsebet had been lost in her thoughts. "What's that?"

"Back on shore, you said..." Fred gritted his teeth. "Uh, you know what, forget I brought it up."

"Oh! I remember now. Yes, at first I was afraid you were going to try finding your own way out of that dreadful maze of a place. I'd have had to waste time searching for you— obviously I wouldn't dream of leaving you to my cousins' mercy. They mean well, but sometimes I think 'clouds' is too kind a term for what their heads are stuck in."

Corvinalias spoke up. His remark was clearly meant for Fred: "*I* wanted to stay."

"So go on back, dodo. What's keeping you?"

The crest on his forehead bristled. "Nothing. What's keeping *you*?"

Fred looked around the inside of the little skiff. The faint moonlight showed him nothing but two people and a bird.

"Speaking of heads, Medame. You haven't got any, ah, weapons. Here. With us. For you to use if you had to, um... kill someone."

"Oh, brother Malfred. You are kindness itself to be concerned for my safety. But I am quite at ease." For a few strokes, she released one of the oars and showed him her sleeve; there was a lump in the pocket, alongside her fan. "This will embolden us, cause villains to fall back in disarray, and smooth obstacles large and small."

"What's that?" A moment too late, Fred remembered the Stone of Protection that he was supposed to have retrieved, with his own magical hands, from the violent white core of the Leet. "I mean, what's that, birdbrain? I'm trying to listen to Medame!"

"Hoy!" wailed Corvinalias.

"I am so, so grateful to you for casting that spell, brother Malfred," said Dame Elsebet, pausing to cradle the chip of limestone through her sleeve, unwilling to pull it completely out for fear of dropping it into the vast unsearchable Denna. The deferential care with which she handled it brought the old sick feeling back into Fred's chest, lodged in a deep place and festering.

She's unarmed, he told himself. I can easily give her the slip later, find my way back to Brewel Hall whenever I want to. And besides, there's no point in going back until after Kestrella's birthday... He ached to let the fierce little Dominelle run her fingers slowly all over his portrait. But even that thought couldn't chase the sickened feeling away.

He watched Dame Elsebet's hands in their fine doeskin gloves, pulling the oars with a rhythmic squeak and splash. They passed only a few other boats; most were skiffs like their own, a few were single-seat leather khayas, but as they came alongside a lighted buoy marking the center of the channel, a barge with a raised cabin flew past them, propelled by eight men pulling like all hells were close behind. Dame Elsebet watched them go, squinting in the pale moonlight. "Men rowing that boat. Most unusual."

"I can row," offered Fred.

"Oh! Please excuse my remark, brother Malfred. These are modern times. Men can...well."

"It's all right. I just, I want to be doing something. I feel bad, somehow."

Dame Elsebet fell quiet and began stripping off her gloves. "You have a noble soul, brother Malfred. Please, wear these." As she gave them to him, Fred saw the mass of blotches that covered her hands. He knew what they were— or rather, what they had been. But then she thrust her hands into her sleeves and he knew better than to ask why her wedding bracelets were so forlorn. From over his shoulder, the gleam of Coastwall's lights touched their little craft, followed by the noise of its night traffic, and finally the stink of its gutters.

"You know what a highcat is like?" said Corvinalias, apropos of nothing.

"Sure. It's like a greyhound with spots. Runs fast, catches antelopes, plays with annoying magpies. So what?"

"You probably know this already— as you are so extremely well read, good brother Malfred of the Order of the Hat, O he who munches down perfectly happily on locusts caught by friends and lets them do all the dirty work and is notoriously stingy with the prayers of gratitude—you probably already *know* that every magpie grows up on mother's stories about King Jo who slew the Cat, and the Seven Cat Wizards, and the Riddle of the Great Cat, all those. You *know* they're practically mythical beings to us. You know that even to touch one is, is, something that gets you marked down in history." The city lights gleamed on the feathers of Corvinalias's neck as he turned to give Fred a sour glare. "It's time *I* had an adventure."

"You can have it later. Right now I'm—"

"Right now you're what? Going back to the Isle of Gold? Wouldn't you rather, and I quote, *rot in the deepest dankest hole of hell?*" The last part was uttered in a mimicry of Fred's voice, so startling in its accuracy that Dame Elsebet thought it was him.

"Brother Malfred! Why would you speak so to Prince Corvinalias?"

"I'm only a Count," said the bird, sullenly.

Fred kicked one foot at Corvinalias, making him flutter a few inches down the gunwale. "Because he's obtuse," he snapped. "Because he doesn't get what's actually going on here. If he'd have just a little patience, and not bring up *his* family and anything that might have happened between *him* and *them...*"

"You're the one who doesn't get what's going on here," barked Corvinalias, shaking his feathers into place and giving them a quick preen with all the self-control he could muster. "I guess even the best of us can wear out his welcome." With a long, bitter laugh he launched himself into the air and started back across the river. "Fare thee well, fool. Some kind of *brother* you turned out to be."

CHAPTER 29

Ata Maroo's fleet sailed not upon any sea, but only the Trade Road and its clay tributaries; even so, her business operated in many and far-flung locations and come evening, some part of it would be honored with her presence, and take on the mood of a naval squadron awaiting inspection by its Admiral. Teamsters grilling their dinner or cleaning the hoofs of their oxen or repairing a yoke would catch a glimpse of her and raise the cry: I see Medame— Medame is headed toward us— straighten your collar, put away those dice, she's here. She was never unjust, never harsh; but if there were any problem— a wagon loaded inefficiently, an ox going lame, a spring or bearing in need of attention— she spotted it within seconds. These were uncommon incidents to be sure, but just as in fleets that sailed the water, there were bound to be troubles now and then.

Tonight, the troubles were within the Ox-Train Queen herself.

Ata Maroo's bull— this one was officially known as Sire 0-6, although she called them all by the endearment "ipo"— loped along the verge of the Trade Road, parallel to Unit III as it lay encamped a league or so from Oldmarsh. She sat in graceful immobility on its immaculately groomed back, the tail of her colorful sarong folded forward underneath her, and she guided the beast with one hand on the golden stripe that ran down the center of its coffee-brown withers. Her hair streamed black behind her, the sunset making its edges glow like campfire coals. Her golden face was serene, but her thoughts were not. Those were filled with annoyance.

Nadima had not returned from that morning's errand to the jail in Silver Bit. From the very first, that girl had been a seven-sided blister on Ata Maroo's pinky toe, but for the sake of her father— owner of a big lumber mill and one of Ata Maroo's oldest customers— her nonsense had been overlooked. But now she had stolen a silver coin, ox number 0-6/57-34, and the stupid man.

At-last-yes, thought Ata Maroo, for in her native language there was a special word for the "yes" that one gives after serious consideration. At-last-yes, this Nadima will be punished, and if it costs me the lumber contract, so must it be. She cannot steal money, or a valuable ox, or the skinny stupid man who looks like God.

Then Ata Maroo was annoyed with herself, for wasting her energy on that silly thought. Again.

Everyone must have a face, she told herself, and there are only a certain number of ways that faces can look. It was simply a matter of time until I saw Him, was it not? And yet, in twenty years of driving freight up and down every road and street and lane and track and cowpath in the Kingdom, she had never yet seen anyone with exactly the big blocky jaw, the great vast fin of a nose, the overhanging brow and the round, forbearing, infinitely long-suffering eyes of her people's God, as depicted on the huge stone heads gracing every island in the Peaceful Ocean. Until He had run into her bull, there in the rain in Good Market.

Unlike the people of the Kingdom, Ata Maroo's people did not believe in the existence of personal gods, or Ye Gods, or a Great God Almighty who is beyond and between and within. Instead they made offering to their kind, patient deity in the form of meat and fruit; he listened to their troubles; and that was all.

This comes of being too long among the westlanders, thought Ata Maroo. Maybe I too am starting to believe I have my own secret god who has come to inspect me.

And then she was annoyed with herself again, for why should she think of her new people as *westlanders* and scorn their religion, as if she still had anything to do with the Peaceful Ocean? She had abandoned those people. She must not think of them, or their stone heads, any more.

But how dare Nadima steal the coin, the ox and the stupid man! Suddenly Ata Maroo was filled with a waspish fury. She raised her feet from Sire 0-6's flanks and let them fall straight down with a thump. The startled bull gave a snort of surprise, bucked a few times, and raced through the camp faster than it had run in years.

CHAPTER 30

Where Coastwall streets and plazas were wide, they were expansive and graceful, fine big open places where the night could play its breeze. But where Coastwall lanes and alleys were narrow, they were cramped and wriggling little pathways that squirmed their way between tall, drunken-looking buildings all of sandstone, buildings so close together that many of them extended arches, like sandstone arms, to brace themselves away from their neighbors opposite. For Fred, tagging alongside Dame Elsebet in the slots of these alleys, only the strip of black sky overhead, and the passing presence of dubious nighttime characters, kept him from feeling that he was bottled up in some kind of chamber.

"It's bound to be here somewhere," said Dame Elsebet, waving her fan. Fred decided that was some kind of nervous tic; it certainly wasn't hot outside, though the crooked sandstone bricks underfoot still radiated the previous day's heat. Or else it was to fan away the stink— that was more likely. It seemed that every other building was a tavern, a squalid tavern with dregs of wine suppurating in the cracks of its cobbles. Shabby cut-rate singers leaned against every wall, ready to regale any passing wench who wanted to hear about herself, and the wenches for their part grabbed at men with impunity. None of them grabbed at Fred, but that must have been because of his scowl. Dame Elsebet slowed down to let him come up beside her, and between them they nearly blocked the street. "I recall the way being almost straight— as straight as any way through this part of the city might be— although it does always seem very different when you are not doing your own navigation. And now it is night, of course."

She had once gone to the Coastwall Station House, she told Fred, in a sedan chair from The Nautilus, a lodging place in this city. "I'd lost my hairpin," she explained. "A particularly beautiful pin which had belonged to my mother. So I decided to go and file a report about it— very daring of me, I think. I was very daring then." She stopped and pointed at a stone arch which looked to Fred exactly like Coastwall's hundreds of other stone arches. "There. Do you see it? The one with the keystone slightly twisted sunwise. If I don't mistake, the Station House was two cross streets and a small jog to the left further on."

It was actually three cross streets, and more of what Fred would call a stagger than a jog, but sure enough when they turned a corner the whole street opened up into a wide, welcoming fan of a plaza, unfolding into a long broad vista of rooftops and towers and lamp posts and even a few trees, rolling downhill to a view of the harbor. The plaza was anchored by a massive sandstone edifice, whose tall bronze doors were held open by marble seahorses. Above its portico was an inscription in the old scholarly dialect Coastwall had once shared with the Isle of Gold: HERE DWELLS JUSTICE.

In they strode, the cool smooth marble floors feeling to Fred like pure heaven after all the rough sandstone cobbles. A wench plied the floor behind them with a mop, cleaning his dirty footprints away.

Two gentlemen were seated at a high stone desk. The young one looked down at them with barely concealed boredom, but the old one jabbed him in the ribs as he sprang to attention. "Good evening, Your High Honor! Get up, sergeant, this is Donn Felip's cousin. To what do we owe the pleasure? Has this fellow been bothering you?" This while he glared at Fred.

"No, not at all. Brother Malfred has been helping me. We are here to see the Grand Constable. Immediately. We will see no one else."

Both gentlemen's faces told Fred they'd come all the way here for a big, fat nothing. "Oh, Medame, I am so sorry. We'll make up a comfortable place where you can wait— sergeant, get on it, there— but unfortunately you've just missed him. He rowed over to Brewel Hall with a squad of officers. Someone there lit the signal to summon him."

"Pocks!" Dame Elsebet exclaimed. "Scabby pocks!" She took Fred's arm.

"Medame?" the old officer called after them, but they were already out on the portico beside the marble seahorses, headed down the hill toward the harbor.

CHAPTER 31

Ata Maroo's bull slowed to a trot, then to a stroll, and finally stopped beside her wagon. She swung her leg over its withers and slid down its side in her graceful, practiced way, smoothing her sarong down behind her as she went. In a long-practiced motion she took a stout wooden staff from the side of her wagon, clipped the end of it to the ring in the bull's nose and handed the beast off to one of the teamsters. "He dirty from road. You groom him down, ah? Wash, brush, comb tail and clean hoofs."

She had just let the steps down from the side of her wagon when something darted in front of her: an express flyer, resembling nothing so much as an angry hummingbird, fidgeting peevishly.

"Another one of these flat things, Medame." The flyer flipped an oblong parcel back and forth as she handed it over. She pulled a wax tablet from her bag and drummed on it with the stylus. "Stamp here— oh, but *you* can sign."

"This for you, ah." Ata Maroo just managed to push a coin into the woman's hand before she flew away. Then with an inward sigh, the Ox-Train Queen took the flat parcel into her wagon, knelt down by the side of her rosewood bed, and hooked her fingers into the brass loops of one of the many storage drawers built there.

The drawer she pulled out was long and deep. It was filled, almost completely, with more of the same flat parcels.

Those furthest back— clearly the ones that had been there longest— were unwrapped. But newer ones still wore their waxed-muslin shrouds, with the stampings and routemarks of the journey they had made: across the blue quilt of the Peaceful Ocean, through the devilish maze of the Herb Islands, around the hidden shoals and frighteningly deep basins in the Warm Straits, through the Midland Sea and up the Denna to the Trade Road. Ata Maroo turned the newest parcel up on its edge and slipped it in front of the others. She put her fingers against the face of the drawer and began to push. But then, for no reason she knew, she changed her mind. She pulled the drawer back open, brought out the parcel, unwrapped it and sat down on her bed to look it over.

And her world flew apart.

It was an *ow pala*, a letter engraved upon a sheet of horn from the mouth of a whisker-whale. *Ow palakk* were the traditional writing surface of Ata Maroo's people, and this one spoke of traditional matters— or rather, of their final and utter breakdown. For it seemed that now, after twenty years of pleading and of writing more and more desperate *ow palakk*, the Ata family had been forced to accept the fact that their only daughter was never coming home, having chosen instead to die in a foreign land. As a consequence, said this *ow pala*— and Ata Maroo could absolutely hear the sorrowing voices of her parents when she read it— as a consequence, soothsayers had determined that, for the very first time in the history of the Hundred Clans, there would be no new Headmother after her. None at all. Ata Maroo's final breath would not go into the wind of the Peaceful Ocean, to be taken up anew by the next Headmother; the chain would finally be broken; the Hundred Clans would become loose grains of sand, cast into the wind of time.

Ata Maroo felt as if all of her innards had been snatched away. Her face turned white and she began to shiver. She tipped slowly onto her side, curled among her pillows like a creature in pain.

"I am the foulest disrespectful excuse for a child ever to live!" she said aloud, in her native language. "And not only that, but witless enough to delude myself that, if I ignored facts, this fateful news would never come." She grabbed one of her pillows and rent it with clawing hands; of course it did not tear, and this only increased her misery. Words failed her and she began, silently and tearlessly deep within herself, to weep.

For twenty years she had maintained— not as a matter of public announcement, but rather as privy information, dropped into the ears of those she trusted— that the only thing keeping her from returning to the Peaceful Ocean, to the big and interesting life of her native people, was the fact that her husband was there, waiting to kill her if she returned. But, she would say, the moment my husband die— my bull and wagon for sale.

In fact, however, as the years passed, Ata Maroo had become more and more entrenched. Her business grew to include not just one wagon and one aurochs, but also the farm where she raised her own breed of incredibly strong, surprisingly swift hybrid cattle; workshops where her vehicles were built and maintained; warehouses where shipments were stored, terminals where they were received and distributed; real estate for future expansion; rich long-term contracts; a pension fund for her teamsters; and more, much more. In theory it all hung on the life of one nasty man somewhere in a faraway ocean. The moment my husband die, I go home.

What a lie.

Because one of the very earliest *ow palakk*— now nearly buried at the back of the drawer— had brought word that her husband had been found, with a poison dart in his back and a harpoon rope around his neck, towing behind a crewless, rudderless boat. As an obstacle, he was gone. But the obstacle he left behind was worse, far worse.

For Ata Maroo, it was bad enough to have run away in the first place, and doubly bad that she had bolted alone instead of taking her parents with her: she had left them behind to face the wrath of the violent brute they had been so unlucky as to mistake for a good man, a good bridegroom for their only daughter who was the embodiment of a ten-thousand-year tradition. Of these acts, she was ashamed. But what word was there for it— and 'cowardice' was not right, as that spoke of fear, when what she needed was a word that spoke of something even deeper and more elemental, of that instinct which makes us recoil from the outcast— what word *was* there for the strange insidious way the years of her silence had of building one upon another, like flows of impenetrable lava, each one making it harder to talk about the one before it, on and on, deepening, never-ending, until there was no point anymore in even unwrapping the *ow palakk*, until the only bearable thing was to put them away unread and work harder, do more, be more, forget?

For just how long she lay on the bed, Ata Maroo was not sure. But when she got up and floated down the wagon steps, it was dark outside. She felt as hollow as a seafoam bubble, and as cold as an island of ice.

Enough of this misery, she said to herself. Breaking with a beloved tradition is a sad thing, but it is no death sentence. In future my people will be a bit poorer, perhaps, in the way of heritage, but they will survive.

That was no doubt true, and reasonable. So why did the thought make her feel obscurely dirty inside? Ata Maroo closed her eyes and pressed her hands into their sockets and tried to be firm.

I have abandoned those people, she reminded herself. I must not think of them any more.

This had once been an easy thing to think. But now it was different. Now it sounded cheap and slimy. She took her hands away and looked at the night for a while, though it was empty.

And then the wind blew. Perhaps it blew from the Peaceful Ocean, through the Herb Islands, over the Warm Straits, across the Midland Sea and up the Denna to her. It blew with a whisper, which was the voice of duty, which was her own voice.

Your chance to do right is not *over*, it said. You simply find it easier not to do it, telling yourself you are ashamed. Damn your shame! What petty vanity! What is it you fear— that your people will mock you? Then be mocked; she who is mocked can still do right. Do you dread that your parents will hate you? Then hate you they shall. But you can be hated, and still do right. Do you recoil from ever showing your face again, back in the land where you tucked your miserable tail and ran away? Then you shall suffer: let the whole world stare at your contemptible face—while you are doing right. And if you happen to die of shame, well, we all must die of something.

She looked around at the glow of the campfires and the shapes of the oxen lying on their chests in the herd. She smelled grilling steak and burning fuel. She listened to fiddles playing and workers passing by and all of it was small and beautiful and clearly not hers anymore. It made her feel a little better, and that little was enough.

"Damona, Boann." she called out to a pair of teamsters. "I have sudden business, ah? Please yoke three good fast team to my wagon."

CHAPTER 32

Dame Elsebet was determined that they would make their own inquiries. "After all," she said, "what do those officers know about it that you do not? You have your mystical visions, brother Malfred, like the one that sent you to me. And you have powers, let us not forget. You cast that cantrip— where is the cantrip?"

"Alas, dear Medame, a magical waterwyrm devoured it. I would have tried to slay the monster, but I thought..."

"Sometimes retreat is the wiser choice, brother Malfred." She patted his shoulder; Fred had to look away.

And so they inquired. For hours. They inquired, they ransacked, they left no stone unturned— some of them literally, for on more than one occasion Dame Elsebet had ordered Fred to help her wedge some cobblestone or another up, using her fan as a lever, because it looked as though it might be a secret hiding cache for something. What, exactly, they were looking to find, Fred didn't know. And truthfully, he didn't care. The only important thing was that Dame Elsebet had no broadspear and no suspicions. His chance to escape would come.

Another thing: it soon became obvious to Fred that Her High Honor, the Domina of Whellengood, might have keen eyes and an excellent memory for locations, but she was hopeless when it came to business with folk on the street. She had no idea who was worth listening to, and who was only wasting her time; they spent wearisome ages questioning beggars, halfpenny topers, thwarted pickpockets and what seemed like scores of other worthless dead-end nobodies. And sailors. Gods, what a never-ending plague of sailors. The harbor was jammed to bursting with ships, and the ships spewed a continuous stream of inebriated mariners who covered the docks in maidenroot spit, wanted to know if the cogwheel on Dame Elsebet's back was some kind of sea anemone, and stared at Fred in almost, but not quite, the right way.

The low point came when he was elbows-deep in a huge pile of torn-up documents they'd found behind the customs office. Dame Elsebet paced nearby, keeping a lookout for trouble, although Fred was far from sure she would recognize trouble if it came. And sure enough, yet another sailor tottered by, stared back at them for a while, then gave a cry of alarm. She rushed over to pluck at Dame Elsebet's sleeve.

"What is it, goodwife?"

"I dropped my last brass penny," moaned the wench. "Did you see it, lady? I think you stepped on it. I need that penny— it's important."

Fred whirled on the sailor and pushed her away. "Pus off, drunkard! We haven't got any!"

"Malfred!"

"It's a scam, can't you see it? Dropped her last penny, my beans. She's just another..."

"There it is!" the sailor pounced upon a tarnished old coin, lying in the rutted street where Dame Elsebet had been standing. When she bobbed up again, she was all smiles. "Thanks, lady. Now I can go pay my shipmate's fine. *Longwing*'s got a right good crew— he'd do the same for me, if I were in jail."

For a moment Fred assumed that— because Dame Elsebet's heart must certainly have leaped into her mouth with the same grateful shock that his had done, upon hearing the word *Longwing*— she would make some sudden outcry or ill-considered move, and chase the sailor away. But she remained calm. Like a stalking highcat.

"*Longwing*? I've heard of that ship."

"She's got a good reputation. Too bad she hasn't got Feathers and me."

"I don't follow you." But she *is* following you, thought Fred, watching as Dame Elsebet drifted off down the waterfront, right at the sailor's elbow. He dropped his handful of paper and hurried to join them.

"...sailed without any warning at all. It's supposed to fly a flag, you know, a sort of..." the sailor was drawing a rectangle in the air with both hands. "Feathers can explain it better. He's good at telling stories, I'm not. I'll bet he's best friends with all the officers in the Station House by now. "

At the Station House— to which the Grand Constable had not yet returned— the sailor paid the bailiff a motley handful of coins and a moment later, her shipmate was with them on the steps in front of the marble seahorses, yawning and stretching the albatross wings tattooed on his arms.

Feathers did indeed have a very entertaining way about him, and his retelling of the *Longwing*'s odd disappearance kept Dame Elsebet on the very edge of her seat: the seat being a woven willow bench under some torches, in the forecourt of a tavern where she had bought the sailors some bread and cheese.

"So this missin' friend of yours. What did he look like?" Feathers asked her, tearing a big chunk from the edge of a bun and stuffing it into his charismatic mouth.

"A gentleman of somewhat middle age, his hair dark gray, his face round and pleasant. He was in the company of ten valiant ladies, and as he boarded your ship, he would have been bid farewell by a very, very tall young man."

"Ten ladies! I wish *I* were that pleasant! Was the tall one a skinny wight with a look on his face like his dog had just died?"

"That's the fellow," said Dame Elsebet. "But did you see the sweet-looking gentleman?"

Feathers shook his head, peeled a slice of cheese off the plate and applied it to a second bun. "No. But I did see your young man gallopin' all over the docks like he'd lost his deep-damned mind. Back and forth to the harbormaster, we were takin' bets on how many trips he'd make. Then he spotted somethin' in the harbor, some kind of rags..."

"They looked like papers," said the quieter sailor.

"Papers, rags. He stuffed 'em in his bag and that was when the thing with the tables happened." Feathers turned to his shipmate. "I swear to my god I had no idea. A fellow gets bad rum, a fellow flips the table, that's natural. Who in the great gray globs chains a whole raft of tables together? Why should I have had to pay—"

Dame Elsebet leaned casually on her elbow. "Please. I don't mean to interrupt, but can you tell me what the procedure is, when your ship sets sail?"

Feathers signaled a serving wench for more cheese. "Sure. There's normally a few stores and medicines and so forth to take on, and cargo to be loaded, although ours is usually just mail. At the end of that, there's a bit of paperwork for the purser to do— an inspector comes aboard and writes out a manifest, the purser signs that nice and the inspector seals it up neat, and he tips his wig and takes it away with him to the harbormaster. Then the barky hoists the old Blue Box and mateys like us, sittin' there in a tavern on the waterfront mindin' our manners quiet as you please, see it and go aboard and away the good *Longwing* flies."

The serving wench set a big brick of golden cheese and a tower of buns between the sailors, and Feathers attacked it with the gusto of one whose belly is full of expired rum that needs mopping up.

"If Yagga forgot to hoist the Blue weeping Box," he munched to his companion, "when the *Wing* gets back in port I'm goin' to make her pay for every one of those mumpin' tables and every bottle on 'em. I'd never have stayed in that tavern so long if she'd kept her hands on the poxy flags where they ought to be, and not down that singer's—"

"Pardon me again, goodwife and sir." Dame Elsebet looked casual, but Fred, sitting beside her, could feel that one of her feet had commenced an agitated drumming. "If a cargo manifest had no sealing wax on it, and no signature, what would that mean?"

"Why, it ain't finished then. Attested, they call it," said Feathers, folding a bun around some cheese. "Not even sure how anyone would get a thing like that. The inspector writes it up fresh, there on board, and they do all the attestin' in the purser's cabin."

"Your purser has his own cabin?"

"Well, usually he shares it with the surgeon, though sometimes the cap'n does rearrange the bulkheads— like if we're carryin' passengers, though we don't do that very often."

"And the purser's cabin, does it have a window?"

"We call 'em portholes, but yes, good lady." Feathers stopped eating for a moment and turned his head on one side. "Is there some reason you're so interested in our paper and our wax and our portholes?"

Dame Elsebet finally lost her composure. "Hijacked!" she cried, pounding her fist on the table so sharply that the empty dishes rattled. "*That's* what Taluca meant with his cry for help! He was in the cabin chatting with the purser and the surgeon, and when he realized there were pirates aboard he wrote that message on the manifest and threw it out the win— hole!" She turned to the sailors. "I must chase down your ship, because the round-faced gentleman was my gift to the King— Doktor Taluca Lively, who Ye Gods sent to help me when I'd lost my mind. He is the price I pay to save my country! He is my magician, unique in all the world!" The sailors stared at her in silence and she explained, "I'm sorry I didn't reveal my identity until now. I am Elsebet de Whellen, Domina of the Whellen Country. Felip de Brewel's cousin."

The sailors' heads swiveled about, looking for the kind of entourage a noble would have with her. There was only Fred, who grinned at them.

Feathers stood up carefully, folding his napkin. "Of course you are, lady. I mean, Your High Honor. We knew you right away. Didn't we?"

The other sailor followed suit. "Oh, yes. Yes. Absolutely, your, ah. High. Ah. Thanks for the food." And they fled.

CHAPTER 33

Ata Maroo's oxen were in their yokes, six of them, well-grown young beasts who could start a mountain off its roots and haul it all day at a brisk jog. Tonight she wanted them to haul only her, on an easy route the animals knew every step of. She would go down past Coastwall, to a place on the shore where she had a big freight terminal and a lot of warehouses. In one of those warehouses was a boat built long ago, covered with dust.

She would drive the oxen herself. There were only a few more things to check, back in her wagon...

"Ow! Oh, pocks. And here I thought I would surprise you, my angel, my diamond!"

She had run into her lover, he of the curled beard and the dark thick eyebrows— the one she privately called the Dolphin, because of his chattering and his constant smile.

"What that smell?"

"Oh, this? This is for us to share. It's a spice-cake ring, do you see, with nuts and sugar and cinnamon. We're meant to have it with coffee, my treasure, and perhaps a bit of that liqueur in the coffee would do nicely. Come, let's climb into your chariot of sighs." He was pulling her by the hand, already up the wagon steps and halfway into bed.

Ata Maroo braced herself at the foot of the steps. "I am on way somewhere. How you get here?"

"I rode my white mule, dear heart. The one who ambles so smoothly. I gave him to your groom— what are you doing?" This as Ata Maroo swung up onto the near-side leader's back and signaled the oxen to pull.

"I told you, I am on way somewhere." She turned sidesaddle on the beast and considered her lover as he wavered unsteadily behind the front seat of the rolling wagon, his collar hanging open and his beard full of crumbs as well as curls. He caught her look and laughed, wiping his hands on the lapels of his robe. "You caught me— I never could control myself. But do stop, my treasure. Stop a while and let me devour something even more satisfying."

Ata Maroo, swaying in the wan moonlight among the sweet grassy-scented backs of the oxen, thought for a few moments and told them, "Whoa."

"Ah! That's it, my jewel! Why bother driving this wagon, when soon the earth will move? Hmmm?" As Ata Maroo climbed from the ox into the wagon and back into her bed, the Dolphin reached out and took her in his arms. He pulled her down beside him and began to kiss her. His lips tasted of rich drink as well as sugar, nuts and cinnamon, and he continued kissing unabated for an impressively long time. But dolphins must breathe air now and then, so at long last he paused and let Ata Maroo say:

"Very clever. As always. But let me ask you important question, ah? Now listen. Would you marry me if—"

The Dolphin sat up so fast that he knocked three or four pillows right off the bed. "I am honored! Imagine our future! So passionate, so prosperous—" Ata Maroo cut him off.

"This not proposal. I am only asking you question. I need husband. But let us say I give up all this, no more business, no more Ox-Train Queen, goodbye. Would you marry me then?"

"Fie, my rose bloom, my nightingale! I care not a fig for your wealth, you know that. I have a bit of something put away myself. Nothing like yours, of course—"

"Ah yah. But imagine all of it gone. Would you go live where I desire?"

The Dolphin surprised her by taking her hand and gazing deeply into her eyes. Perhaps there was more to him than she thought. "Of course I would live where you desire. Whatever you wish, I wish."

"I like that. You mean it, ah?"

"Oh, indeed I do! So when shall the joyous day be? What kind of celebration shall pay tribute to it? And was the...*situation* you alluded to merely rhetorical? Because we really ought to purchase some good residential property and build a few homes, you know— a country place, a city place..."

"Day could be something like tomorrow. We drive all night. And place will be in middle of ocean. On boat."

The Dolphin blinked. "You want us to celebrate on a boat?"

"I want us to live on boat."

He laughed again. Deep and loud, and that made Ata Maroo angry. "Boilsores! I thought you say whatever I wish, you wish."

"Sweetheart. Stop being ridiculous."

"Ridiculous? You not just say you will live where I desire?"

"Well now, I meant within reason. But you want me to live on a *boat*? In the *ocean*? Come on, you must admit—"

Ata Maroo leaped to her feet. "I admit you were pretty good play toy. I liked you, ah? Always laughing and fun time. But fun time is over. Now it is serious time. And you are not serious about me."

"Oh, but I am!"

"No, you are not." Ata Maroo grabbed the luxurious quilt and pulled it from the Dolphin as if ripping a bandage off a wound.

Wordlessly he began to dress. He took his time about it, clearly hoping she'd change her mind. Her mind did not change. When he finally climbed out of her wagon, he opened his mouth and she wondered what he was about to say. But the answer was: nothing. He only took a final slice of cake from his sleeve, to nibble on as he left.

THE DOLPHIN'S EXPENSIVE WHITE AMBLING mule could cover a lot of ground, quickly, but so could Ata Maroo's oxen— if the Dolphin had chanced to be going her way, they might have been forced to travel side by side for many uncomfortable hours. But thankfully, when she rolled down a flap in the canvas cover of her wagon to watch him go, Ata Maroo saw the smooth-striding white shape of the mule turn north. The rhythmic patter of its hoofbeats soon faded away, leaving her to climb back out of the wagon, take her place on the near-wheel ox and start back on her journey.

She felt safe. She knew this road intimately, had watched it become wider and smoother and busier as the years went by. At a word from her, the two highcats jogging under the wagon could attack like darts of golden lightning. Her oxen were fit and sound, and able to guide themselves every step of the way, for the farm where they'd been calved was only a short way beyond the terminal. She had left Fleet Unit III in taut order. And many, many bidders for her business were perpetually lined up, ready to battle one another to the last penny in the comfortable hush of a meeting room at the Nautilus.

She sighed. The Dolphin had been a disappointment. As a husband, he would not have had to do much. Just to be by her side would have been enough: for while it would surely raise a few eyebrows for the Headmother to return with a new, foreign mate, it would at least free her parents from the dreadful burden of choosing her a second bridegroom. The worry of that would kill them, she knew; yet they would suffer a mortifying loss of face if she tried to stop them. If only the Dolphin had agreed! She could have translated his ceaseless chatter as wisdom, or quieted his mouth altogether by keeping it stuffed with nice crisp slabs of roast pork. *But never despair,* thought Ata Maroo, there is still the Sea Otter. And sure enough, there he was, in a shining yellow cube on the road before her.

Ata Maroo recognized his sedan chair from at least a furlong away. The moon was just a sliver, but the yellow silk curtains of the chair were woven with threads of gold that gleamed like mirrors. The yokes on the shoulders of its four bearers were padded with fine soft butter-colored leather, to match their boots, and each of the women carried a torch in her outside hand. Something was strange about the chair, however: drawing closer, Ata Maroo could see that it was hardly moving, sagging in an appalling fashion as if crushed. Its frame was in fact quite severely broken; the bearers' faces were taut with discomfort and exhaustion.

"Wah! You have had accident?"

When the wagon drew to a halt beside the chair, its curtain whisked open and the smooth boyish face of the Sea Otter emerged. His thick, wavy nut-brown hair glittered in the torchlight.

"Oh, I have indeed. A dreadful accident, my dear. This chair was damaged, in a fight over you. And so, it grieves me to say, was I." He turned his head and Ata Maroo could tell he was trying to get her to notice something.

"What you showing me?"

"Oh, only a battle wound, my dear." He pushed back a luxuriant fringe of hair, the better to reveal a slightly puffy, discolored eye. "A trifling incident in which I came face to face with— with that other fellow who has the impertinence to call upon you. I do so hope you won't hold my disfigurement against me."

"No, much to contrary, I like it. In Peaceful Ocean it big honor to have lover fight duel. You win?"

"I certainly would have, dear, but the law got involved and the business ended behind bars."

"Wah! Jail? You call officer to arrest man for wrecking you chair, poking you eye?"

"No, no, dear. I declined to press charges... it really wouldn't do to have this in the announcements, now would it? And as for the eye— well, I would certainly have answered that skinny horse-faced road-pounder with one of the same, if only the officer hadn't left me chained up in the cell."

The light of a bearer's torch flickered upon the wrinkles that bunched Ata Maroo's brow. "Wait minute. *You* were one in jail? In jail with... skinny road pounder? Wait more minute. This happen in town call Silver Bit?"

"It did. How did you ever guess? At any rate, I did it for love of you, my—"

"Did loud girl with big curly hair come to jail?"

"How do you know about all this?"

"It not important." The thought of going back to the Peaceful Ocean before she could find and punish Nadima was annoying in the extreme, but Ata Maroo had her priorities.

The Sea Otter tucked a swath of hair behind his ear and ran one fingertip around his bruised eye. "Well then, since fighting appears to be the theme of the evening, I have a surprise for you: a pair of the Kingdom's very hottest tickets! Come with me, dear, to the prize fights at Micalossa's. Everyone in Coastwall, Oldmarsh, all the far de Brewel fiefs— everyone who is anyone will be there!"

Ata Maroo was under no false modesty about her fame. She knew perfectly well that the tickets were not exactly a selfless gift, but rather that the Sea Otter would benefit socially from being seen with her; however, as she'd been intending to pass through Oldmarsh anyway, she nodded yes. She would talk to him as they went, and get a feel for what sort of husband he would make.

"Come, my dear. Leave those beasts and join me in my chair."

Ata Maroo was sure she heard the chair bearers groan when the Sea Otter said this. But it was a bad idea in many other ways, so she refused. "Nah, that plan have too many problem. Oxen cannot stay alone, what to do with pair of cat, I need wagon— and chair too broken to carry anyhow, ah? Let bearers stow chair on tailgate, put out torches. They can ride oxen."

The smiles on the bearers' faces told her they liked this new plan very much. But the Sea Otter frowned, adjusted his pleated collar and said: "My dear, I insist that my bearers carry lights in this frightful darkness. Why, to think you would be out here alone! I am grateful to whatever fate brought me here, that I might be at your side."

"Ah yah, I have thing to ask you later about being at my side."

"Goodwives! Come!" The Sea Otter clambered out of his creaking, sagging chair, waited while they lowered Ata Maroo's wagon steps, and he joined her— but not in bed, as the Dolphin had. Instead the Sea Otter took one of Ata Maroo's brightest sarongs, covered the wagon's front seat with it, and bid her to sit front and center with him, while the bearers walked beside the wagon with torches. They had not yet begun to roll, and already Ata Maroo could see what was happening: the lights were not to guide the way, nor to flush out bandits. They were there to illuminate the Sea Otter and his renowned sweetheart, so that no one else on the road could possibly miss them. And soon, as they neared Oldmarsh and the road began to fill with traffic, there was quite a crowd of travelers to impress.

ATA MAROO HAD WANTED TO talk to the Sea Otter about their future. But that was not to be. All the way to Oldmarsh he spoke to her about nothing, in voluble ringing cadences no rider in any other chair or carriage or wagon could help but overhear. He painted his flow of speech with liberal coats of "darling" and "my dear," embellished it with a series of ostentatious love declarations, and highlighted it with ebullient greetings for anyone on the road he happened to recognize. So much did he seem to enjoy this trip that, once they reached their destination, Ata Maroo was surprised he didn't direct her to take an extra lap around the herringbone brick forecourt of Micalossa's Theater.

The Sea Otter pulled a few coins from the pocket of his fashionable silk tunic and offered them to the matron guarding the door; when she failed to react, he turned to Ata Maroo with a winsome pout. "Pocks, it seems I need more cash. Have you—? Oh, a galaxy of thanks, my dear. Here, woman! Show us to the very best box."

Slowly, the constant swarm of visitors stopping by their box thinned out; grudgingly the Sea Otter had to stop playing the host, and finally the crowd aimed its attention toward the round boxing ring, fenced about with willow gratings, which graced the stage. A huge chandelier was lowered from the rafters and a team of stagehands hurried to light its dozens of lamps; the cavernous interior of Micalossa's Theater flared with light; and the proprietor, a stout pugnacious wench with a broken nose, strode out and addressed her patrons through a megaphone.

"Good fanciers of fine entertainment! It pleases me mightily to see you all here tonight. Last week's theatricals were widely attended, and last month's display of authentic fire-dancing from the Herb Islands drew quite a reception, but let's be honest: nothing can pack my little showplace like knowing that *Bulldog Pike—*" here she paused for the demented roaring and howling of the crowd; she gave them time to settle down and continued: "—nothing can pack my little showplace like knowing that Bulldog Pike— the Male Mauler, the Ferocious Fellow, the Gentleman Juggernaut— is in Oldmarsh this evening, ready to display his wisdom in the learned art of unarmed combat!"

The crowd surged into frantic motion: thousands of aficionados digging into their purses and pockets for the money that was soon to start flying from hand to hand.

"Some of you thought there would be no match— that no man yet born would venture to set himself up in front of the wicked fist... the merciless elbow... the diabolical knee of Bulldog Pike. But I found him for you, my friends, a true rarity, a veritable nullicorn! Behold him now, do: a fellow with guts enough— or brains so little— that he opposes the immortal Pike for your pleasure tonight!" Micalossa gestured to the back of the stage, and the crowd roared.

"Pus in a bucket," breathed the Sea Otter, leaning over the rail of the box for a better view. "That's the lout who assaulted me, dear!"

Facing the wrong way, and clearly paralyzed by the noise, loitered a freakishly tall, woefully gaunt young man with a messenger's characteristic strip of untanned skin running across the back of his neck. Ata Maroo almost knocked the Sea Otter out of the box, so swiftly did she leap to the rail. "Wah! It stupid man! So where is—" and she spotted Nadima in the shadow of the ring, her purse wide open and one of Bulldog Pike's corner crew dumping coins into it. Ata Maroo's almond eyes grew hard. "Someone let me down to stage! Ah! *Ah!*" She gesticulated wildly, trying to get Micalossa's attention.

The Sea Otter was on her then, physically pulling her back, covering her mouth. "No! Darling! Please don't make a scene— settle down— we have an image to project!"

She rounded on him, enraged at his effrontery. "You very much in love with image, I see that."

"No, my dear! I am in love with *you!*"

"Ah yah? And what if I tell you that tomorrow I will sell my wagon, my terminal and farm and investment? What if I say I will go live in boat on ocean, where no one ever hear of Ox-Train Queen? When I am nobody, will you marry me?"

The Sea Otter took just a moment too long to answer. Whatever warmth was left for him in Ata Maroo's heart cooled to a cinder, and she stood up. "That just what I thought. You keep very best box. It what you really love."

She dashed from the box and dragged, rammed, twisted herself through the crowd. It was exhausting— in those short minutes before the fight began, clusters of patrons knotted together, shouting and shoving, all in a frantic hurry to seal wagers on minutiae such as what blows Pike would deal first, second, and whether there would even be a third; into which sector of the ring the challenger would fall; whether he would bleed over the eye or from the nose; how many teeth would later be found. Ata Maroo had not even reached the stage and already Micalossa was raising her megaphone.

"I present to you, honored patrons, the Challenger. Standing an ell and seven-eighths, weighing eleven Coastwall stones, hailing from that rustic land of the eagle and the ibex— the one and only Elbert... sorry... Egbert? Everett?... the unmistakable Alvert Dragonsson! And now: the one you've been—" Alvert jumped forward and bent to Micalossa's ear, interrupting the introduction of the Champion.

The crowd's impatient growl drowned out his words, but those in the front row saw Micalossa's eyes light up, her mouth hold back a grin. What she'd just heard was pure gold, from a promotional standpoint.

"Attention, friends! The Challenger wishes one and all to know that he is here tonight because he asserts that his opponent, one Bulldog Pike, is not worthy to contend for the favor of a certain lady!"

This was beyond anything the bookmakers had foreseen. The crowd went wild. Alvert was gesturing before Micalossa, explaining still further, his eyes rounder than ever, and Bulldog Pike was shucking off his robe and stomping toward them in his thick brawler's boots. Through the megaphone Micalossa boomed: "The Challenger wishes me not to utter this lady's name. But he wishes to dedicate his performance here tonight to her— in hopes that she will strike Bulldog Pike from her consideration, that she will... how did you say it, good fellow? 'Shun him like a mange-ridden cur'.

"That's what we're here to see! Or is it? Get ready, friends, for the fight of the century! Come up to scratch, gentlemen, because it— is— ON!"

"Get over there," hissed Nadima from behind the willow fence, pointing to a line chalked in the center of the ring. Alvert had never seen the lowlanders wrestle, and had little clue as to the procedure; but Nadima shoved him forward so hard that he stumbled to the scratch line and barely caught himself before he tripped. He gazed down at the Champion, more than a foot shorter than himself and well upholstered in thick muscle.

The fellow tipped his head back and spoke. "Look, mate. Just so we're clear: I don't even know who yer lady is. It's naught but money brings me here to bust yer arse."

"Don't try backing out o' this!"

"Backing out?" Bulldog Pike laughed aloud; his teeth were all obviously false. "May yer god help you, mate." At that moment, a bell clanged. Alvert wanted to ask if it meant the duel was on, but something whipped upward under his chin, and a bright white grid of stars surged forth to blot out the universe. For some reason, a chunk of molasses bun flew from his ear.

The crowd launched into a pandemonium of shouting and a frantic exchange of coins.

"Uppercut! I called it! Pay me!"

"Aw, pus. I thought he'd use that left hook of his."

"I thought he'd use an elbow."

"I thought he'd stomp."

"Boils! Look! That Yondy lad's gettin' up. Sort of."

"*Hurry hurry hurry!* Over here! Every brass you give me wins you two more, if he makes it to his feet!"

"Look *here!* I say every brass wins a silver if he can stand one more punch!"

"Nay, look *here!* Every brass wins a gold if he lands a blow on Pike!"

Deep in the churning mass of spectators' bodies, Ata Maroo was furious. She had almost made it to the stage, was shouting to stop the fight, was protesting that she had never authorized Nadima to put her man in the ring— but Micalossa's Theater was roaring at such a pitch that her shouts were nothing but a sneeze in a cyclone.

Bulldog Pike stood with his scarred, leathery fists raised high. His expression was calculated to beg the crowd's forgiveness for such a brief show. The crowd was staring— not at him, but at something behind him. Waves of fans gasped as one when the stumbling, open-mouthed Challenger threw the wiry loop of his arms around Pike's neck, and pushed one of his thin cleat-soled shoes into the back of the fighter's knee.

It was a well executed move, and might have got the better of some upcountry swain, wrestling outside some goatpath village. But the reigning Champion was not so easily unbalanced. He spun about in Alvert's grasp, and with a slash of the forearm dealt him a stunning blow to the jaw; then he raised one of his thick boots and brought it down on Alvert's left foot.

The nearest spectator gave a blood-freezing howl. The first ten rows all cringed. The whole room groaned in empathy as Bulldog Pike slipped one boot behind his opponent's remaining foot, rammed him in the chest with both hands and sent him reeling, toppling, lying ominously still. Then, amid a great cheering and wailing and gaping of purses the bell began clang clang clanging, ringing and ringing as if Micalossa's Theater were burning down.

Somehow, Ata Maroo managed to reach the stage. She vaulted up onto it, and the guards posted there could not hold her back. She rushed to the far side of the ring, her rage awful to behold. Nadima froze in terror. Ata Maroo shoved her to the boards.

"How you dare? This last straw! You are gone! Tomorrow my clerk send you father letter, call magistrate! If you try to leave town I hire thief-taker!" Nadima lay helpless, clutching the purse full of money to her heart. Ata Maroo grabbed it away. "You get this by thieving— you steal money, you steal ox, you steal man!" She threw the purse into the audience and it was torn apart like a wounded fish amid sharks. "Boilsores, canker, blister, clot! Out of my sight or I call magistrate right *now*!" She turned around to see Micalossa herself. "Where you put the man?"

"Some of the hands took him backstage. My healer gave him redflower sap—" but Ata Maroo was already darting behind the enormous heavy curtain, breaking the bubble of onlookers bent around the remains of Bulldog Pike's opponent.

Alvert was in a cold sweat, mottled bright red and ghastly white under his tan. Blood was spattered across his bitten lip, livid bruises were flaring along his chin and jaw, the fall he'd taken onto the wooden floor had done him no favors, and then there was the grisly matter of his foot.

"Stupid! Leave it on, leave it!" cried Ata Maroo, pushing away a stagehand who was about to tear off Alvert's shoe. "If it broken, you make worse!"

Long ago, near a brackish creek on the lonely plains far to the west of the Brewel Country, a starving runaway girl with nothing to her name but one spyglass, one sarong, and the wreck of a boat she had stowed under some trees, had found an abandoned aurochs calf.

Some misfortune had left one of the calf's feet broken, and though its fierce massive mother had no doubt grieved to leave it behind, nature is merciless. The herd had moved on. If Ata Maroo had not come along on that day, the calf would have become food for a passing longwolf; instead it became the cornerstone of an empire.

The girl searched her new country far and wide, foraging for leaves and grass to feed the calf and wild foods to feed herself. Slowly the two of them limped along, learning new words and places and customs, eking out a hungry toehold on life. She went back and found the boat, took it apart and built a little wagon. While the calf healed, she pulled the load; as he grew stronger, she taught herself how to carve a yoke, how to train a calf. And then one day Ata Maroo discovered that she was the envy of every ox-driver in the world.

No one before her had ever been able to tame the aurochs, that dreaded and celebrated animal, known and feared since the Age of Flint— but this woman drove a full-grown aurochs bull, with a back as high as many a cottage roof and a neck as thick as the oldest blueneedle tree. When it pulled, it pulled not one wagon but a train. When it moved, it cut hours— sometimes whole days— off the length of a typical journey. And it never needed to rest, any more than its owner did, she who brought new thinking and new methods to an old, old craft. Thus was born the Ox-Train Queen.

Now, behind a heavy curtain on an empty stage in a city north of Coastwall, a runaway girl was kneeling beside a broken abandoned creature. *So it is true,* thought the girl, what the old people back in the islands used to say. Everything repeats itself.

CHAPTER 34

YOU'RE REALLY BAD AT THIS, Sweetface wanted to tell the killer.

What's taking you so long, why am I not dead, who is that screaming in my voice? It can't be me. You haven't been able to kill me. You must really be bad at this.

Sweetface's turn in the sickbay had come at last, and he hadn't even been able to walk there. The killer had untied his hands— by that time, they were blood-bloated useless nothings— and tried to get him to walk into the place of execution, but the very thought of it had made Sweetface fall senseless on the deck. He knew too much about what bodies are made from, and what can be done to them, to be brave. In his work he'd learned that healing sometimes caused shocking pain— how much more, then, did being killed cause? Much more. He learned that quickly.

The first time death began to engulf Sweetface, he'd welcomed its thick dark menacing cloud. But the cloud spread and broke and more life, agonizing life, shone through.

Again and again it happened. Every time Sweetface thought the end was upon him, every time the sound of his own shrieks and pleading grew too frightful to endure and the dark cloud hovered almost close enough to breathe, some unmarked spring of strength would flow forth and preserve him. At last he'd decided the killer was inept. And he'd become a little cocky.

Through his agony, he must have shown a glimmer of scorn: the killer stopped, and thought, and did something new. He put down his tools and dragged Sweetface from the sickbay, around the bulkhead, into the captain's cabin where something smelled bad. The killer grabbed

Sweetface's head and shook it until simply by reflex he focused his eyes and saw.

It was dead. It had to be— had to have been. But it was breathing, visibly breathing. And it was begging, audibly begging. Begging for the cloud to come.

CHAPTER 35

"LIFT UP— TAKE EASY, NOW— come this way, ah? Careful! No touch foot! Now lower man slow, put him here."

Ata Maroo had hired a few steady-looking roustabouts to carry the insensate Challenger out of Micalossa's Theater and into the rear court where her wagon awaited. With the solicitous care of furniture dealers moving a valuable piece, they installed him in her great rosewood bed. There, he looked surprisingly small, almost hidden in Ata Maroo's reef of pillows. She wedged several of these around him as if they were wheel chocks, so that he might not roll away, and went up front to the wagon seat. With a gentle command, she drove the oxen out onto the road.

Traffic was heavy. Micalossa's Theater was the center of a near riot, as a curious public swarmed toward it to hear the news, and bookmakers caught flatfooted struggled to get away. Everywhere, Ata Maroo heard people shouting questions to one another about this Challenger. Who was he? Where was he? Why had he ever dreamed of doing such a thing? Was it true that the Ox-Train Queen loved Bulldog Pike? I always knew it, said some. Not anymore, said others.

Slowly, as the Trade Road left the orbit of Oldmarsh, the traffic thinned until once again it was a dark, quiet ribbon of clay and only the occasional cart, or a servant riding shoe leather, passed them by. Ata Maroo called out another command to her beasts: return homeward. Leaving only the force of habit to guide them, she went back inside her wagon.

A wan, faraway hint of light bled through the arched canvas ceiling. The stupid man had not moved at all. It was only when the fleshy block jutting from the middle of his neck wobbled, ever so slightly, that Ata Maroo realized she had been afraid. With a sigh of relief, she brought out a little flintbox, lit the wick of her bedside lamp, and sat down beside him.

First she took the hem of her sarong and wiped the blood from his face. It didn't even show among all the flowers.

Then she pushed away some pillows, found the edge of her quilt, and folded it over him like the muslin wrapper on a long, thin, narrow *ow pala*.

And finally, from the footboard of her great rosewood bed, Ata Maroo pulled a flat little drawer. From out of that drawer she pulled a sharp little knife. She took a deep breath, bit her lip, and slid its gleaming point under the edge of the stupid man's shoe.

"Easy now, *ipo*," she said, as the goatskin capsule sprang open. The colors inside were not as pretty as the ones on her sarong, but just as numerous. She glanced at the man's drugged slack face; it betrayed no sign of awareness at all. Ata Maroo put down the knife, closed her eyes and trusted her hands.

The stupid man's foot was tough, truly, nearly as tough as a hoof, and the calf's hoof was suddenly very fresh in her fingertips' memory. Under them, shapes spoke in translation. Claws became toenails; two toes became five; a muddy coat became wear-hardened flesh— all was plain to her now. She felt what was wrong, and where, and what should be done about it. When finally she was finished with her examination, Ata Maroo pulled out the drawer filled with *ow palakk*.

She was a good carver. She had carved dozens of ox-yokes, maybe even a hundred, perhaps more; and in her youth at sea, she had carved a variety of parts for all sorts of craft. But this was to be her masterpiece, wrought in a new medium. As the hours passed and the wagon rolled on and on, as the sky began to glow and the pink-hot edge of the sun crawled forth, as shadows of swooping birds crisscrossed the white arch of the wagon top, Ata Maroo completed her work. It was a strong, flexible boot made from pieces of whalebone laced together, built to bend in certain ways but not in others, softened inside with strips from her quilt and laced in place with strips from her sarong. *This is like the one I made for my calf*, thought Ata Maroo, although that one had only been made from tree bark and roots. This will hold him while he heals. It will keep him from further harm. It will protect this stone-faced, long-suffering, brave and stupid man, so that he may walk his road again.

THE BEDSIDE LAMP HAD LONG since run out of oil, and Ata Maroo realized that the oxen must be very hungry. They should graze. I should go tell them whoa.

The man remained silent and motionless. Again she was afraid—redflower sap could be dangerous, and who knew how much they had given him?

She went out into the blinking-bright morning and halted the team, took them out of their yokes and picketed them in the common field beside the road. Her cats zigzagged back and forth across the field, hunting hares. The Lantern was showing above the horizon— small and far, but there it was. They would soon be in Coastwall, where she would stop at the Nautilus to sell this life, and go back to her old one. Or was she going back to something new?

Inside the wagon again, Ata Maroo went to a cabinet and took out a tin box with makings in it for breakfast. She took out a brazier and a cup and a tray. She was just making the tea when the man opened his eyes.

The last thing Alvert remembered about the duel was the sticky, disgusting red sap that someone behind the curtain had forced down his throat. Within him the sap had raised a fogbank that obscured all awareness, all sensation. But now, as the fog began to clear, he felt a harsh distant pain deep in the meat and bone of his left foot, and knew instinctively that it was broken.

He had seen flyers with broken feet before: poor sadsters who couldn't earn a living, who tried to run too soon and broke 'em again— who if they were lucky ended up in the care o' the Guild or if they were unlucky ended up lame forever, slow and unwanted, finally starvin' to death. He supposed that's what would happen to him. But then he tried to wiggle his foot and realized it didn't move as much as he'd expected it to. Which meant it didn't hurt as much as he'd expected it to. This realization filled him with surprise, and then he opened his eyes and surprise weren't even close to what he felt.

He knew where he was. He recognized it immediately.

Above him was the canvas ceiling. There to one side was the little shelf where Medame had reached for the diamond-lookin' bottle. All around were her lockers and cabinets, and this soft place where he lay— here came that squirm in his heart again, the one so uncomfortable he wanted it to happen again and again— this soft place was her bed. Her actual bed. And then, with a soft rustling sound of pillows, she was beside him.

"How you feel?" she asked. Alvert stole a quick look around, just to make sure she weren't a-talkin' to anyone else.

"Ah, you cannot speak yet. I understand." And she moved off, a-busying herself about the inside o' the wagon.

Alvert wished he'd said something. He mobilized his tongue, which felt as big as a bale of Khashme wool, and rasped, "Did I win?"

The minute he said it he knew it were stupid. Winners didn't get broken feet. And Medame must have thought it were stupid, too, because she stayed away from 'im. She stayed somewhere where he couldn't even see her, standing at a cabinet doing something that clicked and clanked and scraped.

"No," she said. "At least, you did not win title. Or money. But I think you may be lucky and you foot will heal, if you take care, ah? I have made you special boot." She was beside him again, and she pointed at his left foot with a big silver fork. "I have also made you this. Ginger noodle." She set a little tray over his middle— a tray wi' legs— jammed more o' them pillows behind his back, and sat a-waitin'.

She waited for a while and then she sounded a little sad. "You not hungry? You do not want them?"

As if in reply, Alvert's stomach gave a furious, extremely audible snarl. He was too shy to look at her, so instead he watched the thin wheat noodles, unfolding themselves in a bowl of good beef broth. A few peas floated out from under a slice of ginger. "They smell delicious, Medame." Salty, meaty, sour, sweet. "But I ain't so low down as to go eatin' the only bowl on the table. Please, Medame. They're yours."

He heard her breathe in a little. Then she took up the bowl, and spun some of the noodles onto the fork, and moved her head so that he was looking right at her golden face, right into her black, black, shining eyes.

"If they are mine, I will give them to you as gift. Will you take them?"

Alvert nodded. She brought the forkful of noodles to his lips and he had never tasted anythin' so good in his life. She slipped bite after bite from the fork onto his tongue, and when the noodles were all gone she gave him the bowl to drink from. "Broth has beef," she told him, although he could taste it, "and lemon, too. There is meat and fruit." And then for some reason she seemed very shy, herself, for telling him that. "You want tea, ah?" she jumped up and went back to handling something that sounded like dishes.

Alvert didn't understand. He had lost the duel, Medame had said so. Then why was he here, a-lyin' in her wagon, feelin' all of these wonderful painful beautiful awful things, all a-fightin' wi' one another inside o' him, much harder than ever he'd fought in that terrible willow ring? And then she was wi' him again, giving him a cup o' tea, sittin' so close beside him that he could smell the flower-smelling oil she'd brushed into her hair.

"I... I wish to tell you something," she half-whispered. "You will not understand it. But I hope you will listen. Will you listen?"

Alvert felt like saying: I'd crawl through a hundred thousand hells to listen to you, Medame. But he just nodded.

And then she began talking, in some language he had never heard, a language so pretty he liked just hearing it. Some of its words were melodious; others had a satisfying clack and clang— it was music. But to Alvert's dismay the music turned, deepened, shifted into a sorrowful key. As Medame spoke, her head began to droop, her hair to slip over her shoulder, until it was hanging down in a veil of black shot with a few strands of pure crystal white and behind that veil Alvert heard her breath wavering and when he realized what was happening he nearly dropped his teacup in alarm.

"Medame," he dared to whisper. "You're cryin'."

Her voice was unexpectedly weak. "Wah, it embarrass you. Please excuse it."

Alvert couldn't imagine how to proceed. It seemed wrong to speak, wrong to hold his tongue; wrong to lie there, wrong to move. It was Medame's empty teacup that saved him. Somehow it slipped from her fingers, and when both he and she reached for it, there they were— each left grasping a little bit of cup and a little bit of hand, and neither letting go.

"I, ah... I have," Medame began, and Alvert saw her golden face take on a tinge of red. "I have rude question for you, poor kindhearted broken-footed man. Here it is: how rich you think I am?"

Alvert had never given it any thought beyond a vague admiration. "Why, I don't know, Medame. You've got near a hundred oxen, that I saw. Dozens and dozens o' wagons. And pillows, and dishes, and food, and a crystal bottle, until I lost it." That made him turn red, too. "I'd call you mighty rich—I'll get the bottle back, I promise."

"Never worry about bottle. But tell me truth: you think that really all? You not know about rest of fleet, about farm, about warehouse, terminal, valuation of business?"

Tears of mortification came to Alvert's round eyes. "Oh, Medame! I beg pardon! Oh, forgive me. I didn't mean anythin'. I didn't know. I'm just... a ignorant—"

"I think innocent better word than ignorant. Now will you listen to me, innocent honest generous man? Listen to something serious?"

He would listen till the end o' eternity, he wanted to say. Their hands had crept more closely together; hers now covered his; it was strong like only the hand of a hard worker can be strong, but soft and tender too. He let the cup slide out of his fingers until it was gone, and still she did not release his hand... Alvert realized he hadn't been listening. Medame was saying, "...far away, no more 'Ox-Train Queen'... would you do this for me? And would you go live on boat, in middle of Peaceful Ocean?"

Abruptly he remembered: the duel. The duel! Oh, gods, he'd lost the duel, and he was bein' banished, sent away, shunned like a mange-ridden cur. All the feelings twisting and playing inside of him shrank to ice and ashes. He turned his hand over so that it was a desperate, dying claw, and clung till her eyes opened wide.

Banished to the ocean, he thought. O' course. It was as if she'd seen into the deepest, most private pit of his soul, and decided to turn the place he loved the most into his tomb. He couldn't help but marvel at the harsh justice of it: fair was fair. He had risked, and he had lost. So he gathered all his courage, and sealed his fate. "Aye, Medame. I will."

She let his hand go. So that's it, thought Alvert. He let his raw, grainy, defeated eyes sink shut.

And then he felt her breath, soft ticklish little puffs of her breath, grazing his cheeks and his forehead as she whispered, "Then, ah, there is one more thing. Forgive me, but time so short. I have asked you question. Now there is one last thing that I must know." And she pressed her lips to the thin soft quaking skin of his eyelids— first one, then the other.

No one had ever done such a thing to Alvert. The huge lush feeling of it raced straight down the center of him with a fierce energy and the little tray with legs was in the way, very much in the way. The great golden woman swept it aside and lay full upon him. Her heart pressed against his. His arms moved by themselves, wrapping around her; his mouth drank hers in like scorching spicy *linkapaa*. This was nothing at all like the hasty furtive maneuvers that female flyers sometimes persuaded him to execute behind certain sheds and haystacks, where they leered down and he looked past them— here he was at the glowing core of something vast, here he was floating, here he was magnified. Within the fold of the quilt they pressed together and drew apart, fanning waves of heat, until at last the whole world seemed to stop, and sway, and sigh.

Afterward, a deep exhaustion overcame Alvert. As if from a great distance, he saw Medame reach over the edge of the bed. He made an effort to memorize the twist o' her shoulders, the fall o' her hair, for he would never see them again— the beautiful thing she'd done wi' him was surely her farewell.

"Wait a minute, ah." She rummaged in another drawer and dug forth a dusty leather bag. She loosened the strings at its mouth; a quick shake, and out of the bag fell a little ivory hoop. She slipped its cool smoothness over his finger.

It seemed a bit late for this. He was not her courier anymore. Alvert spun it around his finger, studied its carved surface. "You're givin' me a seal-ring?"

"Ah yah." her expression was nervous, her voice breathless. "You correct, it made from tusk of seal. But this ring not for stamping paper— it is special." She took his hand in both of her own. "If you keep it, that mean you my husband."

He did not answer; he hadn't heard right.

"I hope you will keep it. To show I marry you."

"Marry me? Really, Medame? But why? I'm no one... I can't give you anythin'..."

"You already give more than you can dream. But— ai! I ask again— you want ring? You want *me*?"

He had to swallow a few times before he could say, "I do, Medame."

Then Alvert's bride, the Headmother of the Hundred Clans, embraced her mate the wounded god. She lay against him and gazed up at the peaks and valleys of his numinous face.

"Ah, my good sweet gentle *ipo*, from now on no more Medame. From now on, say Maroo."

"Maroo." He smiled. And he touched her cheek, letting it fill his hand, ignoring the whisk of shyness that tickled his chest. How's a fellow shy about his own wife?

His own wife. He had to think it again, and again, trying to get himself used to believin' it were true. He really might be dreamin'. But dream or no, truth was, he liked that shy tickling feeling. He hoped it would stay forever. It felt like ripples, catching a light that spread and spread on a vast, unfolding ocean.

CHAPTER 36

GRANNY ALMANTREE'S ENORMOUS SERVANT— THE extra pair a weepers the notorious criminal had left aboard her newly acquired smuggling craft to make sure its crew behaved themselves— looked lazily down upon the *Terrier*'s captain and said, "Don't."

"Don't what? You're not here to order me around. On this barky, I'm in command. Mind your tongue or I'll— I'll have you put in irons." It was a brave little speech, and at the end of it the captain had reached out and actually poked the enormous servant right in her protruding gut. But there had been a discernible tremor in his voice, and the *Terrier*'s crew sighed in relief when the enormous servant didn't knock their captain down, but only pushed his hand away.

"Don't go looking for whatever Granny put aboard. I told you, it's a bad idea."

"I'm not looking for—"

"You are. Don't."

The lull that followed was far from silent. The very air around the ship was an overflowing bilge of short-tempered shouting. The sun was fully above the horizon, and from the Lantern high over the city streamed the same tiresome set of flags that had been flying for the past two days: EMERGENCY BLOCKADE. ANY VESSEL LEAVING PORT WILL BE DETAINED.

All of Coastwall harbor was busy trying to put the delay to use. Every wharf was smothered with craft taking on additional cargo, all packed together spar to spar. Most vessels couldn't reach the cranes, so the water between them was thick with overloaded boats. The *Terrier* lay in the midst of this, hemmed in by a wall of much larger vessels— Granny

Almantree's assurance that, when the time came, she would be able to run away unhindered was beyond ridiculous.

One of the *Terrier*'s sailors leaned over the gunwale, looking for a good target. This sailor could spit a gob of played-out flavorless maidenroot nearly twenty feet, more if the wind was with her. She'd already passed the morning by carving what one of the other sailors insisted was an actual bawdy word on the mast step, tormenting the ship's smallcat by repeatedly offering it scraps of smoked fish but then eating them herself, and stealing a wad of slush from the galley with which to grease her pigtail. She was rapidly running out of good harmless ideas. So when a little green-painted rowing skiff, of the sort that landsmen can hire by the hourglass, drew up alongside the *Terrier*, the sailor got her maidenroot ready and was aiming for the dirty, barefoot, bearded monk at the oars when the fellow raised a megaphone to his mouth.

"Hoy, the *Big Rat!* Is your captain free to talk to a lady?"

"Of course not, stupid. Cap's busy gluing the tail back on a blue-arsed ape."

The monk ducked a glob of spit. "Ah. Well, could you— ah, could you go get her?"

And then a brash-looking pigtailed man came to the rail, looked down at the little rowing skiff and said: "I'm here. Is that the lady?"

The monk handed the megaphone to a majestically weathered old woman, who aimed the instrument at the *Terrier* and said: "I am— hush, Malfred, I *know*— I am a person of some resource. I wish to head out to sea at the very earliest opportunity."

The captain snorted and slapped the gunwale. "You and everyone else, woman. Try some other ship."

"I've been speaking to other ships all night— quite a lot of them recommended you. Word is that you are the most accommodating of Coastwall's mariners."

"Ah, well whoever told you that was—"

The sailor who'd been spitting smacked the captain's shoulder and made a wild-eyed grimace at him. "What?" he demanded.

The sailor jerked her head down at the skiff and whispered behind her hand. "You ever seen Whellen Country paper money? No? Well, that's the Domina de mumping Whellen down there, or I'll be a blue-arsed ape."

The captain had never known this sailor to be wrong about anything to do with money. He changed his tune. "Ah, dear lady! I misunderstood. I imagine you're willing to spend a bit on such a request?"

"I am, indeed."

"And to where will you require passage?"

"Now, that... is a subject for discussion. May I request permission to come aboard— what, Malfred? Ah. Excellent point. I know it's not customary, Mesir, but my adviser suggests I ask you to join me in this boat. Will you come down?"

The captain of the *Terrier* smelled opportunity over the reek of the harbor. He came down the man-rope and sat opposite Dame Elsebet while she described the mission she wanted him to undertake: a search, covering those parts of the Midland Sea where a hijacked ship with two nights' head start might have gone. Hopeless. Like looking for a black grain of sand on a gray beach. But it enticed him.

The captain chafed at having to obey Granny Almantree. He'd been making good coin from his smuggling venture for years; now he was expected to truckle to some greedy new owner? Rank raw flux, he'd find a way around *that*— and this job looked like just the way. Sure, Granny Almantree expected the *Terrier* to fly straight for the Herb Islands with whatever contraband of hers was hidden aboard. But the Domina de mumping Whellen, sitting right here in this little boat with him, didn't sound as if she knew much about navigation. It would be easy to convince her they were going somewhere else.

And with a dawning hunger, the captain realized there could be even more to it. A noblewoman with money to spare would be a benny prize in her own right. Certainly, a noble of her rank might come aboard with a bristling great escort of knights and archers. But if she came with just one or two? Why then, she'd have to pay every coin she carried for the privilege of leaving the *Terrier* alive. Or better: her family would pay far more. Or better still: her vassals might outbid the family to *not* bring her back, that they might seize their lands from under her control. It was so brilliant that the captain nearly jumped to his feet and upset the little green skiff.

"Our cargo is still coming aboard, piecemeal. It's supposed to be complete by dawn tomorrow," he assured Dame Elsebet. "I have it on good authority that something will lift the travel ban at that time. At least for *us*, if you follow me." And he winked, binding Dame Elsebet to him in mutual roguery.

"I follow you perfectly. We shall come aboard you just before the dawn. My greatest thanks, captain—?"

"It's best we don't name names, Your High Honor." And again an exaggerated wink. The spark of recognition upon Dame Elsebet's face was the most beautiful thing the captain had ever seen. He was ready to get rich. Granny could go suck eggs.

CHAPTER 37

COASTWALL WAS AN OLD CITY, and though its poor places had spent centuries perfecting the arts of wretchedness and squalor, so too had its rich places grown to astonishing heights of luxury.

Most particularly luxurious was The Nautilus. The Nautilus was an inn— but only in the same way that a masterfully cut diamond is a stone. Really it was a haven where the extremely powerful withdrew to transact their affairs. Only those who met strict qualifications were allowed to set foot in its foyer of red porphyry and alabaster. The late old King, who had made a progress through his vassals' countries every ten years, had been a guest at The Nautilus— it was that kind of place.

The Ox-Train Queen was well known here. One of the miniature portraits behind the manager's desk was of her admiring the herd of beautiful ox-shaped cocoa cakes the pastry chef had baked to celebrate an occasion; many of the orchids in the hothouse were grown especially for her; she had particular favorite rooms and a particular favorite meal. Whenever she appeared at the Nautilus, the Ox-Train Queen felt as though she were visiting the home of a loving relative.

Alvert, on the other hand, had only seen the servants' quarters o' Whellengood and Brewel Hall. Now everything was different. Four strong servants had whisked him lightly up to a vast airy room that was but one chamber of a comfortable suite. A dulcimer-drummer had come to stand under the balcony and play soothing music, and a great copper bathtub had been set just inside the balcony's open doors. In this lay Alvert, submerged to the neck in clouds of soap scented like juniper, eating slice after slice of fresh-baked herb toast spread with honey and oil. His booted foot stuck out over the edge of the tub and rested upon a padded velvet bench.

“This water smells about a thousand times better ’n the hot pools in Devil’s Dale,” burbled Alvert. “And there’s no sharp rocks.”

“Alvie, *ipo*, let me help you wash away road dust.” Ata Maroo scooped up some hot water and rubbed it into his short velvety nap of hair that felt like a newborn calf’s ear. Everything about that was just so wonderful, she did it again and again. She kissed his forehead and it tasted faintly of the mountains.

A discreet knock sounded at the door, and she hurried to accept the extra-long robe the Nautilus’s tailors had quickly put together. “The rest of your husband’s wardrobe will be ready soon, Medame Ata,” murmured the servant, with an expression that told her the Coastwall gossip mill was already busy grinding.

In a few hours, the doors of the largest room of their suite would close upon an unprecedented gathering of the capital city’s financial elite and by the next morning, she and Dragonsson Ata Alvert would be on their way up the coast. There they would launch the boat that would take them... well, not exactly home. Had this become her home? Ata Maroo did not really know. She was melancholy, and a little bit frightened, but the deep wretched corrosive feeling that had been with her for so long it had formed a callus on her soul was gone.

A crash sounded from Alvert’s balcony. “Whoops,” she heard him say. “I’m all right. Just need more toast.”

CHAPTER 38

MEANWHILE, ACROSS THE INTRICATELY PLANTED formal garden in the most exclusive courtyard, Fred craned his neck to glance out of his own balcony doors. The barber's shears instantly froze. She had never yet made a mistake, even on the most fidgety patron; the Nautilus did not condone incompetence. Likewise, the maid shining Fred's smart new half-boots paused to let him uncross his legs. "Ugh, again the sour notes," he groaned. "If that fellow doesn't tune his dulcimer soon, I'm going to tell one of you to go over and tune *him*."

"Very Good, Mesir Murd," said all the servants together.

There were a lot of them, and the more the better— an empty room would have crushed him flat the moment its red lacquer door closed. Instead Fred had surrounded himself with a maid arranging flowers, a valet pressing his closely-tailored new silk shirt and brushing his fine new doeskin breeches, a cook busy making rice rolls of cold braised eel and sea herbs, an old matron with hands of steel standing by to give him a massage, the barber, the bootblack and, as a final delicious touch, a Fool. Fred made the Fool stand in the corner and do absolutely nothing. He was only there because— why the hell's holes not. Dame Elsebet, in contrast, had not wanted anyone in her room at all. "In my case, *not* having any maids is a luxury," she'd said, and Fred had shrugged at that, thinking: whatever wheels your barrow.

The barber handed him a mirror, and Fred examined himself. All in all, he didn't look too terribly much the worse for half a year of misery. Sunburned, yes. Hollow under the eyes and with a few more wrinkles, undoubtedly. Bitter cynical expression from being booted out of his home and turned into a friendless vagabond who eats lizards? Check. But the haircut and the shave, the bath and Oh Ye Gods yes the sweet sweet slugs of *real* Sherry Lorroso, those had done him a power of good— it would have been the world's worst decision not to have taken

Dame Elsebet up on her offer of this room, these clothes, this delicious return to normalcy. And come the dawn he'd make some excuse, miss the sailing of the *Big Rat* or whatever that nasty little ship was called, and make his way back to Brewel Hall looking like a gold penny. He'd banter wittily with Felip de Brewel, trade a few remarks about The Theater with Dame Irona, tell Petir to go read a book and then ask Kestrella whether she'd like to render his figure.

"And now, fellows and goodwives," he announced, standing up and turning an exuberant series of handsprings across the silk carpet and finishing with a back flip and twist right into the deep, soft, clean feather bed, "I am going to sleep like the dead. Until dinnertime. Gather round and I'll show you how it's done."

CHAPTER 39

Corvinalias was bored.

There, he'd said it. He was bored. The de Brewels' garden was interesting enough, the first few dozen times he'd flown up high to look at it, but it wasn't the real Brewel Country, just a model. And the highcat had been a wonder, for most of a day, but he soon realized that the creature was never going to leave Brewel Hall. In fact, it spent far more of its time curled up in one corner of Dame Irona's sleeping platform than doing anything else, and Corvinalias's efforts to understand its language had reached no further than deciphering what might have been extremely distant cognates for "yum", "chase" and "tired".

Now the golden hour had begun. Even the charred remnants of the tearoom looked beautiful. Kestrella was giving some of Petir's friends a carriage ride through the garden, and the rest of the family and their party guests were off somewhere laughing over gossip, crying about the terrible, terrible burglary, stuffing their faces or playing cards or Ye Gods knew what these people filled their time with. It certainly wasn't adventures. Corvinalias yawned, dropped from one of the trees into the stone gazebo, and gave the highcat a little kick. "Buddy," he told it. "Come on, let's do something."

The cat only licked its paw, rubbed its face and said "Tired."

The sound Corvinalias made was a multi-tonal combination of groans from three Uman dialects, magpie both ancient and modern, monkey, gull and albatross. He zigzagged to the top of the tree, took its very tiniest uppermost twig delicately between the claws of his hind and main fingers, and let himself sway with the breeze.

The sun sank lower, lower. The Lantern stood out plain against the horizon and inside of it the light came on. Smells of Uman cooking, farm dung, ashes and water blew by. In the fake little country below, flashbugs began to twinkle. Kestrella and Petir's friends came back, leading the horses, dragging the carriage and carrying one of its wheels. Corvinalias shot the sleeping highcat one last look and launched himself out of the garden, toward the city.

Corvinalias crossed the broad brown Denna with the last rays of the sunset. The jam of ships was still there, now studded with lamps and safety lanterns, the miasma of Uman cursing and ill-temper rising from it thicker than ever. Aboard one ship, some sailors were fighting over possession of a frowzy-looking parrot, which was so drunk it fell off a yardarm and disappeared into the harbor. Corvinalias did not want to get involved. He flew on.

In the spire of a dilapidated church, a crew of bats began shrieking out one of their tedious, needlessly detailed work songs. Corvinalias had no wish to overhear 365 different names for the mosquito. He flew on.

A little girl driving milk cows home to their owners squealed and ran to chase down a runaway calf. Porters on the street dropped their loads and ran to help her. A little boy ran to steal the things the porters had dropped. A dog ran after the boy and bit him. Corvinalias shook his head and flew on.

High over the knotted innards of Coastwall he flew, as the tableaux beneath him changed like seasons from poverty to security to comfort to wealth and then back again. In the better areas, lamplighters and street cleaners came forth to do their work, like dung beetles. In the worse ones there was only darkness and stink. Corvinalias studied the paths of canals to see where they went, and the tributaries of the Denna to see where they came from. There had to be someone down there who was getting ready for some adventures.

One of his landmarks, now well lit and still quite clearly visible, was a huge inn with many red and white brick walls separating an array of beautifully planted courtyards. Behind it, a series of paddocks stretched away from the stables in rolling strips of dark grass. Horses, mules and cattle leaned out the windows of their stalls, turning their ears to bear on a couple of long golden shapes that zigzagged back and forth across the paddocks, leaping the fences between as if they were not even there, coming together to roll around, clasping each other with their front paws and beating each other with the hind ones, then breaking apart and zigzagging some more. Corvinalias stopped his wings and spun down for a closer look. *Two* highcats?

"Chase!" he shouted, and the cats looked up, to where he perched on the edge of the stable roof.

"Chase! Chase!" agreed the cats. "Chase chase chase!"

"Tired?" Corvinalias asked them. "Yum?"

"Yum." The word was full of assurance that later on, someone would give them yum. Corvinalias decided to check the inn for their owner.

He was surprised to find that one of the rooms he peeked into had Fred in it— but then again there were a lot of other Umans in there with him, so he'd be fine. He was sitting up in bed, stretching and rubbing his eyes and smelling very clean, looking much as he had before his people pushed him out of their hive on the Isle of Gold. But Corvinalias was through with that blister. He flew on.

He passed a room where a family was doing some kind of foreign praying. Another where a man sat drinking and reading a letter and crying. One where a mother was rocking twin babies to sleep. And one— a particularly large one with a balcony and floor-to-ceiling windows wide open to the warm night air— was so crammed with shinies that Corvinalias crashed right into the extended windowpane as he soared by, gaping.

The lady, the group of gentlemen, and the archers gathered inside turned to see what had made such a thump and squeal.

"It's all right," said a gentleman. "Probably only a bird." And they turned their attention back to the mountain of papers in the center of the huge bleached whitewood table around which they sat.

Corvinalias clung to the brick and sandstone wall and laid his spinning head on the windowsill. Those in there, now, *those* were shinies all right. No embroidered flimflam, just rank upon rank of carts marked with the seahorse-and-scales of DeCoastwel Bank, their lids unlocked to display box upon box of neatly sorted coins. Not many silver ones. Mostly gold. The piercing gleam of them set his heart racing. "Yum," he groaned faintly.

The lady looked up. "That my cat?"

One of the other gentlemen said, "I will go check on your animals, Medame Ata," and an archer stepped away from the door to let him.

Still a little shaky, Corvinalias used his beak and claws to creep over to a balcony. He flung himself over the rail, sat up on the marble floor and started to preen.

"Get away with you!" someone scolded him in a thick Yondstone accent. "Bad luck thievin' critter! Shoo! Ain't I already had troubles enough wi' one o' your kind? I ain't a-goin' to let Maroo have any troubles, pus clump it!" And from the dim comfortable interior of the room jutted the tallest Uman Corvinalias had ever seen. Well, maybe that Yondy oaf Fred had dragged into the barn was as tall as... this is him! Isn't it? Corvinalias rolled away just in time to avoid a swinging bath-brush.

"Magpie Guild sent me," he squeaked, scuttling behind a potted plant. "Some wight's message bag got lifted not long ago. I'm supposed to find the owner and tell him it's been dealt with!"

The fellow stopped swatting. "Dealt with?"

"Affirmative," Corvinalias said in a bureaucratic monotone. "The bird responsible has been punished under the directives of Act 2172, Subsection 504, part X."

"Ah," said Alvert, bending down from his enormous height for a better look at Corvinalias. "Part ecks, is it? That sounds pretty bad. Ecks is what they put on the front o' your flyer's license if you get sacked." He hobbled onto the balcony, leaned his handsome teak cane against a chair and sat. There was a white linen stocking on his left foot, and some kind of interesting boot contraption over that.

"I got sacked," he continued mildly. "I thought that were the end o' the world. But now... I think I'm dreamin', to say the truth. Never thought I'd ever have such adventures."

The feathers of Corvinalias's crest stood up and he dared to hop onto the arm of the fellow's chair. "Did you say 'Adventures'? Please confirm. As an envoy of the Guild, I am authorized to participate in adventures."

CHAPTER 40

DOKTOR TALUCA LIVELY STRODE THE length of this big boat they called the *Longwing*, from the rear end of it all the way up to its pointy front, with the bold confident steps of one who sees everything going perfectly.

He took up the tail of his robe and wiped his hands as he strode. Sunlight was rapidly fading, so an onlooker could not have seen the color of his garment, or the much darker color wicking itself to the shoulder of each of his sleeves, or the similar color smeared all over the wooden floor of this big boat the *Longwing*. But there were no onlookers. There was only Doktor Lively, who turned his face upwind and drew a deep breath of his favorite sharp, rusty smell— an operating-table smell, a slaughterhouse smell.

That last fellow had been a funny one. Lively had liked him. Well, maybe not liked, exactly; inferior people weren't worth liking. But the fellow had been interesting. For one thing, he'd borne somewhat of a resemblance to Lively himself, with his round sweet face. And he'd been a surgeon. That was a kind of healer, wasn't it? Too bad the fellow hadn't known any spells. Lively would really have enjoyed talking shop with him, but in over twenty years there had never been anyone for Doktor Lively to talk shop with, or at least if there were, once such a fellow had met the Doktor he didn't talk— or indeed live— for long. It was dull and tiresome, being the only worthy person among inferiors. But when you thought about it, that was unavoidable. It was lonely at the top.

Lively strode the deck a bit longer, spotting leftover parts of the Longwing's crew here and there as the sky grew dark. He kicked these overboard, stopping to admire a few that had been particularly gratifying to craft. He was in truly top form now: the practice had done him good. Too bad he hadn't thought to ask Sweetface, or the purser, or that inspector, to make notes. Lively shrugged and began to climb carefully down a set of stairs to the room where he'd hidden the knights.

Surely, he thought, some of them will know how to make this boat go in the right direction. That was another thing he hadn't thought about— how all the ropes and things worked— but he was not particularly worried. The details would iron themselves out. Worry was for inferiors, not for such as he. And once he reached the Isle, a few hours' more work would put the world and all its potential right at his masterful fingertips.

CHAPTER 41

IF THERE WAS ONE THING Fred couldn't get enough of, these months past, it was meals.

The eel rolls his cook had made him were gone. The sherry Lorroso, gone. The candy pastilles in the Stewen crystal bowl on the inlaid onyx table, gone. He rejected the notion that eating so much might bring back his former, frankly plebeian build: If I ever looked as though I could dig a ditch, he thought, that wasn't food's fault. It was the deep-damned job, was what did it. As a garden hermit, he intended to let himself become spectacularly intellectual and as fat as a winter bear.

And so, the moment he woke up to the setting sun, stretched and scratched and doused himself with lavender-scented water and had his valet dress him up in his new clothing, Fred's plan was to go find some more food.

As it happened, he didn't have to search at all. A knock sounded on his door and one of his servants opened it to reveal Dame Elsebet, tapping lightly on the red lacquer with the handle of her fan.

"Please invite brother Malfred to sup with me," she told the servant, but brother Malfred was right there.

"Sup! That's my new favorite word."

"Why, Malfred— you look, look..."

"Gentlemanly? Fashionable? Handsome?"

"...not much like a holy man at all. Although of course I'm sure it makes no difference. When our gods visit us they disregard appearances, isn't that what the scriptures say?"

"You mentioned some food." Fred straightened the fall of his breeches and, feeling as though something more were required of him, hastily added: "Yes... so the scriptures do say."

"Let us go to The Taproom. We can make ourselves some sandwiches— I really cannot face a big, proper meal. Besides, simplicity is the mark of virtue." Again, the sort of pause that made Fred think he ought to respond in kind.

"Oh, yea, verily."

THE TAPROOM AT THE NAUTILUS was made up as a replica of a typical countryside hostelry: a great fireplace which in winter would have been lit, but was now filled with an artful tableau of cast-iron cooking implements; tall-backed wooden settles with the very gentlest rearward slant, so that they were more comfortable than the genuine kind; a hanging chandelier full of lanterns whose oil was sweetly scented; and in the middle of the room a butcher's block featuring a great crisp-crusted roast of beef, from which patrons could carve their own supper, in the hearty fashion of villagers.

Fred heaped a towering pile from the rare end onto several slices of marble rye, poured a generous cascade of horseradish cream over the top and, remembering his manners, cut another piece of bread and a chunk of roast for Dame Elsebet.

"Why, thank you, brother Malfred," she told him when he set these down before her. Her voice was brimfull of the utmost sincerity, and there came that weird unpleasant feeling to bother Fred again. He hurried to staunch the feeling with great gulps of beef, but the things she said really weren't helping.

"I really do thank you. From the depths of my heart. If you hadn't been there for me when I got that awful message, I don't know what I would have done."

"Oh, you'd have thought of something."

"I understand you've taken a vow of modesty. But I salute you, dear man. I cannot imagine how, how, terrifying— how utterly mind-reeling— it must have been to dive into the Leet. I used to be a diver in my youth, you see." She looked a bit self-conscious as she pointed to the wall near their table.

Fred stopped chewing for a moment. Among the charming old posters on the walls was a hand-tinted bulletin engraving of a damsel with her arms upraised, preparing to dive from a high bluff. Her muscles stood out in plateaus of pink and gold and the wind lifted the dense flag of her honey-brown hair. The damsel's eyes were dark and deep. And familiar. All at once Fred recognized her. He wasn't sure he could swallow his latest bite.

"That bulletin was issued when I made the world's record dive at a place in Yondstone called Heaven's Heights. The record has been broken since then, of course. Many times. I was only nineteen, still such a daredevil..." Dame Elsebet's voice began to falter. "...soon to... marry..."

"Are you all right?"

She had closed her eyes and was whispering to herself, breathing in an odd rhythmic fashion. Fear gripped Fred. The young King did things like this. He wanted to grab her and shake her before it was too late and she slipped into some kind of a paralysis— but it was all right. She was only praying, or something. She opened her eyes and seemed a bit embarrassed about it and Fred began to wonder if maybe he shouldn't try slipping out right now.

Dame Elsebet's smile was crooked, timid. "Doktor Lively taught me how to do that. If I feel it happening, I just do the breathing and the visualizations." Very gently she fixed her gaze upon Fred's and said: "By 'it' I mean madness, Malfred. If I hear the— thing. If I see its shape. It's my own fault, you see, that my husband and my father were killed. No one else can possibly be blamed. And afterward, I had to be tied down— tied down and guarded. Lorenz was forced to act as Regent for five whole years. And those horrible bouts kept plaguing me, off and on, until Doktor Lively came.

"Even if the Doktor had no magic power at all, he would still be the dearest thing in the world to me, because he helped me finally banish my madness. But his healing spell is something different. That spell is the only bargaining chip I have— thank Ye Gods my country had the peace and prosperity to support the Doktor in perfecting it!

"It is a miracle to me, Malfred, every day I count it as a miracle, that during the regency of my sweet gentle harmless loving baby brother, the poor boy did not find himself the target of some usurper— some traitor. Thank the Great God Almighty that Doktor Lively could heal me, so that I might do my duty and not foist it on Lorenz. It would have destroyed him eventually, you know. Ruling takes a certain... hardness of heart. Even if he could have spotted a traitor, I don't think he could ever have..." and she pantomimed the *kuaga-losha*, the second of the three broadspear cuts.

Inside Fred's fine new cordovan half-boots, his feet began oozing sweat. A drop ran down his back. The weird feeling was mixing with fear to create a truly hideous combination. He heard himself saying things, random things.

"But you! You, ah, you are good now."

"Not so very good. I'm still terrified, to be perfectly honest, that this plan we have with the ship..."

"Aha, yes, the Rat Dog."

"...that our plan to search for Doktor Lively will come to naught. The other day at my feast, Lorenz said something to me: he said we'd only know the outcome, when the King tells us whether there will be any more de Whellens. My brother has already dropped his nobiliary 'de', you know. He is plain Lorenz Whellen now. He doesn't have to worry about things like traitors, and whether the King will be pleased..."

"He'll be pleased." Fred didn't know why he said that. He had no idea whether the King would be pleased. If he'd ever known whether that kid would be pleased or not, his life would have been easy. "You can bet on it, good lady, like fire is hot and water's wet and birds have flappy wings..."

For the first time in as long as he could remember, he felt clumsy. As he got to his feet it was like swimming through mud. But the door wasn't too far; he could make it. And at that thought, something made him blurt out: "...as for me I really want to say I never intended any, uh, that is! I never really wanted to ah uh! I didn't ever mean to..."

"Brother Malfred! Are you speaking in tongues? Having a vision?"

"Yes! Yes! That's it. I'm seeing..."

What was he seeing? Over Dame Elsebet's shoulder, coming through the delightful huge rustic doors of The Taproom at the Nautilus, was a deputation of bankers, a magnificent giant with a cane, and... Ata Maroo. That's what he was seeing.

"Malfred, ah! You changing so fast I hardly keep track of you! First you monk, then you Fool, then you vagabond and now— oh. Good evening, You High Honor." Ata Maroo bowed deeply to Dame Elsebet, as did the bankers and the giant. And Corvinalias. *What?* Fred shot the bird a look, but the look didn't land. The magpie was not concerned with him anymore.

"Good evening, Miss Ata. I regret that I was forced to leave Whellengood before our meeting regarding the… the… oh dear, I cannot recall."

"Railway, Medame. If you still wish to discuss it, these gentlemen now in charge." She indicated the bankers. And then she aimed the full broadside of her attention at Fred.

"You interesting man, Malfred Murd. The other day I really thought you down on luck, but maybe that only pretend play, ah? Maybe you have fun tricking me, like funny magic trick you do back at inn in Good Market." She paused to chuckle and Fred didn't even have time to think *Oh my god don't let her say it* before she said it. "Maybe King did not sack royal Fool after all, ah? Maybe you just pretending to be vagabond so you gather new joke material." Ata Maroo's laugh bubbled forth deep and warm and hearty; her filed teeth showed, making her look like a friendly panther.

Fred meant to run for the door, he really did, but he glanced back at Dame Elsebet and her face was a clammy greenish white and instead of running he was paralyzed, hearing her say:

"Brother Malfred? What does she mean, royal Fool, vagabond, magic trick, joke? Brother Malfred. Malfred. *Murd!* Answer me!"

"It's nothing! She's crazy! You know what, I just realized I should go and…"

But Dame Elsebet was the one closer to the door. She was standing up. Her timidity was gone— her face was turning from pale to red, her eyes from frightened to furious. She had been born to rule a country and her voice rang out with undeniable authority: "Stop him."

Involuntarily the bankers, the giant, even Ata Maroo moved between Fred and the exit. Dame Elsebet advanced upon him and she did not look old. She looked eternal.

"So you find me a ripe target for mockery?"

"No no no I don't..."

"So you think I am a mere lunatic, who can be toyed with for the sake of some base jape?"

"I don't! It got out of hand! I only wanted some money!"

"Money? You schemed to extort *money* from me? When I am in desperation, with the future of my people at stake?"

"See, when you put it that way, it sounds really bad..."

"So you are a confidence trick man! A criminal! No, I will go further: you are a traitor."

Joke's on you! Babbled some waggish sector of Fred's brain. Good luck chopping me up without your broadspear!

"You are a traitor of the very ilk who might have undone my brother. Thank all Ye Gods, it is I with whom you have chosen to interfere. I know how to deal with you."

And Fred couldn't help but follow her eyes to the butcher's block in the middle of the Taproom. The great roast was flesh pink and blood red and the carving knife protruding from it was a long, gleaming, supple, finely sharpened blade.

Fred's knees buckled, just as they had back in the combat arena at Whellengood. He saw Dame Elsebet reach for something, raise her arm. Fred's ears were split by a frightful crash.

A crash. A metal-sounding crash. From his sprawled spot on the floor he could see what had happened: she had snatched the Stone of Protection from her sleeve and hurled it into the fireplace, with its artful tableau of cast-iron cooking implements. She turned and glared down at Fred and he could almost feel the blast of her scorn.

"Very well, Fool. Yours is the last laugh, after all. I know *how* to deal with you, but I find I cannot do it. I have larger things on my mind, or perhaps I am an old weakling now after all. At any rate I don't need your pathetic fake spells or your filthy little rock anymore. I am my own Stone of Protection, sir, and have protected my country for forty-five years, no thanks to the likes of you." She addressed the others. "Get him out of my sight."

The Nautilus's security crew were already upon the scene and as they dragged Fred away wave after wave of that sick, sick feeling rolled over him. His heart was simultaneously exploding, and crushed. He could hardly breathe. Everything was going jagged and colorful but also grainy black. Just the way a throbbing white boil reaches its bursting point, something in him burst.

"I'm sorry!" he wailed, though by now he was out of The Taproom and Dame Elsebet couldn't hear him at all. "I'm sorry, I'm so sorry, I never wanted to hurt you, I didn't mean for any of this to happen, I would never have done it if I had known, I regret it, I wish I'd never thought of it, I was just afraid to stop, I'd give anything to take it back, I'm sorry!"

Tears were rushing down his face and after he was thrown out through a discreet rear door, the dust of the alley stuck to their wetness. He lay in the dark and cried. Rats skittered by and a stray dog stopped to lick the back of his head.

Dame Elsebet hadn't heard any of Fred's apologies, but he didn't find that important. He didn't want to bother her ever again. If that meant he had to keep on feeling sad for the rest of his life, so be it.

He sat up against the wall, caressing his beautiful half-boots and the embroidered cuffs of his smart silk shirt and the dirty knees of his handsome breeches. They were the last things he'd ever have to remind him of her. Soon she'd be gone, and who knew whether she'd ever find who she was looking for, or make it to the Isle, or whether the King would listen to her.

And at that thought, the sickness was with Fred again— only now he no longer wanted to chase it away. Now he knew what it was.

During the night he drifted through the alleys of Coastwall more or less at random. His mind played little part in where he went; this decision was left more or less to his legs, which consistently chose the easier path— that is to say, the one that led downhill, and so at length he arrived on the waterfront as the third day of Coastwall's blockade was dawning.

The blockade brought both agony and opportunity. No one knew how long it would go on; decisions about whether to offload a consignment and send it overland were difficult to make; many a ship's owner was alternately outraged to hear that his vessel was no longer needed, and pleased to discover that someone else— with perhaps a less perishable, but more profitable cargo— would be using it instead. Scribes lit the lanterns of their booths early to find flocks of customers already waiting. Taverns were roaring full around the clock, and taking on extra staff in the throwing-drunks-out line. Longshoremaids and stevedores prowled the docks with coins tearing out the seams of their pockets, and light-fingered brats flittered close behind them.

There was confusion, and commotion, and cover.

Fred sat in a shadow and considered the Big Rat.

The dumpy little carrevelle was the only ship going where he wanted to go. Or at least, that smarmy captain of theirs had assured him of it. Fred didn't see how it could possibly leave Coastwall, but then there was a lot he had never seen, so maybe the smarmy fellow would turn out to be right.

There was really only one thing to do, and it would be a ticklish thing, because the very sight of Fred would be repulsive to Dame Elsebet. He had to make absolutely sure she would never know he was aboard.

He watched the harborful of masts and yards jouncing up and down, side to side, until he was dizzy. The Big Rat wasn't too awfully far away. With some flips, with some leaps, with some judicious inching along the intervening ships' spars, he could probably fall right into the harbor and drown.

How did people actually stow away? Stow. That's what they did, they got stowed. Fred watched the dumpy little carrevelle: in the thin silvery light he could make out sailors climbing casually as acrobats, rigging a boom with a rope snaking down from its extremity to a barge, where a string of wagons held some kind of big cubes.

These cubes were wrapped in cord and burlap, each one stamped with the weight "20cwst." and a guild emblem, a pair of shears. A stevedore scrambled among the cubes, measured them with her striped staff and shouted to the sailors aboard the Big Rat to bring that scabflappin' whip and sling closer, damn it, can't you see these blisterscratchin' bales of greasy fluxin' wool are down *here*, not flyin' up on the boom like your sweetheart's lousy britches. Four at a time, the stevedore fitted the bales into the sling's pyramid of rope and rode with them, directing the sailors to winch them inboard and lower them down hatches into the Big Rat's hold.

There was a rhythm to it. Fred watched a few of these trips and gauged the timing, which direction the workers were likely to be looking, where the rapidly rising sun would cast its shadows, and then, taking a deep breath and trusting to luck, he ran down the dock, vaulted onto the barge, scurried to one of the wagons and hid in its box.

No one saw him. No one except the stevedore, as the whip lowered her into the wagon and she stepped down off the triangular wooden base of the empty sling. Fred pressed his finger to his lips, gesturing for silence, and then pointed toward the ship. She raised a foot at him.

"Please!" he whimpered.

The stevedore signaled for a break. "One minute, here! Got a damaged bale!" Then back to Fred. "Right, rich boy. Why should I risk my job for *your* stowaway beans?"

"Uh, because... because..." Fred couldn't think of anything to offer her, other than the obvious, but she was a fine hardy good looking wench and probably didn't lack for options. Yet his eye fell upon the back of her hand, where a single sad half-finished rose crept from between her fingers.

"...because if you put me aboard, I'll give you a magic spell. One that'll bring back your betrothed."

The stevedore looked as if Fred had hit her with a boom. "Bring Jergen back?" she whispered with trembling lips. "You're lying."

"It's written down," said Fred, rummaging in the broad flap pocket at the front of his shirt. "You can take it to any scribe. Take it tonight and have him read this out loud and watch, if your betrothed doesn't come back that means a... a monster ate him." And he seized the hand with its aborted wedding bracelet, turned it palm up and into it thrust the crumpled page of the cantrip.

The stevedore stared at it for a moment with teary eyes. Then she shoved Fred into the middle of the sling and said: "Keep your head down and once you're in the hold, get out from between these as fast as you bleedin' can." She maidhandled three bales of wool onto the base around him, rolled a fourth one over the top and gave the whip rope a pair of sharp tugs. Then up, up soared Fred, across the water and down into the belly of the *Big Rat.*

THE STEVEDORE HAD CONTRIVED TO leave a small gap between the bales, and through it Fred squirmed out of his woolly prison before the rest of the great stout bricks closed in around him. The hold, the orlop, and the underdeck were all places that brought such a horrific new perspective to the very concept of "indoors" that he was utterly reckless with terror when he burst out upon the main deck. A few sailors did notice a wild-eyed, rich-looking stranger, but they just assumed he was somehow connected with the captain's special passenger— the *Terrier* was, after all, a barky where things weren't always on the square; plenty of its doings went best with a blind eye turned upon them. Within moments, Fred was well hidden inside a surprisingly clean and new little boat he'd found, hanging from some davits on the starboard quarter.

The top of the boat was open to the sky. It was a surprisingly beautiful sky, with fluffy lamb-like clouds catching the colors of the sun. Fred could hear sailors' feet on the deck, caught the sound of a voice that could only be Dame Elsebet's, saw the silhouette of a sailor going up the mast nearby... yipe. That was too close for comfort. He looked frantically around for something to hide under, but found only something to hide *in.*

There was no time to be picky about it. Under one of the thwart seats was a locker with sliding wicker mesh doors, and Fred slipped inside. His heart was racing and his breath was short, and even though he kept his face close to the wicker, hiding in that locker was a pure threesome triplet of all hells brought to earth. He could feel the deep-damned thing wringing him in its woven embrace. He kicked out frantically, and his foot hit something that gave a muffled metallic clank.

Curious, Fred reached down to the vicinity of his boots and his hand closed on a squeaky-smooth flat wooden board. He pulled the thing up close to his face and studied it through the dappled light and shadow of the mesh.

It was a pair of old-fashioned pewter drinking cans, much like the ones he'd seen in the treasure room at Brewel Hall. But these cans were firmly riveted onto a varnished wooden plaque, with their mouths inclined sharply toward one another, about to clash together in a hearty toast. Crude silhouettes of a man and woman were carved into the plaque between them. A wedding souvenir. But what was it doing in a boat locker? He held it closer to his eyes, examining it for clues, and took a sniff of it to see if he could tell what kind of whet the bride and groom had once drunk to each other in.

He was earnestly trying to imagine it, when with a jolt of pleasant surprise Fred realized that he had briefly managed to distract himself from the terrifying crush of his hiding place. But only briefly— the moment the thought had formed, the crush was back and he couldn't help letting out a single, agonized gasp.

Gasping, gasping, he couldn't stop gasping...

Wait.

He *had* stopped gasping. He could most definitely feel that he had stopped, after just the one. He even held his breath a while, to prove it to himself. So how was he still making the noise? Or if not him, *who?*

It took Fred about a minute's hard concentration to figure out what was happening— or rather, it took him a quarter of a minute to figure it out and the other three quarters to convince himself he wasn't insane. The *cans* were doing it. *They* were gasping.

The mouths of the pewter cans were angled exactly so that Fred's last gasp bounced from one to the other, echoing endlessly. It was as though a barman making a brandy flip were pouring sound, instead of liquor, back and forth between them.

Magic?

Fred wedged his hand between the cans, covering one of the pewter mouths. After a final echo, the gasp melted away into silence. The locker resumed its inimical crush.

But now, Fred was ready for it. Into the cans he whispered the words he longed to hear. When he slipped the wedding souvenir into the deep, wide front pocket of his shirt, the words were muffled almost to oblivion by the noise of the harbor, but he could feel them. Right there against his heart. He held them close, and closed his eyes, and prayed— in his own way, without plan or piety— prayed Dame Elsebet wouldn't see him slip off this ship once they touched the Isle of Gold.

CHAPTER 42

The Domina of the Whellen Country is aboard my ship!

I repeat, gloated the captain of the *Terrier* privately, Elsebet de mumping Whellen is aboard my mumping ship, right this mumping minute, and if what Granny Almantree said is true, then the moment the last batten is wedged over the last hatch we'll be flying for the Isle of Gold as if...

He looked about him and sighed. *As if there weren't any other ships cramming this harbor,* he felt duty bound to finish. But there they were, and it was ridiculous to think there was any way past them. Still, at least he had his own special prize aboard and she was alone, alone, delightfully deliciously completely alone.

The sailor who'd first identified Dame Elsebet strolled casually past him. She did this at least ten times a day and somehow he'd never managed to tell her it was a breach of discipline, that there should be no one on the quarterdeck but him. Somehow he felt like the odd man out: the *Terrier* had never really observed discipline. It might have been better if they'd had something resembling uniforms, or at least badges of rank. But all the captain had was his dignity, and he exercised it by not replying to this sailor as she murmured, "I get half. Because without me, you wouldn't even have known who she was."

The blattering hoot of a conch shell sounded. The captain felt something warm behind him. It was Granny Almantree's enormous servant, back from her quick run to the head. She poked the captain in the ribs and said "Cargo's on. Get ready."

His temper was short and he let a little bit of annoyance creep in when he snapped, "Ready for what?"

A shout of alarm sounded from down the harbor, closer to the Lantern. Someone started ringing a bell. More shouting and then the pandemonium took hold in earnest: fire. A wall of fire. A half dozen ships were burning, thick oily black smoke already surging up out of them, flames from their holds so high it caught onto their sails, and the flames in their sails catching onto tarred cordage, and the cordage burning through and swinging free and taking the fire to still more ships. The enormous servant breathed down into the captain's face. "Tell 'em to get moving," she urged him.

"Prepare— weigh—" stammered the captain. But Granny Almantree wanted it done quicker.

"Cut and run!" roared the enormous servant, and to the captain's distress his sailors all obeyed her. Down rolled the twin lateens and square foresail. Away went the cut end of the cable. The wind even began to blow. And it was the hour of the tide, the great brackish heart of the Denna gushing out with irresistible force. Somehow miraculously unscathed, the *Terrier* slipped past all the mayhem, past the shadow of the Lantern, past the oddly deserted customs hulk, past the mole-eyed lookouts on the breakwater, past the suddenly somehow temporarily inattentive navy, and out into the brandy-black Midland Sea.

CHAPTER 43

THE *LONGWING* HAD BEEN BUILT for speed, not luxury. Her hull was as sharp and slender as the leaves of the victory lorro that had once crowned heroes on the Isle of Gold. So what little she had in the way of cabins were small.

But they had been built with care for all that, and now Lively found it difficult to make the knights pull open their sliding white-oak door.

First he'd tried simply knocking. No reply had come from within; he was very much surprised at that, for he'd chosen his escort party with great care. The special position he held at Whellengood let him observe its people very closely, and over the years he'd learned which of them made useful tools and which did not. Up until the moment he knocked on the door of the late captain's cabin, Lively had thought these ten particular swords fit right in the palm of his hand. But no one had answered his knock, and that had annoyed him.

When knocking failed, he asked them. He put his mouth up to the gap around the edge of the door and shouted, although shouting was usually not his style. So unnecessary. He never had to shout; he had other, better options. But the oak was thick so he had cleared his throat, wiped some dried spittle from his lips and barked: "Open up, Ladies. I've cleared the coast."

When this, too, brought no reply, Lively kicked the door with all his fury. The door hardly rattled, but Lively's foot made a nasty sound. He didn't have to pull off his boot to know what had happened; he spoke for a while and then the foot was all right, but his mood was not. His mood had turned decidedly bad. "I don't like this, Ladies," he howled back at the cabin as he went off to search through the *Longwing* for a hammer. "I have the strangest feeling that you're forgetting who invited you."

The carpenter's maul was a big hardwood mallet and it was meant precisely for striking down bulkheads such as the one that formed the wall of the cabin. Not that Lively knew it; he didn't swing the maul at the neat little corner wedges holding the bulkhead in place, but directly into the center of the door. At the first blow the door rattled and groaned. At the second, a whole panel of oak flew out of its place with a yelp of tearing splinters and left a sudden window, through which Lively could see the knights clustered as far from him as they could get.

The front one, there. He wanted to twist her craven face. But Lively put a cheerful lilt into his voice instead. "Come on, let's stop this silliness. It's time to come out."

"We prefer to wait till we land."

That one, too. The one with her dagger out. She'd get it next.

"Now, now, now. I won't bite."

"No, but you might *stab*."

"Gods damn you wenches! Did you think this was going to be a lawn party? I'm offering you the chance to be my personal guard when I become..." Lively poked his arm through the hole in the door and felt around for a hasp or a bar or whatever was holding it shut. He couldn't find anything. "Damn it. You know what, I'm not offering that anymore. Now I'm offering you the chance to stay alive. I'll count three to see who wants it. One... Two..."

Just as Lively's fingers finally closed around the little catch that secured the door, one of the knights sprang from the group, her marbled sword gleaming, and sliced off his arm.

Two of Lively's former fingers clenched with enough strength to hang on, and as the arm dropped toward the painted floorcloth, it had enough leverage to turn the little catch; when he stepped through the door all he had to do was pick the arm off its place as though it were a hat on a peg. He raised the pumping red stub which remained at his elbow, jammed the pink bone of the arm against it, and spoke again as he had spoken to his foot. No more blood. No more seam. In seconds the arm was whole, and Lively was flexing his fingers to test them, and he was among the knights brandishing his hammer. What *had* he been thinking? He didn't need guards anymore. No, what he needed was some last-minute practice.

CHAPTER 44

How vast the sea is, marveled Dame Elsebet, how truly mighty. With a sigh, she allowed that if this were the field plowed by the de Brewel seahorse, then perhaps that creature was stronger than her Heart of Stone, after all.

The wind and sea did in fact feel like a single creature, with an equine quality to its moods. They moved the ship in ways that made her feel as though she were riding rough country, following her pack of hounds to unexpected upward leaps and downward drops, sideward shies and wary slowdowns and surges of enormous unleashed power. The sky was bright, and full of clouds that looked as substantial as sheep, watching the hunt gallop by. It was alternately picturesque and awe-inspiring, so much so that she could almost— *almost*— push aside her terrible anxiety over what they might soon find. Would Doktor Lively be safe? Unharmed? She dared not think the word *alive*, but worry needed no words.

After they'd lost sight of the land and watched the tip of the Lantern retreat below the horizon, the sailors had busied themselves with their maritime tasks, which included gambling on throws of various dirty, ancient coins, a modest round of bare-knuckle fights, boiling some lumps of wan flabby meat to create a perfectly repellent-looking meal, and, every so often, minding the ship.

The captain had assured Dame Elsebet that they would soon begin the agreed-upon task of combing the sea for Doktor Lively. In the meantime, she might visit his cabin for a sip. "It's only sailors' grog, my highly honorable Lady," he had said with a wink, "but it would please me very much to drink it with you."

And so she'd accepted, ducking slightly as she passed through a pair of doors the captain told her was called a companionway, down a short flight of steps that was really more like a ladder, along a passage and into a wooden room with a slanting wall of windows that really was quite beautiful, reminding her as it did of the glass wall in the Grand Salon at Whellengood. But then this in turn reminded her of how the lightning had destroyed her symbolic tree, and she caught sight of her own reflection in the hourglass sitting on the table: the face of someone old and frightened.

The captain smiled a little, perhaps to cheer her up. It was a rascally smile, a foxy kind of smile. Dame Elsebet waved her fan slowly and studied his face. She decided it was the teeth.

He offered her a small wooden mug and raised one of his own. "Here's to a rich country indeed," he said. "Your Whellen Country." And he gave her a bold rascally look.

"Why, thank you, Mesir," said Dame Elsebet. "It is kind of you to show me this handsome view. The windows add something that the open deck hasn't got— a sense of scale, I imagine. Of proportion."

"Yes. Proportion is key, isn't it? Keeping the relative size, the relative *value*, of things in mind." The captain strolled casually toward the door of his cabin and found Dame Elsebet there just a step ahead of him, examining a barometer that hung on the bulkhead. He tried reaching for the latch, but she was blocking it, having turned around to examine a small ivory carving on the bulkhead opposite. The captain clenched his foxy teeth and indicated a bottle, a cut lemon and a sugar bowl on the locker in front of the stern windows. "Please, do help yourself to another whet of grog."

"Thank you, but I am so clumsy at cooking. If you'd like, you can make it for me," replied Dame Elsebet, fanning languidly and staying right where she was. The captain shook his head.

"I think I'll wait, your High Honor." And he jammed himself between her and the exit. "I think I'll wait to see what kind of value people assign to your safe return."

"I beg your pardon?"

"I said, I think I'll wait to see how rich your country really is. You're in *my* country now, Medame, and I have outfoxed you. You are my prisoner. You'll pay me all you have, and so will your family, if you ever want to leave my ship alive."

Dame Elsebet paused in mid-fan. "That sounds like a threat. A death threat."

"It is," said the captain, showing the knife in his hand. "You'll do as I say. Because I have this."

"No I won't," said Dame Elsebet. "Because I've got *these*."

She put both hands to her fan, twisted it. Its silk pleats gave way and left her holding two bronze sticks.

Twinstaves, the captain realized a moment too late. One of the staves whistled toward his hand and sent the knife flying with a fleshy-sounding crack. Before the captain could yelp, the other staff crossed his temple and he dropped like a brick.

Dame Elsebet threw the knife out a porthole. *Assess the situation*, she imagined her trainer Lady Verocita saying. Her mind raced back, back, searching for clues as to what position she was in.

The captain had used the word "my", she recalled. Repeatedly. My prisoner, my ship. Had he been acting alone? Then she might bluff her way out of trouble. But what if this were a crew of pirates, all expecting shares of a ransom? If so, then she was in a very bad place.

And yet: she'd once enjoyed bad places. Had she not plunged into many a shadowy cave after the firewyrm, armed only with a torch and a short-shafted broadspear? Had she not ridden down a bhabairus and lanced the brute in the very gateway of its lair, moments before it ate that poor little boy? Dame Elsebet's heart began to race with an old familiar joy. Hunter against monster, she against it, her favorite sport, until—

In a corner of her mind piled high with debris of the past, a great menacing form began to stir, standing taller and taller, turning, turning and opening its jaws. Her fingers trembled around the twinstaves. In memory, she heard herself shrieking in a desperate bid to attract the pale form's attention. Still it grew, grew, and raised twin mauls of dark hooked blades... she had not remembered so much of this in fifty years. Frantically she breathed and chanted. This was no time for madness...

On the deck of his cabin, the captain gave a final twitch. She turned to look: his foxy dead face was bloodied, but all of it was there; his neck and shoulders and chest were intact. At the sight, Dame Elsebet gave a final effort of mind and hurled the pale form back into its abyss.

Quickly she dragged the captain's body to the stern lockers and shut its broken hand in the lid. She threw the bottle down on deck, scattering a mug and a few slices of lemon beside it for good measure. Then she slipped her twinstaves back into her sleeve and floated up the stairs, through the companionway, and out into what would prove either a safe hiding place or a battle.

"Goodwives!" cried Dame Elsebet. "Something's happened— it's the captain— there's been a dreadful accident!"

CHAPTER 45

Corvinalias had been disappointed to learn that the two highcats were not coming with them on their adventure.

But then, they didn't belong to Ata Maroo anymore; neither did the oxen; neither did the silver-gray wagon with the white canvas top. She had sold them all to the newly formed Trade Road Company for more shinies than there were leaves on a summer tree, and those shinies were to live at DeCoastwel Bank until she decided what to do with them.

They'd left Coastwall with the dawn, not in any big fancy wagon but in a two-wheel cart pulled by Ata Maroo's bull alone— and damn it three layers deep if that beast couldn't *move*. Every time Corvinalias thought he'd flown far, far ahead of the cart he turned around to see it coming, with the bull kicking up road dust as it stepped out in a long-striding racing trot. The twelve mounted archers' horses had to lope to keep up with it. The highcats were not used to this kind of traveling, and instead of trotting with the cart they sat up behind Maroo and Alvie, one on either side of a teak chest full of shinies for the road.

"Chase?" Corvinalias had asked them. Who knew when he'd ever have the chance to talk to a mythical beast again. How unfair. The cats had no word for what was happening and only shook their heads.

For nearly an hour they rolled on like that, until they reached an earthwork with a gate in it, a gate with the emblem of a cloven hoof, and Maroo had jumped out of the cart and hugged each of the guards at the gate with an expression Corvinalias didn't really understand. But it was obvious enough to him that everything inside the gate had once belonged to Maroo. Every barn, every warehouse, every loading dock and every boat dock on the creek that flowed out into the sea. The archers formed up around the teak chest and watched as workers rolled open the doors of a warehouse on the creek to launch the weirdest boat Corvinalias had ever seen. It was like two boats with massive upside-down sails joined together by a house, and it barely fit in the creek. But soon it was at the breakwater where Maroo's freight terminal ended and the Midland Sea began. Maroo finished hugging all of those people, and giving most of the shinies away to them, and she said a bunch of words he didn't understand to the highcats and handed their leashes to one of the people who was, for some reason, crying. Then Maroo stood with her bull for a long, long time, whispering in its big ear, and finally she joined Alvie and a small crew aboard that weird boat and that's how they got to where they were now. Out in the ocean. Corvinalias looked around and saw a whole bunch of nothing. This was an adventure?

The house in the middle of the big weird boat was comfortable enough, and the fish Maroo caught and grilled up for their midday meal were tasty enough, and the little four-stringed lute she strummed on afterward had a pretty enough sound. But the ocean was just as boring as it had been when Corvinalias journeyed to the mainland with Fred. Back then he'd at least had something to do: talk to his pet, get to know him. This time around, Maroo and Alvie were busy pushing their faces together, and in the end they withdrew to one of the rooms of the house and let down the canvas flap that made the door. Corvinalias tried asking the crew where they were and what they were doing, but all they did was gab to each other in seafaring lingo— about what, Corvinalias could not guess, because the ocean was just a big vibrating blue-black disk of nothing.

Finally he'd had enough. He swooped into the house and squirmed under the edge of the canvas flap, tail first.

"Hoy! You two! Are you doing something I don't want to see? I'm not into that nature stuff— just want to ask you a question."

"You can look, bird. What you want?"

Corvinalias bristled his whiskers in exasperation. "Right, so tell me: what kind of blind-goose adventure is it I've been roped into, here? I've seen this place before, you know— a big salt lake, whoopee. A few albatrosses come by every now and then and tell you their shaggy-dog stories and that's all. Your yodeling partner there distinctly told me this would be an adventure. So when's it start? I could have stayed back in Coastwall and been a mythical beastmaster!"

To his great annoyance, Maroo began to laugh. Not a rude laugh, but clearly she knew something, and that got under his feathers. He screeched, and she stopped laughing, but still she was smiling and Corvinalias switched to a growl.

"Wah! Calm you self, bird. I was going to do this later— Alvie, *ipo*, we have all time in world, ah?— but now is good a time as any. Let us see if I still have team after twenty year." And she rose from her pallet of pillows, retied her sarong and strode out onto the platform surrounding the house, then down onto one of the big canoe-shaped boats the house rode upon. She opened a hatch and drew out a waxed-canvas bag, and from the bag a tangle of cordage. Corvinalias couldn't help but feel a stab of curiosity. "What's that?"

"You will see." Maroo brought out a strange-looking wind instrument and before putting it to her lips she said: "Ready now, bird? You good at imitating sound. Listen please to *this* sound."

Ye Gods, it was loud. And bizarre. A squealing, buzzing, crackling, cryptic howl.

"You got it? You can imitate?"

"Let me try." Corvinalias practiced while the crew covered their ears and made painful faces. At last Maroo approved.

"All right, bird. Now this what you do. You see good?"

Corvinalias puffed up with pride. "We magpies can see all kinds of things Umans can't."

"That perfect. All right, you fly out in ocean, ah? Sky full of cloud today, but you look for different kind— small one that pop up, puff puff, here and there close to water. When you see small cloud, you go fly down and look for little black mountain under it."

Corvinalias tipped his head to one side and gave his new pet a hard glare. He had heard of hunting the shortwolf— it was a stunt Uman-beings liked to pull, where they would send the butt of their joke out on some impossible errand.

"You want me to find small clouds. That pop up. With mountains under them."

"Ah! Maybe I should have say island, not mountain. Little black island come and go, so you watch for moment when it above water. Then you make sound you just learn. You can do this?"

"I suppose so. What is that noise, some kind of spell?"

"With luck, you will see." Her smile had mischief in it, and that was mildly interesting. So even though he was pretty sure all this would amount to nothing, Corvinalias set out on his shortwolf hunt. He skimmed the surface of the ocean, he rose high on a bulge of warm air, he looked in every direction and saw a handful of ships, but otherwise a whole lot of not much... and then suddenly, off in the distant greenish blue, there it was.

One cloud. Two. He aimed for the closest one and flew arrow-straight toward it, watching as it moved across the surface of the sea, appearing and disappearing. It was a tiring flight, through wind and sun, and when Corvinalias got there his heart was pounding. But he swooped down low, caught his breath and let loose with the strange new sound for all he was worth, determined to at least have tried.

The little island bulged out of the water so suddenly that he had to dodge. It got really big. And bigger. Bigger. A long, shiny, unbroken ridge, the size of a boat and still growing. Corvinalias was just about to quit hovering in the wind and get the pocks out of there when the island rolled on its side and he beheld the massive face of a sea monster, black marked with patches of white just like his own.

It blinked at him with one big, wise eye and replied to his call with a blast of sound so huge it rang the ocean like a bell.

Corvinalias was aghast to see a blob of his own dung fall on the creature's cheek. *Forgive me, great being,* he said inwardly. It'll wash off. I didn't mean to— you just— you just— words failed him.

Now the creature was speaking, saying something at great length in a vast explosion of bursts and crackles. Replies sounded through the water from all points of the compass, until Corvinalias found himself hovering dumbstruck over six of the animals. They drew great breaths that nearly pulled him into the nostrils on the crowns of their heads and, as if they had planned this forever, dove and rushed off through the folds of the ocean toward Maroo's big weird boat.

CHAPTER 46

"IT WAS MY FAULT," MOANED DAME Elsebet, standing outside the captain's cabin as a knot of sailors rushed to the scene of the accident. She didn't have to fake her expression; just hearing herself say those words, the very same words she'd fought for years to come to terms with, was disconcerting in the extreme. She breathed deep and went on: "he was reaching into the locker when I, oh my fool of a god, I sat on the lid..."

"... an' the pain a breakin' his hand musta made him flail around like a gaffed fish an' whack his head on the table leg," one of the sailors finished for her. Dame Elsebet nodded, dabbing her eyes and sidestepping toward the companionway doors. She didn't want to spend any more time below than necessary, trapped in a narrow hallway with so many wenches much bigger— and younger— than herself. Especially that enormous one who breathed through her mouth and never said anything.

On deck, the afternoon sun made her blink. The deck was checkered with the shadows of clouds. She no longer had her fan to fidget with, though its staves were waiting in her sleeve; she could only loiter about near the mizzenmast, looking as remorseful as she could, studying each and every hand aboard the *Terrier* for signs of being in on the late captain's plan. None of them showed any such sign, and Dame Elsebet was just on the point of letting her nerves relax, when the last one strolled up to her and said, "Poor Skipper. Some kind of bad luck that was for him, to hit his head right on the corner like that."

"I am devastated. My, my deepest..."

"Save 'em. None of us are likely to miss him much. In fact, I like it a lot better this way, because now I get all of it."

"All of what?" She watched the sailor's hands. Her eyes. The direction she was facing. They spoke to Dame Elsebet and told her: *She's got someone coming up behind me.*

"Of the big fat ransom I'll ask, for you and your little sticks."

The sailor lunged forward, clearly meaning to grab Dame Elsebet's sleeve and stop her from drawing her weapons. But instead, Dame Elsebet whirled backward to face a second attacker, about to club her with an oar. She seized its splintery handle with hands wide apart, twisting it as she spun, levering it neatly from the attacker's grip and turning it to bring the broad end back down upon her in a long, fierce, unbroken slice. If the oar had been a broadspear, the second woman would have been split into the two diagonal pieces of the *ina-losha* cut. But even an oar was more than enough to hurl her senseless to the deck, while Dame Elsebet swung her rear leg out to reap down the sailor who'd threatened her.

From his uncomfortable place inside the locker of the new lifeboat, Fred heard an uproar, running feet, and the dull meaty noises of impact after impact. Why were the crew shouting? Were those shouts turning into screams of panic? Was that Dame Elsebet's voice he heard, ringing out loudest of all?

Forgetting his new resolve never to trouble her again, Fred sprang from the lifeboat. Even as he shouted her name, he could tell his help wasn't needed. Dame Elsebet was gripping and raising and swinging a wooden oar with violent fearful precision, her foes already lying scattered in various stages of destruction, and the cries Fred heard bursting from her were not screams of distress, but shouts of joy and even peals of genuine, delighted laughter.

But the moment she saw him, her exultation died.

THE SIX MIGHTY SEA CREATURES swam faster than Corvinalias could fly. He had to push himself to keep up, because he wanted to hear Maroo's reaction to his success. From far off he could see her jumping up and down on the platform of her boat like a giddy little girl, joy shining upon her face. In fact she couldn't wait for the sea monsters to reach her: when they were within sight she leaped into the ocean, not even pausing to take off her sarong. The creatures surged toward her, the largest two in the lead and the smaller ones hanging back. Corvinalias circled overhead to watch as she spread herself across their giant faces in the biggest hugs she could make, patting them and talking to them in her native language. She took her time with the largest two, who then in turn appeared to introduce her to the others. Alvie and the crew hobbled to the edge of the platform and stood looking on in wonder.

At last Ata Maroo swam back to the boat. "Everyone start handing down those ropes, ah? They are yoke for what we call cloud whale— oxen of my people. This the team I drive from Peaceful Ocean, twenty year ago! They have made new home in these waters and had four calf— one every five year, that is not bad!" Now the cloud whales clustered around the boat, nudging it with their flippers and their tails, and opening their mouths to show huge pink tongues, neat rows of conical teeth and, in the case of the adults, upper and lower pairs of long, outward-spiraling ivory tusks. All six whales chattered endless streams of crackling, squealing noises, careful to keep them hushed so as not to hurt their tiny mistress's ears. Behind the wall of their cicada hum, Corvinalias could distinctly hear one whale whistling "Ipo, Ipo, Maroo" and another one imitating Corvinalias himself, repeating in perfectly correct magpie, with his very own Isle of Gold accent: "Wait till she sees these! Now *this* is an adventure."

"I want to go find more of them!" he pleaded, fluttering around Maroo as she swam to the bow of her craft and stretched out a configuration of ropes, floats, and chains as if it were a huge kitten's-crib. With a squeak of excitement one of the adult cloud whales plunged its head into the loops, expertly hooking them in its tusks. The other one jostled its mate aside and did the same. They could hardly wait for Maroo to put out a second yoke; two of the calves had tusks just barely long enough to catch the loops and they shoved their parents aside, eager to attempt the maneuver, while the youngest ones nipped sullenly at whatever ropes they could grab and tried pulling them.

"Cloud whale like to do whatever it see other doing, ah?" Maroo pointed out. "This what let people drive them in first place, many thousand year ago. But what will I do with more whale? I do not even have enough yoke for whale I have. If I do not make more soon, there will be family argument." Sure enough, one of the younger whales had bitten its sibling and they dived under the boat to scrap like huge puppies.

"Please? *Please?*"

"All right, bird. You not need my permission! Go fly, go look. But I tell you six whale more than plenty. This how my family made living back home— shipping business, same like Ox-Train Queen. Four whale can pull raft of dozen barge each bigger than this—" she jerked her thumb back at her boat. "I tell you I do not need bigger team. You go look for something else."

The magpie trilled in excitement. "You mean there's more? Hurray!" And he soared up into the chubby white clouds, higher and higher into the dome above the Midland Sea, until he hung on a breath of wind, looking down upon a vast grid of waves. Corvinalias wanted to sift the sea. He wanted to learn what other magical things it held. How could he ever have thought it was empty? Now he realized it was a field filled with life, with creatures burrowing under its sapphire and emerald surface to pop up and sparkle in the alien sun. Suddenly, the person he'd been before was too small. He was embarrassed to recall that he'd thought a couple of cats were anything to be excited about. Or a wandering Fool. Ye Gods, *he'd* been the fool. Below him, people rode across all this majesty in little wooden boxes, dimly touching the face of a limitless being, without ever knowing what was all around them. Saps. If only they knew. If only—

Corvinalias didn't actually know much about ships, but there were a few in his field of vision and something was definitely wrong aboard one of them. The people on board were swarming around like ants whose hill had been stepped on. He spiraled down for a closer look.

The moment he recognized Fred, shuffling along one of those beams they tie sails to, and someone menacing him with a whip— well, he'd never, ever flown so fast. His lungs nearly turned inside out. He almost couldn't explain it to Maroo. But somehow, he did.

"Come in cabin now, bird," she said as he lay gasping on the platform. When he didn't move, she scooped him up and carried him into the house. "Hold tight, crew! Alvie, get away from edge, ah? Everyone get ready: whales about to pull."

CHAPTER 47

DAME ELSEBET HAD SEEN FRED, and nothing could fix that. Not even the part where one of the injured sailors staggered to her knees, threw a loop of rope around his neck and threatened to feed him to a shark unless Dame Elsebet dropped her weapon.

Of course she hadn't dropped it. Fred wouldn't have dropped his either, if he'd had one. He completely understood why she'd kept on swinging the oar, in ever wilder fury, and he would have loved to keep on watching her except that she really was very, very tiny all the way down there on the deck a hundred feet below.

Fred had scrambled up the mainmast to escape from a short pock-scarred wench who'd sent nine strands of stout scratchy knotted rope whistling past his face. At first it had seemed like a good plan: back in his glory days a few months ago, he'd earned a second-level Fools' Guild certification in Funambulism, having demonstrated "(Level 1) reliable skill in traversing a taut stationary rope of opposing core and lay, and/or a taut stationary wire cable of zero-twist construction, as well as (Level 2) reliable skill in the performance of at least three recognized acrobatic stunts and/or recognized classical dance steps in the course of such a traverse". But to his dismay, the swaying yard turned out to be far trickier than any tightrope. Looking down, Fred could see ocean underneath him, not a stretchy net strung over a straw mat. And that sailor with the cat o' nine claws was really used to being up here.

Fred had reached the end of the yard. The cat whistled again and a scorching blaze of pain erupted across one of his arms. He staggered, slipped and crashed down around the yard in a panicked hug, the wedding souvenirs in his front pocket nearly crushing his breastbone. He yowled in agony, closing his eyes tight and bracing himself for another lick of the cat.

At that moment the ship jolted in a motion unlike that of the sea, and an unearthly grating, clanking, squealing noise resonated up through the mast, the yard, the bodies of all aboard.

"Pus, what was that?" said the sailor, frozen with the cat held high. Then the ship jolted again— in the opposite direction— and off the yard she fell, to what fate Fred didn't know.

All he knew was that there were sea monsters in the water.

What else could those things down there be? Two— no, three— no, six of them, black and white and gargantuan, making that unearthly sound, overriding even the panicked screams of every soul aboard the *Big Rat.* The monsters paused for a moment and gathered in a circle, as if they were a throwball team deciding on their next play; they plunged straight down into the waves.

A moment passed.

And then three enormous missiles of black and white shot like geyser blasts from the waves on the far side of the ship, spray peeling from their flanks, their jaws opening wide to clamp shut on mouthfuls of yards and shrouds and sails.

At the same time, on Fred's side the keel was surging up out of the depths, a great stinking haystack of shells and weed. The beasts on the yards fell down with all their colossal weight, pulling their catch along with them; the ones raising the keel flung it clear up out of the water; and the *Big Rat* capsized like a gigantic toy.

The yard upon which Fred lay traced a long, majestic, perfectly quarter-circular arc. It happened slowly enough that he could see the tiny figures below him rush toward the high side of the deck; watch the new little lifeboat go hissing down, as a whole deckful of unsecured objects went floating free. He had time to rub the fresh pink welt on his arm, take a deep breath, and pinch his nose shut before he slipped a few dozen feet down the yard, picked his spot and dropped into the brandy-black sea.

CHAPTER 48

AND NOW WE GO BACK in time.

Back to when Dame Elsebet's hair was honey brown, when wyrmlight lanterns did not yet illuminate the streets of the Whellen Country, when Lorenz de Whellen still lived at the family home. On a particularly hot and stormy day in a hot and trying summer, the foresters at Whellengood found a stray monk. And Dame Elsebet, out riding to try and quell one of her bouts of madness, felt an instant bond with the poor frightened young man.

He had a kind, round, pink face and a pronounced limp. During a crisis of faith he'd leaped from the high wall of his abbey and hobbled away in despair, and when the foresters found him he was weeping. Weeping, because he—a peaceful man, a man of the Gods— had killed a bandit who'd attacked his lonesome little camp.

He'd fought hard. Too hard: afterward, all his prayers had been powerless to save the wounded bandit's life. The monk now considered himself beyond redemption, not only a deserter but a murderer. He vowed never to let his brothers look upon him again, and refused to reveal his name, though it was soon learned that an abbey in the fiefs of the faraway Vonn Country was missing one Brother Taluca Lively.

The bandit, meanwhile, had been none other than the notorious Three-Thumbs Booker, recently escaped from a Coastwall prison. Although rumors had gone about that Booker was dead and fed to the fishes of the broad brown Denna, clearly he'd been Lively's attacker. True, he had fallen into the campfire and burned off his face; yes, his hands were somewhat mangled from the struggle he'd had with the monk, trying to gain control of a knife. But he was positively identified by the presence of his namesake, a third thumb.

Brother Taluca Lively wanted to die. Dame Elsebet knew just what that felt like. She talked to him. And from the moment she swept the poor young man to her heart and held him like the son she would never have, she experienced miracles. Miracles such as how Lively made her madness go away, all culminating in something no one in human memory had ever yet managed to create: a true, reliable magic spell. It took over twenty years of work in library, laboratorium and infirmary, but Lively did it. He perfected the spell, earned a Doktorate Magistre of Healing, and became the treasure Dame Elsebet meant to offer the King, in return for the future of her people.

That was one way to look at it.

Here is another.

Watch as a man much feared for his violent temper is outlawed and driven into the wild forests beyond the far fiefs of the Vonn Country. See how he camps in the forest, hunting and fishing the best he can, which is not very well. See the man's anger grow fiercer and darker day by day, until one hateful morning an animal comes to graze just inches from the ash of his fire.

The animal looks like an antelope the color of a moonlit pearl, with a vast cape of mane and a long, spiraling beard brushing the earth. It reaches out its black leather nose, touches the sleeping man, breathes its sweet breath upon his cheek. It is a nullicorn. And an old, old legend, which no one really believes, says: should a virgin pure of heart touch the beard of a nullicorn— the wishes made then will come true.

The man by the dead fire is not asleep. No one has ever loved him. And his heart is pure, pure depravity. He seizes the beard of the bawling nullicorn, pulls it to the ground, and shouts out his wishes while he breaks its neck.

Later he kills a monk, too. He finds that a bit more exciting than killing the nullicorn, but now the man sees that he has a problem. There are people in this forest— the monk proves it. So he hurries to think of a plan. Watch the man's face: it is interesting. No one would ever guess, to look upon him, that he is such an evil man.

He thinks: a big wet dead body like this one will not burn. So I must disguise it. No, he thinks, I am not a skillful enough butcher to make this look like another antelope. It will always look like a man. He is worried. If people see this, he worries, they will think I am a bandit like the notorious Three-Thumbs Booker, and put me in prison, and I may not be able to escape like Booker did. Now watch the man's face light up, as he has his idea.

I will wear the monk's smock and boots, he thinks.

No one can see through leather, he thinks.

A big toe looks very much like a thumb, he says out loud.

Watch carefully as the man cuts a little bit from the flesh of his hand, just to see if his wishes are true. Look at his smile. Surprisingly sweet, is it not? And so, when the people do come and find him, he is ready. He is the nameless monk who killed a nameless bandit. And by the time the people have counted the bandit's thumbs, and decided on a name for the monk, he is already the pet of a high noblewoman who is damaged in a way that he can heal and rebreak for ever and ever.

CHAPTER 49

A PECULIAR STRING OF CRAFT SCOURED the Midland Sea.

Wind and current made no difference to the double-hulled Peaceful Ocean catamaran, and the broken-masted old carrevelle, and the neat new little lifeboat, all lashed together in a train. Cloud whales powered them: four in harness, and two more racing back and forth under the waves, scouting.

Dame Elsebet and Miss Ata sat on the forward edge of the catamaran's platform, drinking tea and watching the huge triangular fins on the whales' backs saw the water. From time to time Miss Ata looked through a spyglass, or played some order upon a bizarre-sounding signal pipe, or explained some detail of the luminous sea to her husband, who Dame Elsebet thought might have been the twin of the messenger she had sent to report the sailing of the ill-fated *Longwing*.

"If *Longwing* anywhere on these waters," Miss Ata assured her, "Whole or wreck, we find her."

In the carrevelle, a pair of stout matrons guarded the entrance to a lower deck. Those of the *Terrier's* former crew who'd survived the capsize had been relieved of their weapons and locked in the orlop. One wench, almost as tall as Miss Ata and twice as thick, had been concealing eleven daggers, garrotes, poison needles, and throwing wheels. She'd seemed strangely unconcerned at giving them up, muttering only that her granny wasn't paying her for no pirate wheeze; the rest had been similarly disspirited, and had gone tamely below, taking with them a spitting, hissing smallcat and the late captain's stash of rum.

In the new little lifeboat was Malfred Murd. Exiled jester, erstwhile monk, onetime magician, and formerly almost a figure model, occult scholar and garden hermit. He had lost one of his handsome cordovan boots. He sat slumped on the thwart seat, hardly seeing the ocean, listening to the meditative breath he had put into one of the Twin Cans so that it might repeat for him. Why not? Breathing worked for... for her.

He could hardly bring himself to think Dame Elsebet's name. She would have done so well without him. At least he'd managed to cry out for her forgiveness; although she hadn't heard him, that cry had lanced the awful boil that had been making him sick inside. It had let out some of the guilt. But there was still plenty of guilt left, guilt for what he'd done to someone else.

Fred wiggled the toes of his bare foot. That was the one. The foot that had cost him everything, the one whose arch had finally given the young King the kick in the ass he deserved for twenty years of torment.

At the time, Fred had really believed it was torment, injustice, even cruelty. Why, just because he was entertaining and active and witty and afraid to ever be alone in a room, had he been dragged from his dull small prison to a bigger, fancier, infinitely more prestigious one? Why, other than to attend on that blank-faced maddening inscrutable wet blanket of a boy, with his noises and his fidgets and his fits? That one who, no matter how Fred tried to cheer him up, stayed cheerless, who no matter what kind of friendship Fred offered him, was unfriendly, who never realized that *brother* wasn't just a name for a monk— that what the old King had brought him really could have been a brother, if only that brat had been the slightest bit interested.

Of course now Fred saw it as if from outside. And from outside it looked terrible. Boy or man, prince or king, Enrick couldn't help how he was. He couldn't see or understand how the years had slowly soured his Fool's playfulness into resentment, mockery, outright contempt. Everyone else saw it, though. At the end of his life even the old King had seen it. At this thought Fred hung his head over the gunwale of the new little lifeboat, and groaned and strained, but the guilt did not pour out of his mouth and into the sea. It would have to come out in words. But when?

Aboard the catamaran, a bell clanged. Supper. The rope that tethered Fred's boat to the big craft hauled him under its lee while he sat, listening to the Twin Cans in his pocket and saying no word to anyone. No one said any word to him. Ata Maroo threw him down a full leathern bottle of water, and a slice of roasted fish, and turned back to her guests on the platform.

"We see it! We see it! We see it!" Corvinalias came screaming out of the clouds, with a buzz in his voice that Fred had never heard before. "Zzzkkkcccttt and Krrreeejaaakgkgkg spotted its keel, and I saw the topside. It's just to the west of us! Everyone hurry! It's the *Longwing* for sure— albatross figurehead and all. But not under sail. Just drifting."

"Come aboard, fool," ordered Ata Maroo. "I will drown no one, not even you." She pulled him aboard with her tough farmer's grip and turned her back on him. That was as it should be.

While Ata Maroo furled the sails, the catamaran accelerated to a truly staggering pace. The cutting edge of each bow plowed up a tall furrow as translucent as the windows of Whellengood Hall, tipped in a split hiss of spray. The little lifeboat bumped and leaped as though it were a frenzied trout. Behind them even the dismasted *Big Rat* was flying, a great white bone in her teeth. Swiftly a speck on the horizon grew, took shape, showed sagging yards and untrimmed sails and a long black aimless hull. At the taffrail, above white finescript reading LONGWING, COASTWALL stood a single figure. A man. A man with dark gray hair and a round pink face. A man whose call of "Help! Help!" brought Dame Elsebet to tears.

"Help is here, Taluca!" she shouted up to the *Longwing* as the whales pushed and pulled the ships expertly into position. "We got your message!"

"What message? I mean, I sent several messages! Which one was it? What did I say?"

"The one written in plainhand on the back of the papers. 'Send Help'."

"Ah, yes. That one! Thank Ye Gods it reached you."

Under the *Longwing*, the whales were shooting back and forth, squealing and growling. One of them poked its face up above the water and uttered a long, peevish-sounding trill. Ata Maroo stared down and said, "Unusual number of shark around this ship."

"I'm going to come down," shouted Doktor Taluca Lively, heaving a man-rope over the side. "There's no one else aboard. The— the pirates hidden in the hold came up and killed them all. And threw them into the sea. That's why there are so many sharks." Suddenly he too burst into tears, heartbreaking tears, the deep tormented sobs of someone who has looked into the face of unspeakable barbarity—

On a stage, finished Fred's gut. *In a play.* But no one had asked him, so he kept silent.

"I send someone up to search for survivor," insisted Ata Maroo, and motioned to one of her crew, a sailor who had clearly survived the blisterpox. The sailor threw a grapnel up over the *Longwing's* gunwale and was aboard before Lively could figure out how to use his rope. The look on her scarred face when she returned was one of absolutely genuine horror. She shook her head to say no, no others— although her eyes remained in some far-off region from which they might never return.

Ata Maroo turned to Dame Elsebet and said softly: "You hire *Longwing*, Medame. You wish us to take her in tow?"

"Oh, no, don't!" cried Taluca Lively, and Dame Elsebet held him as if he were her child, patting his back as he sobbed. Her face said: burn the pocking thing for all I care. Ata Maroo directed her whales to move the train of craft back out into the open sea and leave the *Longwing* as salvage.

"We are for Isle of Gold now, yes?"

Dame Elsebet nodded.

Fred couldn't take it anymore. He had to speak up.

"So. Dok. Where'd the pirates go?"

Lively gave him a reproachful glare. Dame Elsebet balled her fist at him. Fred wished he didn't have to keep talking, but he did— someone had to prove this Doktor wight was as fake as a paper wig. "I mean it. Did they just sail away?" He pointed back at the *Longwing*'s boats, all still neatly stowed. "In what? Did they have another ship with them, hidden in the hold? Or did someone come and pick 'em up for a pirates-only jamboree?"

For a moment Lively seemed not to have an answer. But then he pushed himself away from Dame Elsebet, tearing at his own face and hair, and roaring in a voice wracked with pain:

"All right! I admit it! I killed them! Me, a healer, sworn to a sacred oath! Me, once a holy man sworn to the gods!" Dame Elsebet had to seize his hands and squeeze them till her nails drew blood. "I killed them! I admit it! I knew... exactly... how..."

The fellow's final breakdown was so pitiful, Fred was sorry that he felt compelled to say "Oh? Exactly how?"

Dame Elsebet thrust Lively into Ata Maroo's arms and stomped across to throw her shadow over Fred.

"You are out of my favor, Fool, and on very thin ice. Cease your disruptions immediately."

The majority of Fred would have been more than happy to take her advice. Yet somehow, again, his mouth rebelled. "But... there's something phony about that wight."

"How dare you! A liar such as yourself!"

"Right! You see, that's the thing. I mean, it takes one to know one. And I'm telling you, Your High Honor... he's... there's something, well, fake..."

Dame Elsebet tore off her marbled steel crown and hurled it at him. Though it splashed into the sea, she didn't care. Her attention was pointed at Fred alone, pointed like a blade, and she said: "Hear me now, you piece of trash. I didn't kill you before. But I will do it yet— though not in front of a good man who has seen too much killing. Once we touch the Isle of Gold, you run for your life, traitor, charlatan. Because if I see one square inch of your hide, I'll find a spear to stick through it. You have my word as the last Domina de Whellen."

CHAPTER 50

TALUCA LIVELY WANTED TO BE there already. Why was it taking so long?

The Isle of Gold was right there in front of them. The sun was behind it so it didn't look golden at all. But the King lived there, and those Prophessors were there— the ones he'd been writing to. In a few hours it would all be over. He would be the new King, and what he said would go— not just at Whellengood, but everywhere. What power he'd have! But he had to get there first. *Faster, you mindless rank reeking brutes,* Lively told the cloud whales under his breath. Move yourselves or I'll take white-hot coals from that tea brazier and jam them down those holes in your heads. Then you'll really spout clouds, won't you?

But these thoughts were distractions and Lively knew it. There was a big problem. That woman was here. Gods damn it all, hadn't he worked hard to make sure she wouldn't follow him? He'd sailed on the very day of her scabby feast, he'd left her a pile of fake spells that might have got her drowned. For a moment, Lively considered that going aboard the ship and sailing early might have been a mistake. But no. Waiting had made him antsy, and anyway what difference did it— suddenly he remembered Sweetface. Was *he* the one who'd written the message? The message that somehow, against all odds, had brought that woman here? Oh, how he wished he could take Sweetface apart again. He'd do it slower this time. That would teach him.

What's wrong with me, anyway? Lively reproached himself. He had only reproached himself a handful of times in his entire life. There had been no need. He was not one of the inferiors. Except for his one flaw— that woman. How Lively hated her!

At first, she had been perfect. He could make excellent use of her: rich as all hells, and easy to twist because— having somehow managed to get both her precious new husband and her dear old Da mauled to death before her eyes, on some moronic ice-bear hunting expedition— she was broken inside the head. Broken people were the best tools. But after a few years Lively noticed that she'd broken something in *him*.

Anyone else, he could kill. He didn't have the silly squeamish trouble with killing that inferiors did. So if anyone got in his way, or had something he wanted, he could get rid of them. Easily. Except, for some reason, when it came to that woman. He couldn't kill her. Some days, he could barely even hurt her. On the worst days, he even felt compelled to heal her a little bit.

This weakness had made him no better than her slave. He'd wasted years scribbling who knew how many thousands of pages with her mumping scholars. He'd helped build her miserable machines. He'd poured forth his own sweat, saving worthless lives in those wretched infirmaries of hers— although every now and then he *did* manage to take a few patients apart.

It had been torture. Yet somehow, through it all, he'd managed to perfect his repair spell— and what was better, to create the secret one. The one he would unleash today, if only those brutes pulling the boat would hurry... *and,* whispered his self-reproach, if you can get rid of your flaw.

Because what if that woman were to interfere with the plan? What if she tried to stop him, physically stop him? He would be crippled. It would be a nightmare. Triumph would turn to disaster. At the very moment when the world should see his mastery, instead they would see his impotence.

The misery of it swam up so strongly before Lively that he covered his face and knelt, rocking forward and back. The platform vibrated to a hurry of feet and then— oh damn her, damn her in a thousand torn pieces to every corner of every hell— she had her arm around him.

"It's going to be all right," said that woman. "I promise. I'll stay right by your side."

CHAPTER 51

AND SHE WAS, SHE *WAS* right beside him. She hadn't lied. Lively was in agony: he'd had to stand waiting while that woman said goodbye to all those inferior nobodies—hugged the huge Eastern wench with the viper teeth, shook hands with the skinny giant who needed his ugly face punched some more, and bowed to a bird. That had been the most ridiculous of all. Bowed to a bird! If it had been up to Lively, he'd have crushed that babbling pest's head with his thumb.

But finally those nobodies had sailed away, and then that woman had said: "Thank Ye Gods, Taluca— no, thank the Great God Almighty— that your journey is made. Let us go to the King then, and do what we must."

We?

"This isn't a 'we' thing, My Lady," he insisted, struggling not to bite his own hand, tear the limb off a tree, grab a rock and hurl it. "It's something I must do alone, remember?"

"I remember, Taluca. But since then I've had second thoughts. Now I feel as though my sincerity will shine through much more strongly if the King actually sees me kneel. I won't speak a word, I promise. I will simply be there for you."

The gravel footing beside the dock crunched as Lively turned on his heel. He began walking up the path. And she followed him, damn it. Lively began to trot. He was not a trotting kind of man. It tired him. Still she followed, kept on with her tiresome bleating. "I don't understand. Why *shouldn't* I come to the Palace with you? I'll admit that my being here is unexpected, but—"

Scabrous pox, reeking flux! She won't shut up! The fever in Lively's brain rose and rose. Was he even on the right path? Of course he was. He'd memorized the map of the Isle; this was the way. So where the reeking pus were his confederates? He'd spent over a decade writing back and forth to those wretched spotty bookworms, convincing them that his political movement would benefit them, making sure of their support. If those nobodies really wanted their rewards, they would have met him here.

"My Lady, I will... wait, let me catch my.... ah. I'll tell you once again why I don't advise you to join me. Simply... put... I'd prefer you to let me... handle this myself. Some things are best spoken of... man to man." He bent down, hands on knees, panting. They'd stopped beside some windowless brick sheds. He didn't like the look of them— they looked old, abandoned. *Was* this the way? Where *were* those fellows?

"I won't speak a single word. I'll only kneel and—"

"I don't want you there!"

Damn it— Lively knew he'd used too loud a tone, too sharp a vocabulary. He tried smoothing it over, but the words were hard to bring forth. He was too agitated. He almost didn't manage it. "My apologies, but can't you see, My Lady? I don't want to upset you! Things might end up being said... that could get ugly, disturbing..." On the nearest shed, a sign painted in the Isle's outdated dialect read: ADRESATURE PERR ESTRACION D'ORRO. Equipment for extraction of gold. Gold miners' tools. Pus! This was the wrong way, after all.

"Well, I assure you, nothing could be uglier than the thoughts I've endured these past—" her last word turned into a yelp of surprise as Lively grabbed her wrist and whipped her through the open door of the shed. She was caught off guard and her arm hit the iron doorframe, bending backward; a dull pop sounded from her elbow.

And then— *oh clots*— the sight of that woman's white face, of her wet eyes and clenched teeth, they hurt him. Why, why must he endure this idiotic, meaningless suffering?

Now that damned woman was smiling a brave little wounded smile, and that made it even worse. Through a blur of nausea Lively heard her say: "It's all right, Taluca. You can make short work of this. Say the words, my dear."

Lively gulped air until he could steady his voice. He spoke— of course he spoke, he couldn't resist her, she was his downfall— and the healing came, but it was imperfect. Boils, *boils!* He was losing his touch. Would it affect the other spell, too?

"What's wrong with me?" he wailed.

When that woman touched his cheek and said "There now", the last shred of Lively's self-control parted ways with him. He loosed a great animal howl and seized her with both hands, as hard as he could clench, wherever he could grab, muscling her into the shed with a strength newborn from the womb of rage. He moved blindly but at the very last moment he managed to assert a personal desire: to grasp her damaged arm and whip it again, as hard as he could, so that the noise it made against the shed's doorframe wasn't some craven little pop but a delicious belting snap that seemed to hang in the air even over the clang of iron as he slammed the door and threw the lockbolt.

He'd done it. He'd hurt that woman. Lively braced himself to pay: his flaw would make him pay. And yet, as he waited, panting, listening to the moans of pain and the feeble scrabbling noise from behind the door, he felt... nothing.

Slowly it dawned upon him that this last outburst must have burned his flaw away.

He marveled at this. He couldn't help rejoicing, shouting out loud. He had never felt better in his life. If he had known how to turn a somersault, he'd have done it. His prospects were boundless, his future was bright. Why did he ever doubt himself? Worry was for inferiors, not for such as he. Now nothing could hold him back, nothing ever again!

On to the Palace! Surely this road led to it— on the Isle of Gold all roads led to the throne. And so Taluca Lively, the healer who would soon be King, hitched up the tails of his cloak and, puffing with effort, took off running.

CHAPTER 52

CLOSE BY THE DOCKS ON the northern shore of the Isle rose a steep stony bank whose footholds Fred knew well from years of scrambling. The moment the catamaran touched at the dock, he was up those rocks and gone. Underfoot, the scratching of dry grass and the intricate rolling and jabbing shapes of pebbles took him back to youthful days. Hopping over the hedges. Zigzagging through the stiles. The expression on Lumpy Lettie's face when he slapped open the gate of the kitchen garden and darted through.

Only a scattering of the help were about their business. The Palace seemed cold and hollow. A brittleness hung about, something akin to fear but without any definite object.

The audience room was empty. The feasting hall was empty. Even the family apartments— empty. Fred raced through the Palace in a blur of anxiety, the walls and floors and ceilings chasing him through every room. From his pocket the Twin Cans kept up their meditative breath, but its power to soothe him was wearing off. At last Fred arrived in the nursery, where a dome filled with colorful mosaic birds and beasts rose above the crib of the King's only child, born one year to the day after his marriage to Margadet de Vonn.

Hundreds of pounds of stone animals, on the verge of collapse, growled down upon him. But otherwise nothing seemed terribly wrong. True, the little Crown Prince's favorite blanket was in a state far more rumpled than the nursemaid usually allowed. But everyone made mistakes. They let the blanket hang over the edge of the crib; they left the pillows turned on the wrong sides; they left the Prince's tiny crown lying on the rug...

No. That, they did not do. The blood pumped by Fred's racing heart turned cold.

"Enrick?" he called.

When there was no reply he took a breath and tried again, louder.

"Enrick? Margadet?" A drop of sweat ran down his forehead, dripped from his nose. "Hoy! It's, ah, it's me. I'm back, ha ha. And I'm starting to think that something's... uh..."

Now everything *was* terribly, definitely, obviously wrong. So wrong that Fred bolted from the nursery and made for the saferoom.

The Royals had a saferoom— a sort of personal keep— down in the deep sandstone bowels of the Palace. The Isle of Gold had never been taken, but if some terrible barbarian navy were ever to overwhelm its defenses, that was where the family would hide. Fred was privileged to know its location; in fact, he and the young King were the only people in the past hundred years to have crawled through the long, dirty tunnel of the saferoom's secret exit. He steeled himself for a final plunge down a staircase like a huge meat grinder, through a pair of doors like fearful scissors, and then— he was among a group of strangers.

It was odd that they were all men; the household guards were nowhere to be seen. Instead, these looked like scholars— fairly young ones, though some had spectacles on and many were dressed in Prophessors' robes. They milled clumsily about, clearly ill at ease with their brand-new daggers.

Fred's arrival disturbed them. One of the strangers shouted at him, demanding to know if he were an associate or householder of Enrick Castramars. That was another shock: no one outside the family ever addressed the King by his given name, much less appending that of the royal House as if it were a commoner's surname.

"Hoy. Cheeky prick. Have you forgotten how to say 'His Majesty'?"

The impertinent fellow's face flared red. But before he could reply, a Prophessor Fred had seen at levees once or twice jumped in, pointing at him.

"Why haven't you secured this fellow? Of course he's an associate of the Castramars tyrant, you idiot. That's his Fool, or keeper, or something. He's one of them. Secure him!"

The impertinent fellow unlocked the saferoom door. It took him, the Prophessor and two other men to hurl Fred bodily inside.

"Fred I told you to go away forever," said the King.

Being in the saferoom was like hovering beyond time. Though the furnishings were perfectly clean and new, they were long out of style. The tapestries on the stucco walls showed portraits of royal ancestors who'd been dead for years before Fred even came to the Isle. One of them looked a lot like the King, who sat on a bedstead covered with nubby gold silk, slightly apart from his wife and the baby.

The King had grown a natty little beard during Fred's absence. It was as blue-black as his hair, neatly trimmed to a point. Fred wanted to shout into the man's face but he couldn't risk having him shut down right now. So instead he drilled a stare into the tapestry ancestor's dark-blue eyes. "Well, forever's a long time. Hoy, Enrick. Listen. Those men outside..."

"Fred you kicked me in front of people. I want you to go away forever."

"About that. Listen, Enrick, please. I want to spend all day telling you how sorry I am. But I can't waste your time, do you understand? Something really bad is happening right now. And you need to—"

"I want you to go away Fred."

So far the King's wife had said nothing. Like many blind people, Margadet de Vonn had a patient, serene nature; she held the baby tightly against her ruffled bodice with one hand and with the other one, she touched her husband's arm. He squirmed a little but didn't shy away. "Sweetheart," she whispered. "I'm going to talk to Malfred."

"No don't talk to Fred he kicked me in front of people I sent him away."

Fred addressed the Queen. "Margadet, who are these people and why did they move you here?"

"Don't talk to Fred!"

"Hush, hush, hush." Margadet stroked the King's arm with firm linear motions. "I won't talk to Malfred. I'll talk to you. What did the Prophessors say, sweetheart? Tell me again why we were supposed to come in here."

"The Prophessors said they discovered a volcano and it is about to erupt and when it does the air will be poison so we are safe in the safe room where the air isn't poison."

"And tell me about how they claim to be some kind of political movement, with backing from influential gentlemen all over the Kingdom, intent upon setting up a new regime."

"You just said those things why do you want me to say them again you just said them."

Fred took a deep breath and turned away. Time was wasting. He took a chance and spoke directly to the King. "Listen. Enrick. Something's really, really wrong with this whole setup. The wights out there, they have weapons..."

"Of course they have weapons they said when the air is volcano poison there will be riots so of course they have weapons you kicked me Fred I want you to go away."

"I will!" Fred clapped his hands together, so loudly and suddenly that both the baby and the King flinched. He strode to the door. "Let's see if they'll let me go, shall we?"

"They won't," murmured Queen Margadet. And a tear pooled in the corner of each of her doll-like eyes.

The door had been changed: the big bronze lock that used to be on the inside of it was no longer there. Fred was pretty sure it was on the outside, now. There also was no door handle. His fingers shook as he pawed the filled-in hole where it had been. He turned toward the pitiful lonely family behind him and said: "The secret exit. Behind the tapestry. Go. Go."

The Queen leaped to her feet, steadying herself on the King's shoulder. "Show me where!"

But her husband remained stubbornly seated. "The air will be poison and there will be riots and it is safe in the safe room."

The Queen clenched her jaw and strode around the bedstead, letting the edge of it guide her; she moved faster than most people would expect and knew exactly where the wall would be. Probably she could hear it. She reached out; the moment she touched one of the soft tapestries, she grabbed a handful and tore it down. Her voice now had an edge of ice. "Is it here? Or behind another one?"

"Oh, gods. It's gone." Fred marveled that he could possibly feel surprise. Of course the secret exit had been bricked over. The kind of people who herded kings and queens and little princes and damned fools into saferooms and moved the locks to the outside wouldn't forget to brick over a secret exit.

The King *was* surprised. "That's strange it was there once I know it was there once did someone take it away that's strange."

In the midst of terror, the human mind sometimes inserts moments of delirious beauty. Whether it does this out of mischief, or because the gods inspire it, no one knows. On its own whim, Fred's mind suddenly chose to show him a painting of Dame Elsebet de Whellen. There she stood outside the saferoom door with her broadspear. In this imaginary artwork, the path of its blade was represented by a band of the most perfect crimson— not even Kestrella de Brewel's studio assistant could have ground such a lovely color— and the intricate turning of the band's contours was a fascination in and of itself. In sinuous loops and figures of eight, the painted broadspear slashed the conspirators down as if they were just so many sheaves of straw; Dame Elsebet's face was corrugated with righteous rage; her hair flew loose in a comet of white. And for the final, perfect touch the imaginary artist had let drops of crimson fall upon the painting, here and there as fate willed them, as if to bring it all to more visceral life. Fred had never imagined anything more beautiful.

A grinding sound came through the door as it unlocked. It swung open to reveal not Dame Elsebet, but that magician of hers.

A cluster of men hung behind Lively, who entered the saferoom with a decided bounce in his step. When he saw Fred he froze. "Who's — aha! The one-boot fop from back in the boat! Ahhhh. My mistake, not watching you— I thought you were a nobody. But you obviously know these—" and he gestured with his head, unable to even utter the word *people*. He looked around as if puzzled. "The ventilation in this hole sounds like someone mumbling. Hoy! Majesty!" Lively's movements were big and fast. With no preparation whatever, he strode up to the King, loomed over him, stared right into his face. "At least, I'll call you 'Majesty' for a few more minutes. You know what this is about."

The King's foot began to bounce on the floor. "It's the volcano they discovered they moved us here to keep us safer from the air when the air is poison the Prophessors explained it all weeks and weeks ago weeks and weeks they explained it all weeks and weeks ago." Now both feet were drumming rapidly, uncontrollably, and he spoke as if racing through a book. "A dormant column of magma was recently discovered at the juncture of the two stone formations with which the Great God Almighty formed the Isle of Gold approximately ten thousand human lifetimes ago which... in the timespan of gods... would amount to..." with the stranger crowding him, the King was starting to melt into catatonia.

Lively's round face bunched together in irritation. He raised his hand. "Get away from him!" Fred burst out, coming between them.

Lively slapped Fred instead. "What's that, fop?"

Fred didn't give him the satisfaction of flinching, though his ears rang as he replied: "I said get away from him. Are you deaf? Maybe you could heal *that*."

Lively dusted off an ugly little laugh. "Oh, so my fame has preceded me. Ah, if only I hadn't promised myself I would keep this part strictly business. I would so very much enjoy rearranging you. Maybe I'll do it later. Pen! Ink!" He drew a small sheet of heavy paper from his sleeve; behind him, one of the conspirators brought out an inkhorn and began cutting the point of a very large quill. When the quill was ready, Lively dipped it and pressed it forcibly into the King's hand. The wrong hand, noticed Fred. This wight knew nothing about the King. "Hoy, Castramars! Pay attention, now! Do you hear me?"

The King managed to gasp "How dare" but he was slipping away. Fred had seen this thousands of times. Soon no power on earth would be able to prove he was listening.

"You will read this paper aloud and sign it! I said, do you hear me?" Lively thrust the paper at him, but the King didn't react.

"Leave him alone!" cried Queen Margadet, and the baby began to twist and fuss. Lively gave a full-body spasm of rage but willed himself into a calm.

"Very well, eyeless grub. I will read it aloud. I wrote it, you see— but of course, these words are meant to come from your simpleton husband. Eh-hem." He drew an oratorical breath and read:

"Lively, Lord, I hand my crown to you.
My orb and mantle— yea, my scepter too.
The holy potion poured upon my head:
I wish its holiness to you instead.
This gleaming Isle of Gold is now all yours;
the coin that flows to me will change its course;
and —"

The knot of men behind Lively had been quiet until now. Suddenly one of the Prophessors stepped forward. "I must object, Doktor Lively! That part about the transfer of wealth was never agreed to. If you recall, ours is not a mere coup. It is a popular faction intent upon meaningful reform."

"Your faction is no longer of any interest to me. *I* am intent upon enjoying the fullest possible use of my powers."

"But Doktor Lively, any powers inherent in the Crown would not transfer to you personally. The powers of a lawfully constructed State, even one stemming from— hoy! Let go of my hand."

"I have two very personal powers. Let me show them to you. To *all of you!*" Spit flew from Lively's snarling mouth as he clamped the Prophessor's arm under his own, twisting the sleeve of the man's robe into a tourniquet. Moving expertly along with his prisoner's agonized flailings, he broke the fingers one by one, tore them away to show the stubs of bone, dangling from sinews that writhed in and out like worms.

Lively had to raise his voice to be heard over the fellow's howls. "My first power is the power to heal. Bear in mind that I can heal far, far worse wounds than these— why, just recently I put my whole arm back on. I've reached the point where I can usually heal a severed head. As well as many other interesting configurations. Hold still, swine!"

At this point Lively crushed the Prophessor's maimed hand and its detached fingers all together in his own, uttering a string of noises unlike any human language. They were strange and intricate and not very loud. Within moments, the wounded Prophessor's fingers were back upon his hand; although they folded in all the wrong directions, the swelling fled from them and the bruises faded away. Yet Lively didn't release the Prophessor. Instead he glanced over his shoulder at the scholar who had been preparing the quill pen.

"Ah, but you're asking: what is the second power? It can't just be the power to kill, because, well, everyone has that, more or less. No, my second power is far more subtle." In a flash, Lively snatched the scholar's little ivory-handled penknife and jabbed its tip into the healed Prophessor's shoulder.

Now Lively he uttered another bizarre string of sounds.

These sounds were ugly. More than ugly: malevolent in the extreme, like curses wailed by damned souls being boiled in pits of corruption. Lively showed his teeth and said: "It's the power to make even the very smallest wound fatal." Indeed the wounded Prophessor seemed to have lost all his strength; Lively hurled him easily against the wall, where a tapestry fell over his face. "Check him in five minutes or so— you'll be a believer. Ah-ah!" He pointed an accusing, slightly bloodied finger at some of his conspirators, who seemed about to run away. "Run off and I'll find you. Then you'll experience my second power for yourselves."

Fred found himself thinking of Dame Elsebet again. How proud she had been of this monster. A jolt of worry cramped his heart. Where was she?

"Does *she* know about the second spell?"

"You mean the old lunatic from your boat? You must be another pet of hers. Her precious baby." At this, he glanced at Queen Margadet— she had inched closer to the door. "You!" to one of the scholars. "Grab that wench. And *her* precious baby. Do it now or I jab you!" Back to Fred. "Of course she doesn't know. The second spell is my very own secret. But if you're a friend of that woman's, I have some very sad news. She's gone all to pieces. Little tiny ones, all over the beach. Even I can't heal *that*. So sorry."

Fake, thought Fred. It's a lie. Somehow, instinctively, he knew it. Wherever she is, she's alive.

"This needless violence must end!" cried one of the older Prophessors, who stood conveniently near the door. "I repudiate you!" and he took a stand against the violence by turning sharply and running away; most of the other conspirators followed him.

Lively was left with only a bare handful of his most rabid supporters, men with the unmistakable signs of madness written in their faces. For the moment they clung close to him, but their number was small. Lively turned to them and said, "I command you to—"

And then from the gold-covered bedstead came a voice, deep but weak.

"Prophessors I am still your King that villain does not command you. I do I am still your King. I command you Prophessors: I command you to kill him."

The men turned wild eyes from the King to Lively, who chuckled and said, "Nice try, simpleton, but they figure the better deal is to stick with me. And they're right, since— *hoy!*"

The man who held back the Queen must have loosened his grip, because she broke free. She could hear exactly where the door was.

Gripping the Prince against her heart, she sprang for it, but Lively was quicker; he tore something out of her grip, shoved her sprawling out of the saferoom and into the corridor. When the Queen hit the stone floor, her hands were empty.

"You fiend!" she screamed, turning back into the saferoom, her sightless eyes filled with an unearthly rage. Her throat erupted in a primal roar: "Give— me— MY— *SON!*"

Lively had listened to hundreds, perhaps thousands, of death screams and fought off many a desperate victim. But Margadet de Vonn surpassed them all, hurling herself upon him with animal ferocity. Trying to protect his face from her she-bear claws, Lively almost lost his grip on the baby. Trying to fend off her kraken arms, he almost tripped over a low table covered with porcelain figurines. Had the Queen not been as blind as a firewyrm in full blaze, he might have failed to regroup and kick her away. But somehow he managed it, and held the wailing baby away from her by one leg.

"Oh? This? You want this? I'll give it back. But first, some magic."

Booting the Queen back onto the bedstead, he turned to the family like a showman and revealed the penknife that was still in his hand. He jabbed its point into the sole of the baby's foot and uttered that string of hideous noises. The baby fell abruptly silent. Lively gave a bark of laughter and hurled the limp child into the Queen's arms.

"There! Take your spawn, grub. Too bad you couldn't see my trick— but I believe you might have heard it. Now your mate will sign the transfer of power. Or else I won't say the healing words." He snatched the inkwell and the pen and advanced upon the King wearing a rictus of determination. "Is it a deal, Castramars? Answer me!"

The King stared ahead in glassy silence.

Fred wanted to leap to his feet and forge the signature. Why did Enrick have to go into one of his fits now, with time passing, precious time? The Queen rocked the silent baby; the scholars wavered; the world began to decay. Then, in a voice so dim and distant that it seemed to come from the bottom of a mineshaft, the King spoke again.

"You have only three men left. They want to kill you."

"Oh, that makes me sad. They won't, though, because what they want more is their reward. And I have to be alive to give it to them. So sorry."

"I can reward them if they kill you."

"But then what about that thing there? If my men obey you, it'll die."

"He's not a thing!" roared the Queen.

The King swayed back and forth, his face a mask of eerie composure, as if he were unraveling a knot. "This paper of yours you don't need it. Once we're all dead you'll do whatever you want paper or no paper." A cracking noise sounded from the King's hand: he had crushed one of the porcelain magpies from the knick-knack table. Streaks of red grew between his fingers. "Even if I made you King you'd never heal my son his very existence is a threat to you. You will not let him live even if I sign this paper even if we do hear you say the spell it will be a fake one. We are doomed to die and so is our son he is doomed no matter what I do. I cannot save him but at least I can rid the world of you. So Prophessors. As your King I command you: kill this monster. Kill him."

Fred was in awe. Enrick, he thought, why did I never know your mind could do this? The royal order had broken through to Lively's madmen. They were drawing their knives: in moments, their master would die—and so would the infant Prince, and so would Enrick and Margadet, who might continue to walk the earth without their child, to talk and breathe; but really they would be dead, gone forever into an inescapable place deeper and more pitiful than any hell. Fred gazed at one of the conspirators' knives— and time spun down to a glacial pace.

True enough, nothing any of them did could make that monster heal the Prince. But there was something Fred could do to make that monster heal *himself*. And what healed him could heal others.

Fred was far from Lively and the knick-knack table was in the way. Yet he felt his strength gathering for the most precise, explosive acrobatic leap he'd ever made in his life. He reached into his pocket with one hand, prepared the other one to flash out and grab; and though he knew it was foolish, he was a fool and that's why as he coiled himself and bounded forward, he yelled "HOCKA, BOCKA, DOMINAKA!"

The confusion it caused was just enough. Fred cleared the knick-knack table as if he'd been a flea. He grabbed the nearest conspirator's knife, plunged it into Lively's barrel chest and twisted its rosewood handle.

Every figure in the room stretched into motion. They seemed to be falling inward upon him, or perhaps exploding outward away from him; Fred supposed that their faces must be a sight to behold. But he concentrated only upon Lively's.

The monster had to look down to make himself believe there really was a blade protruding from his heart, with some inferior clinging to it. When he saw beyond a doubt that he was wounded, he balled his fist around Fred's, pulling out the knife; the shock on his round pink face melted seamlessly into a stony jut of indignation. His narrow nostrils spread and his upper lip began to rise. *Now.*

With his free hand Fred drew the Twin Cans from his pocket. Lively's eyes rolled downward, trying to identify the objects, as he spoke the weird words of the healing spell. But Fred held the Cans right beneath his mouth— the healing spell went directly into them and began repeating itself. Endlessly, flawlessly.

"Catch!" yelled Fred, flinging the Cans to the King. They hit him in the forehead but it was all right: the Queen heard them clank to the floor; she kicked them to safety under the bed. Fred turned to the frozen conspirators and cried: "Now! Kill him *now!*"

The monster cursed him with some foul-sounding imprecations, but the game was up. His onetime minions fell upon him in violent bloodlust, tearing him apart to vent their guilt and fear. He managed to heal himself a few times— for as long as he still had a tongue— but then he could heal himself no more.

Fred staggered against the wall. He had a terrible stomachache. He clutched at it and the pain flared hot, wire-taut, unbearable. He looked at the slick, red wetness on his hands.

The knife Lively had been holding.

Those ugly curses.

The second spell.

He tried to speak, but instead his whole body shook. He fell.

From his spot on the floor, he could see the King and Queen— although they were sideways, and partially blocked by the knick-knack table. They were huddled together around the Prince. But were they holding the Cans to the child? Were they in time? Did it work? Fred wanted to ask all of these things, but he couldn't make a sound.

A ring of strange indifference began spreading from his wound, as if his flesh didn't care to stop the damage, wasn't even going to bother trying. The ring of apathy grew larger still, invading his lungs, making it hard to breathe.

His field of vision began to blur and flash. The noise of the room faded down to a hiss. The air became too thick to draw in, too heavy to push out.

Then Fred closed his eyes and turned inward, toward his own unexpected, yet suddenly familiar god.

CHAPTER 53

PAIN. HEAVEN HAD PAIN. WHO knew?

But then Fred thought twice. If there was pain here, it might be… you know. He looked around for clues.

Above him hung a cloth, woven with a coat of arms. Red and yellow stripes, a white lozenge and a magpie— a motif he'd known well, when he was alive. There were more cloths arranged around him like the walls of a pavilion; they must be bedcurtains. Though he was closed in on all four sides, and above, Fred didn't care anymore. Let the silk ceiling fall in on him— what does it matter when you're dead?

"Mesir?" came a whisper. Fred ignored it. After a pause it repeated: "Mesir."

A second voice whispered "He's sleeping, idiot."

"How do you know? What if he died again?"

"He can't keep dying forever. Eventually it'll take. I mean, look at his little Highness— he went back and forth a few times before he got better, didn't he?"

Fred groaned his throat clear and rasped, "Nedward is better?"

Maybe he shouldn't have said anything. With an eye-spearing flare of light, the bedcurtain swished away. Ow. The Queen's own pink-cheeked maids stared down upon him with great satisfaction. "He is," one of them said. "And it looks like you'll soon be well enough, yourself. Call in the healer!"

At the word "healer" the nearest maid pressed him back down against the featherbed and told him it was all right.

This healer was no veteran of evil. In fact he looked very much like Petir de Brewel. He stood in front of the window grinding musty sweet spicy things in a mortar, and didn't bother with any chit-chat. When at last the grinding was completed, the healer came over and rolled back the white linen bedsheet, then unfolded his patient's infirmary gown. Fred wanted to complain about the intrusion, but one look at the black and green streaks fading about his wound made him grateful just to be alive.

The healer painted the herbs on with a brush made of more herbs, apologizing whenever Fred flinched. Then he bundled him back up, let him sip something fizzy through a wheatstraw, and withdrew. Fred slept some more and awoke later to let a maid feed him soup. But in mid-sip, he remembered something.

"Dame Elsebet de Whellen!" he cried. "Where is she?"

"De Whellen? Probably in that traitor country, whipping her slaves."

Fred sat up and his belly seared with pain. "You mean she went home? She left?" he pushed away the next spoonful of soup.

"Went home? No. No de Whellen ever came here. Now open the mine... heeere comes the pony... Ah! Your Majesty!" The maid sprang to her feet, dropped the soup, and disappeared.

"Hello you saved my son," said the King, and Fred could tell he was making an extra-special effort to look him in the eye.

The effort proved exhausting, so the King turned to look back out the window as they spoke, and Fred turned toward the silk wall. This was more like it, more natural.

"I used to hate you Fred for a while but somehow I don't want to hate you any more."

"Thank you, Enrick. From the bottom of my heart." Fred gave an ironic smile. "I know that isn't so far down. But I — I have so much to say. When I'm better I'll say it. From now on, I want to be the right kind of brother." He struggled to sit up. "But listen. There's something urgent—"

"Sometimes when Da was alive I wanted to ask him to send you back I used to want to ask him to send you back but then when it was my turn to be King I couldn't ask Da anymore so when it was my turn I could only ask myself..."

"Uh, Enrick..."

"Fred you know it's my turn to be King since three years ago so now you have to not interrupt me see Fred I've learned to stick up for myself."

"But..."

"It feels good to be King it actually feels good really if it gets too tricky I ask Margadet to help she is really smart Fred I have to tell you it feels good to ask Margadet some people say don't ask her she's a woman so she only knows to fight and work and have a baby but Margadet is really smart so I tell them I don't care and I ask her..."

"Speaking of a woman..."

"...and Margadet had this idea that I give you a boon I had never heard the word boon Fred have you ever heard of a boon I never did but Margadet says they do it in her country they give someone a boon to say thank you it is whatever the person asks for then they give it that is a boon you can ask me for anything Fred like titles or land or anything Margadet and I want to give you a boon because you saved our son and what is more we have the healing spell now thanks to you we have it forever and we Oh! Fred no don't get up the healer says it isn't time please lie down where are you going? Fred?"

CHAPTER 54

THREE DAYS.

Dame Elsebet was becoming weak. Her tongue felt huge, her skin felt loose and baggy, and her head throbbed constantly.

Summers on the Isle of Gold were hot, but the equipment shed was thankfully cool and dark, except where gaps in the roof let in some sunlight. By a stroke of luck, on one afternoon the gaps had also let in some rain. Dame Elsebet had trapped the precious water by spreading her not-glass scarf below it; she'd squeezed as much of its wetness into her mouth as she could, then licked the smooth fabric dry. But she would much rather have kept on using it as a sling: her arm was a mess. It was unnaturally shaped and frighteningly discolored, and in one area certain sharp things stabbed agonizingly close to the surface. Still, she consoled herself by remembering that she'd seen far worse injuries in Taluca Lively's infirmary.

She tried not to think about Lively. She tried not to guess why he'd attacked her; she tried not to wonder where he'd gone, or when he'd come back. She especially didn't want to think too much about that last point, because she was afraid she knew the answer.

So he hated her. But why? And what had become of his plea before the King? No, don't think about that.

Does anyone know I'm here?

Three days.

The sun was making its turn toward evening of the third day when Dame Elsebet heard feet: horse and human.

She began to shout. The search party heard her, thank all the gods that were and ever would be. When the thick iron door of the shed swung open, she surged out and seized the water bottle a maid offered her; while she guzzled from that miraculous fountain of life, Dame Elsebet wouldn't have noticed it if lightning had struck the earth a foot away. But by the time the water was gone, she definitely noticed the sedan chair that had come along with the search party.

From behind the closed curtains of the chair a man's voice said, "Your High Honor. It's me."

Dame Elsebet wiped her mouth with the back of her good hand.

"*You*. I promised I'd kill you."

"You did. But listen. You can't— see a square inch of my hide, can you?"

"What's your point, traitor?"

The man in the chair squirmed and whimpered a little. Then he said, "Well, what I mean is, then technically we can talk. Without your having to stick a spear through me. Ahhh!"

Dame Elsebet tore back the curtain of the chair. She twisted the fabric and snarled. "Now I've seen your damned hide. And I stand by what I said—what's funny, traitor?"

"I just realized it's all right. Even if you do see me, you don't have to keep that promise. If I remember, you swore it as 'the last Domina de Whellen'. Didn't you? I think those were your exact words."

"What about my words?"

Fred really was afraid of her now, to tell the truth. She showed every sign of climbing straight into the chair and tearing at him with— what was wrong with her arm?

"Well! Ah! It's just that you aren't the last Domina de Whellen anymore! There are going to be plenty of others, in the future. Dominas and Seigneurs, and all the rest, because now your family's title exists in perpetuity. I took care of it."

"What do you mean? Don't you dare lie to me, sir."

Fred slid to one side of the chair, though clearly it was difficult for him. He patted the empty spot. "Please. Your High Honor. Sit with me, because I'm afraid I've gone and made the King angry again and I'd really prefer to take my time getting back to the Palace with you. I have a strange, ugly story to share along the way."

Dame Elsebet stepped warily into the vehicle. "Does it have anything to do with that fellow who was my healer?"

"It does."

"Is something wrong with your... oh, dear gods, Malfred."

"I see something is wrong with you, too."

"So when you warned me about him..."

A silence fell. The bearers lifted the chair.

The summer evening smelled of golden dust. Beside them the mounted archers' gear jingled, their horses puffed and snorted, and from time to time a magpie chattered in the trees. At last Dame Elsebet turned to Fred and whispered, "Will I have to sharpen my broadspear for that fellow who hurt us?"

Fred covered her good hand with his own. "No, Medame."

"Oh, thank the heavens for that. You know I'm not quite so young anymore."

The Heart of Stone Adventures continue with

POWER'S PLAY

and

DOOM'S DAZE

Sign up for my newsletter
and get updates at

evasandor.com

Printed in Great Britain
by Amazon